N

wo

"Wouldn't

now, Mr. Kandelin."

Brett's reply stopped the lawman's companions. Even the hostler turned from what he was doing. "You wouldn't run, Marshal. I found out about Ortiz. He promised to buy my cattle if I delivered to him down here, and I brought them down, and that son of a bitch is one of the rebels or whatever you call them, an' he's going to come up here to take my cattle. Marshal, you want to sit on your butt, you go right ahead. I'm goin' to find Mr. Ortiz and yank him inside out."

No one said a word until Brett was leading his horse out of the barn. One of Severn's companions, a lean weathered and lined older man called up front. "How many men you got?"

Brett turned to answer. "Two."

Also by Lauran Paine
Published by Fawcett Books:

THE HORSEMAN

THE NEW MEXICO HERITAGE

THE GUNS OF SUMMER

THE SHERIDAN STAGE

THE CATCH COLT

THE YOUNG MARAUDERS

THE BANDOLEROS

Lauran Paine

FAWCETT GOLD MEDAL • NEW YORK

A Fawcett Gold Medal Book
Published by Ballantine Books

Library of Congress Catalog Card Number: 90-93135

ISBN 0-449-14663-4

Manufactured in the United States of America

First Edition: October 1990

CHAPTER 1

Heading South

They left the corral yard at mission San Miguel before sunrise—not, as would normally be the case on the south desert to avoid the heat—but rather because the next town, called Coyotero, was their destination, and they'd been on the trail a long time.

Although the south desert was reduced to bare essentials most of the year—earth, horizon, and sky—in springtime, a period of brief duration, it was one of the most beautiful places on earth. There were flowers, grass, a sky of cobalt blue, and air so pure a man could see to the farthest curve of the world.

The three drovers were wearing coats when the sun arrived. Sunrise on the south desert was unlike anywhere else. The sun jumped over the horizon, flooding thousands of miles with golden light in two seconds.

The cattle grazed along as they'd been doing for weeks, without being pushed, making no particular attempt to drift. It hadn't been a hard drive, just a long one, and because the gray-eyed man who owned them wanted to avoid unnecessary weight loss, thus far they'd been close to water and comfortable bedding grounds.

Once, there'd been a thunderstorm complete with lightning, but that had caused the only interruption. It had required two days to bring the animals back to one place so the drive could be resumed.

The dark man wearing an old forage cap and a blanket coat was tucking his first cud of the day into a cheek when he raised a gloved hand and said, "Smoke."

Both his companions stood in their stirrups. It was indeed smoke, and probably had been around before sunrise, but until daylight they hadn't been able to see it.

The dark man said, "Hell of a distance," to which the youngest of the three men, who looked to be no more than twenty, wondered aloud if the smoke wasn't rising somewhere down over the border in Mexico. None of them knew exactly where the border was, and, in fact, none of them had ever before been on the south desert.

The graying man with the turned-up collar said nothing until he'd completed a study of the smoke. It appeared to be some kind of soiled, greasy cloud, spreading and increasing in height as it burned until it had to be visible for miles.

The man's name was Brett Kandelin. He'd been free-grazing cattle for many years. He sold them on the hoof, and his entire existence to this point centered around cattle. Therefore it was reasonable for him to consider everything, even the distant smoke, in relation to his cattle. "If that revolution down there is still on, an' if that smoke's rising over some town or battlefield, I hope to hell it don't have anything to do with the gent who contracted for these animals," he exclaimed.

Neither the dark rider nor the youngest one said a word, but the sudden idea that all their work might be for nothing occurred to both of them.

Before reining west to keep some cattle from ambling too far, Enos Lee, the dark man, said, "If that's a battle, it's one hell of a dead serious one."

After the dark man's departure, the young rider, named Hale Barlow, became more than ever intrigued by the smoke. "Most likely a town caught fire," he said, looking at the weather-bronzed graying man at his side. "Wouldn't be no battle, would it?"

Brett Kandelin gazed at Enos Lee. "You never saw one?"

"No, sir. If it's a battle, why don't we hear no cannons?"

The older man thought about that for a while before replying. "I don't know. Maybe Mexicans don't have any. Or maybe they haven't come up yet. Old feller told me one time years back Mexicans hauled their cannons around on big wooden sleds."

Hale's eyes widened. "Don't they have wheels?"

Brett smiled as he turned back to watch the smoke. "All I know is what the old man told me. I don't know any more about Mexes than you do." The smile faded; Brett Kandelin returned to his unpleasant thoughts.

The man who had contracted for his cattle had been a Mexican, farer than most Brett had seen, and much fairer than his two companions, one of whom was a pockmarked, very dark, beefy individual who never smiled. How the buyer had known where to locate Brett he hadn't said, and Brett hadn't asked. Free-grazers roamed the land following the grass. They owned nothing but skinny cattle they'd buy in late winter and graze through the spring and summer, making as much weight gain as possible before selling off, holing up during winter, and striking out to do the same thing again the next year.

It was a nomadic existence. It was also a risky one, what with more and more livestock men taking up land and defending it any way they could, including using gunfire, especially against free-grazers.

Over the last few years it had been increasingly difficult to free-graze, and although Brett Kandelin had seen the handwriting on the wall that far back, it was the only way he'd ever made money with cattle. So he had continued to free-graze. But it had occurred to him a year or so back that it wouldn't be much longer before he'd have to quit. In fact, on the drive down across the south desert he'd wondered if this hadn't ought to be his last free-graze drive.

Hale Barlow reined away eastward to lead some cattle out of the thornpin. In the opposite direction, the dark man had his drifters back where they were supposed to be. Neither he nor the cows had any difficulty. After so long on the trail, cattle could tell when a rider was coming their way and would dutifully go back to join the herd.

The distant smoke had risen and spread until it threatened to obscure the sun. Whatever was beneath it was feeding flames at a great rate. Brett was sure of one thing: It wasn't a brushfire, not this time of year, when everything was green and full of moisture. The longer he watched it, the more he wondered if it wasn't, indeed, a town.

They had been told at Mission San Miguel that their destination, the town of Coyotero, was the only inhabited community on their southward route, until they crossed over into Mexico.

Brett squinted as what seemed to be a sprawling town firmed up faintly in the distance. He looped his reins, removed his gloves, and built a smoke. If that was Coyotero, he'd fulfilled his end of the bargain. The man who'd contracted for the herd, whose name was Gil Ortiz y Duran, would be down there waiting. He would have riders with him to take over the herd for wherever he intended to go with it, and he would have the money. Except for those huge billowing clouds of smoke everything appeared to Brett Kandelin as it was supposed to be.

Hale had gotten the cattle out of the thornpin thickets, and the dark man was slogging along on loose reins behind the animals he'd also turned back. The morning was perfect: cool, fragrant, tranquil. If the town ahead was Coyotero, the long drive was finally about to end. That thought conjured up another one: Should this be Brett Kandelin's last year as a free-grazer?

He hadn't made up his mind by the time a sprawl of adobe and wood, with a few tin roofs to reflect sunlight, was only a few miles ahead. Brett beckoned his two riders.

The cattle were in good feed, which wasn't unusual; they'd had good feed most of the way south. But ordinarily, this close to a town, local stock men of one kind or another—goats and sheep had seemed to predominate the farther into the desert they'd gone—had fairly well overgrazed the countryside.

The cattle, sensing a lull, slowed their onward progress

and began to fan out a little while keeping an eye on the three horsemen. They hadn't been allowed to stop this early in the morning in weeks, but as the horsemen swung off to palaver, the cattle eyed them less and concentrated more on food.

Enos, whose interest in the distant smoke lingered, said he thought it had to be at least twenty, maybe even fifty miles southward. Brett told them he would lope ahead to scout up the town if they would mind the cattle, allow a little drift but not too much; he'd fetch back some supplies after he'd hunted up the Mexican named Ortiz-Duran.

Both of his riders smiled, less over the prospect of something besides beans, spuds, and wild game than because they were at the end of the trail.

They remained beside their horses, watching Kandelin ride away. Enos shook his head, beat dust off his old army forage cap, and said, "I think this'll be his last drive." At the raised eyebrows this remark brought, he added a little more. "I been with him four years. It's been gettin' harder an' harder to graze over the land." He smiled at the younger man. "Everythin' has its time. He knows that."

"He hasn't said anything," Hale stated.

Enos, twice the younger rider's age, was indulgent. "He don't say a lot of what he thinks. It's his way. Did I ever tell you how him an' me come together?"

"Something about some trouble in a place called Eden?"

Enos laughed, which made the strong white teeth particularly noticeable in his dusky face. "Eden? It wasn't no Eden for me. I'd come in after a long, dry ride and put up my horse, which they treated real well, an' went to the cafe for dinner, but mostly for water." Enos paused to gaze at the distant figure of a horseman. "He was eatin' at the counter. When I sat down, the cafe man come along lookin' cranky, and when I asked for a quart of water before the meal, he said they didn't want niggers in Eden and there wasn't no black water, neither."

Enos shrugged slightly. "I reckon I should've expected it. Eden wasn't too far from Texas. . . ."

"What happened?"

"Brett sat there eating. There was a few other gents at the counter. None of 'em looked up, just went on eatin' until Brett pushed up off the counter an' as that cafe man walked past he never raised his voice. He just said, 'Friend, you ever been real thirsty? No? Let me tell you somethin' about bein' thirsty. Everything's the same when there's no water. Horses, cattle, birds, an' men. You don't never refuse a drink of water to anything. Anything at all. Get his him quart of water.'

"That cafe man was a heavyset feller with eyes the color of wet clay. He stood a while lookin' at Brett, while along the counter no one moved or ate; they just sat there like crows on a fence, waiting. Me, I'd have got up and left, except that I couldn't, not right then, so I sat like the others, waiting.

"The cafe man started to growl something, and Brett pointed a finger at his face. "You get *me* a quart of water, friend. *Now!*' "

Hale was intrigued. "Did he get it?"

"Yessir, he got it, and with all of them watchin', Brett pushed the bottle down to me. Not a sound, mind you, and I emptied the jar. . . . But I got to tell you I'd lost my thirst, an' as soon as it was down I commenced sweatin' like a studhorse."

"What happened?"

Enos's white teeth flashed again, but the smile was rueful. "Brett paid for his dinner, paid for mine, and sat there until the cafe man'd fed me an' I'd eaten it all. But I wasn't near as hungry as when I'd walked in. Then Brett jerked his head for me to follow, an' we went outside."

"That's all? That was the end of it?"

Enos's reply was delayed. "Yessir, that was all of it. But after he took me out to his camp, he told me if I went back—sure as gawd made little green apples—they'd hang me. So I helped him drift his cattle, an' we been together ever since."

"Four years?"

"Four years, Hale. Sometimes he cooks, sometimes I cook. But he ain't much of a cook, so the last couple years

I been doin' most of it. For a while we had a wagon, but lost it in a grass fire. Since then we've traveled light. I've wished we'd get another wagon, but we never have. . . . Tell you somethin' about Brett Kandelin—he don't like to argue. He figures things real good, makes a decision, and that's it. Not exactly stubborn, mind, but once he's got a bone in his teeth he don't often turn it loose. Well, you been with him since his drive began, you'd ought to have figured him out."

"Some," Hale Barlow said, "but not like you have. He's likable, ain't he?"

Enos laughed. "He is that. An' he's a bad man to cross. Like I told you, he don't like to argue. I guess because when he argues he gets mad." Enos rolled his eyes. "I've seen him mad a couple of times, an' I'm here to tell you I wouldn't want him mad at me. . . . Well, we better scatter out or they'll drift to hell an' gone."

"Enos?"

"Huh?"

"Where's he from?"

"I never asked, Hale, an' he never said. He don't ask personal questions, an' neither do I." The dark man eyed the younger one for a thoughtful moment before speaking again. "We been about eight weeks on the trail. When he hired you on back up yonder he didn't ask nothin' personal, did he?"

"No."

"And the three of us had some laughs, some scares, got soaked to the skin a few times, and missed a few meals, an' we're still together, ain't we?"

Hale Barlow smiled. "We better go check the drift," he said, and turned to snug up his cinch before riding eastward.

Enos Lee leaned across his saddle seat, watching the younger man for a while, then wagged his head, grinned, and rode in the opposite direction.

There was a stage road a mile or so east of Coyotero that was layered in dust from use and seemed to angle southward from the north. It was the spindrift of tan dust that told Hale Barlow there was a vehicle traveling ahead at a fair pace.

Although he was curious about the road, he turned back with the cattle.

Far to the west, Enos Lee was sitting his saddle, skiving a corner off his Kentucky twist and alternately looking in the direction of the town and beyond it, where the billowing, dirty-looking smoke was being borne away by a wind of its own creation. Below, at the source, the fire that had been feeding it appeared to be decreasing.

It still puzzled him how one of those mud towns they'd seen since riding into the heartland of the south desert could burn. Wood burned, but adobe didn't.

He got into the shade of a dense, thorny thicket, loosened the cinch, and hunkered in shade, watching the cattle and waiting. With nothing else to do, he thought about his conversation with Hale Barlow, who was a good range man despite his youth.

He also thought about the possibility of this being his last year with Brett Kandelin, and the prospect was not a happy one. Four years with someone, through more trouble and discomfort than a man could shake a stick at, could not help but forge a bond.

CHAPTER 2

Coyotero

The town of Coyotero was in most ways typical of the Southwest. The oldest inhabited places couldn't have died if they'd wanted to in a part of the country where water determined all activity, two-legged and four-legged. Coyotero straddled an extreme rarity in the south desert, an underground source of water that, at certain times of the year, rose to within eight or ten feet of the surface. It caused varieties of deep-rooted vegetation to remain green and flourishing even after the full force of summer arrived.

In its earlier existence, Coyotero had been a *rancheria* for hundreds, perhaps thousands of years. Vestiges of prehistoric occupation were commonplace.

Centuries later the casqued and mounted Spaniards arrived to forever disrupt and desolate a very ancient way of life, and to establish one of their permanent posts where there was good water. From these posts they launched expeditions of exploration, encouraged by the belief that there was a Fountain of Youth—and cities where gold was as common as dirt.

Next came the Mexicans, less talented in the arts of conquest and, therefore, more often than not the sacrificial sheep against the ferocity of the Indians.

The Mexicans were originally part of the great explorations, used as workhorses for the Spanish expeditions. They came first as a trickle, then as a stream, and finally as a flood tide, and while their graves, marked and unmarked, told their own tale of sacrificial sheep, they never stopped arriving. So in the end, while they lost many to Indian skirmishes, the Mexicans still outnumbered their enemy.

Finally came the pale-eyed people, on big horses and in the vans of large, ponderous, almost indestructible wagons. They did not, originally, plan on settling but came instead to trade down in *Mejico*. However, in the few rare places like Coyotero, where there was water, they made their homes. And that fairly well completed the eons-old disruption and displacement of the dark-eyed people.

As Brett Kandelin rode at a dead walk down the very wide main thoroughfare of Coyotero, he could see the living artifacts—the largely distinct variations of humanity as well as the less distinct products of centuries of cheerful miscegenation. He'd seen enough of these desert communities lately to recognize the separatism that invariably existed. On the west side of Coyotero was Mex town, a barrio inhabited by people who had maintained their own way of life even after the serpent and eagle of the Mexican flag had been replaced by what they called "the bloody gridiron." The barrio was complete with a dusty plaza, in the center of which stood a large water well, bricked up all around to a height of several feet to prevent accidental drownings, particularly of children. The rough surround of buildings central to the big, dusty plaza included residences—usually no more than one- or two-roomed *jacales*—little stores with porches to provide shade, and a cantina.

On the west side of the main road through town, but also throughout the business district, was the world of the gringos, an altogether different community within the overall community.

Brett left his horse at a massively walled adobe barn with a low roof. It was run by a gringo with a mouth full of gold teeth and the perpetually laughing eyes that showed venom in their depths.

There was activity on the west side of Coyotero. Groups of people in earnest conversation ignored him as he strolled up to the only hotel, called Casa de Leon—House of the

Lion—a thick-walled, massive structure with the appearance of a barracks, which, in fact, it had once been. A small, intense collection of people on the full-length porch didn't even appear aware of his presence until a dark-eyed, burly man turned almost irritably to ask if Brett wanted a room. When he was told that was a possibility, the burly man said, "Come with me," and went briskly down a long, gloomy hall with doors opening off it on both sides, flung one door open, and gestured. "Two bits a night, friend. For one person." The burly man pointed. "That back winder is nailed shut." The implication was clear enough; the hotel's proprietor had figured out a way to prevent one man from renting a room, then sneaking his friends in through the back window.

As Brett nodded and handed the man a silver dollar, he said, "By any chance you know a man named Ortiz-Duran?" He was answered with a quizzical look from the hotel proprietor—the first lesson in Brett Kandelin's south desert education.

"You're new down here," the burly man stated. "If you wasn't you'd know Messicans use both names of their parents. In other words, the father's name would be Ortiz. That'd be his proper name. Then they use the letter *y*, which means *and* in our language, then the mother's name. You see? Your man's name is Ortiz. That's the name you use. The rest of it you don't use, unless you write him a letter. . . . And no, I don't know him." The burly man paused. "What about him?"

Brett had taken off his riding gloves, tucking them under and over his shell belt, when he replied, "I'm supposed to meet him in Coyotero."

"What for?"

Brett's gaze cooled a little. "You ask a lot of questions, mister."

The burly man's retort was almost fierce. "We got reason, stranger. Where you from?"

"Up north."

The burly man considered that before speaking again. "Didn't you see the smoke? Hell, we could smell it since yesterday. There was a hell of a battle down over the line. Right now folks are sweatin' bullets about which side won."

Brett went to a chair to sit down. "How far over the line, friend?"

"No farther than Ciudad Morales . . . Ciudad Morales is a fair size town about ten, fifteen miles from here. Coyotero is about six miles from the border." The burly man studied Brett's calm expression for a moment before continuing. "It don't matter a hell of a lot which side won, but if it was the *federales*, then maybe they'll go back lookin' for another of them Messican route-armies the *pronunciados* got. Maybe. An' maybe they'll come up over the line. If the *bandoleros* won, sure as hell they'll come up over the line, especially if they was routed. Messican army units aren't allowed by law to come up here any more'n our soldiers are allowed to go down there. But with *bandoleros*—they ain't soldiers, anyway, they're revolutionaries, mostly brigand bands—if they won, places like this town could be right in their path. They take everything: horses, weapons, liquor, cattle. They plunder and rob and kill folks for the hell of it. . . . You know what *ley fuga* is? You don't. That's when they get drunk and stand in the roadway an' make people run for their lives—and shoot 'em in the back as they're running. It's sport with them. They make a circus of it."

The burly man paused to mop off sweat before also saying, "This Messican you're lookin' for, this Ortiz, who is he?"

Brett had no difficulty answering the question now. The burly man's obvious agitation was very convincing. "He contracted for a herd of cattle I brought down here. They're ranging a few miles north. Ortiz, whatever his name is, was to meet me in Coyotero, pay for the cattle, and take 'em over."

"This Ortiz . . . Was he a Mex soldier?"

"I don't know. He was wearin' regular clothes when we met up north. He had a couple of other Mexicans with him. All we talked about was the cattle, the price, and where I was to deliver them."

"He didn't mention the revolution?"

"No. We just talked cattle. . . . My men and I saw the smoke, but that was all. If it was a battle, how come we didn't hear guns—cannons and the like?"

"When did you get down this far?"

"This morning."

"The battle ended yesterday. It sounded like the end of the world. There was noise until hell couldn't have held it all. Then there was the smoke, no more cannon fire, a little rifle fire, until this morning, then just the smoke. What we're worryin' about is . . . sure as hell *someone* is goin' to come up over the line. They've done it before. Since I been down here I've seen it five, six times, an' when they leave, mister, there's nothing left. Dead bodies everywhere, fires, chaos, and devastation like you never seen in your whole damned life."

Brett rose from the chair. "You got U.S. Army posts down here?"

"Yes. Thirty miles east. We sent three riders for help yesterday morning. You think that's good? Mister, if it's *bandoleros*, believe me they'll be here, murder everyone in sight, an' be gone before our army can even get close." For a moment the burly man stood eyeing Brett Kandelin, then bleakly wagged his head. "You sure picked a hell of a time to come down here." The burly man had a sudden thought, and swore. "Cattle! That's what they come for. They've ruined their own country, ate up or killed their own beef. If it's *bandoleros*, they're always hungry. Gawddammit, if they got any idea someone just arrived here with cattle, that'll be all they'll need."

Brett replied quickly. "I can turn back," he said, and the burly man darkly scowled at him.

"What the hell good would that do? All they got to do is know they're cattle up here, an' mister, they ride like a whirlwind. You couldn't get away before they'd overrun you."

For a moment the burly man was silent, then he said, "Our lawman's named Bill Severn. He ain't no army general, but he's gettin' things organized as best he can. You ought to talk to him. Maybe he knows your Ortiz." The burly man paused again, then shoved out a thick, powerful hand. "I'm Jess Eames."

Brett shook the hand. "I'm Brett Kandelin."

The burly man walked out of the room, the degree of his agitation epitomized by the fact that although he was wearing an old shell belt and holstered Colt, he moved like someone unused to such things.

Brett returned to the porch and leaned on an upright for a few minutes, gazing at the groups of anxious people, all armed and one-third of them, like the burly man, wearing guns they did not seem at home with.

He saw a small band of armed men down in front of a particular thick-walled building sandwiched between two structures of more recent vintage. There was a tie rack in front of the adobe building, with saddled horses tied to it. Someone long ago had crudely painted one word on the north side of the building: JUZGADO.

Brett made no sense of the word, but above the front of the *juzgado* was another word, this one in English. JAIL.

He started down the west side of the very wide main thoroughfare in that direction, and arrived there as most of the armed men out front began to move away. Brett had the impression that the men were moving to implement some kind of plan.

When he entered the jailhouse, a large older man looked around from a tiny iron stove where he'd just filled a cup. His gaze was something between irritability and anxiety.

Brett introduced himself, eyed the big, older man's shirtfront where a worn, dull badge was pinned. Then he explained his situation, mentioning the cattle and ending up by asking if the town marshal knew anyone named Gil Ortiz y Duran.

He did not get an immediate reply because a rather wild-eyed, sweating, balding man barged in, ignored Brett, and said, "Bill, there's somethin' goin' on over in Mex town."

Marshal Severn nodded. "Yeah, I know."

"Well, for crissake, they could be organizin' to join the *bandoleros*. We got to do something."

The big, older man went slowly to his desk and sat down, holding the cup of coffee. His gaze was stone-steady as he said, "They're as scairt as we are, Slade. *Bandoleros* kill our Messicans just like anyone else. Maybe even quicker. An' I've already done something, so you don't go off half-cocked and stir up more trouble. We got enough already. Stay out of Mex town. Pass that along. Keep out of there."

As the wild-eyed man rushed back to the roadway, Marshal Severn sipped coffee. He eyed Brett over the cup's rim and seemed about to wryly smile as he put the coffee aside and leaned big arms atop the old desk. "You sure came here at an interestin' time, Mr. Kandelin. How far from town is your herd?"

"A few miles. And right now, I'm thinking about going back, get them turned north, and hightailing it out of your territory."

The big man gently wagged his head, saying almost exactly the same thing the hotel proprietor had said. "You'd never make it, amigo. If they're *bandoleros*, an' I'm bettin' my life they are, there'll be an army of 'em. You'd do better to stay right here in town. You got riders?"

"Two."

"Mr. Kandelin, they'd ride right over the top of you. If it was horses, I'd say you might make it, but not with nothin' as slow moving as cattle. . . . Ortiz, you said? That's a pretty common name. Where was you to meet him?"

"Here. In your town. I figured to just ask around until I found him."

The big man sipped more coffee, hung fire for a while before speaking again, and this time he actually did smile. "Seems to me it's goin' to be a matter of timing for you. Maybe Ortiz is here . . . and more'n likely he isn't. Yeah, I know a man named Ortiz. Right now'd be a real bad time for a strange Mex to come ridin' into town. Either way, Mr. Kandelin, whether you find him or not, if you don't get it done before evening, I'd say he's not here and likely won't be coming, an' by then we should have word of what happened down yonder around Ciudad Morales." The large man's smile widened as he saw the pained expression on the younger man's face.

When Brett said, "Maybe they won't come up here, Marshal," the lawman continued to hold his cup of java and smile.

"Maybe not. Maybe one chance out of a thousand they won't."

Severn finished the coffee, shoved the cup away, and studied Brett Kandelin. "Where you from?" he asked in an almost casual way.

"Up near the Colorado–New Mexico line."

"That's quite a distance. Been a long drive, has it?"

"Long enough, Marshal. Too long if we rode smack-dab into a war. I talked to a feller named Eames a while back. According to him, if *bandoleros* come to your town, there'll be an army of them."

Marshal Severn calmly inclined his head. "That's sure likely. You ever been this far south before, Mr. Kandelin?"

"No."

Bill Severn leaned back until the old chair squeaked. "You know much about Messicans?"

"No."

"It don't make a hell of a lot of difference which they are, in federal uniforms or wearin' crossed bandoleers, except that if they're Mex regulars there'll be a little discipline. Hopefully enough for their officers to keep 'em from runnin' wild and chargin' up over the line like madmen. But if it's regulars, with *rurales* among 'em, nothing'll hold them back. If they're ragged-pantsed *bandoleros*, there's no discipline, no order, just a hell of a gang of kill-crazy Messicans on horses shootin' at anythin' in their way, includin' their own companions. An' after battles, whether they get fed or not, they get liquor."

Brett eased back in his chair, gazing at the older man. "What are *rurales*?"

"We don't have anythin' like that. They're constabulary troops. Some folks call 'em red flaggers, because when they ride into a place they usually are carryin' a red flag. That means no quarter. Messico's a big country, mostly rural an' dirt poor. There's always some son of a bitch puttin' out a *grito*. That means a call to arms, to revolt. What it really means is plenty to eat and drink, plenty of killin' an' plundering. *Rurales* are supposed to patrol the countryside. They're a law unto themselves. If they sniff out a revolution in the making, they have that red flag. They round everyone up and shoot them. If there are red flaggers among the federal troops, no matter who won that battle down there, you can bet your boots no matter who comes chargin' up here, *rurales* won't be far off."

"Government troops?"

Marshal Severn's smile returned, without a shred of humor in it. "Amigo, you got a lot to learn about the country down here." He rose, still smiling. "If you find Ortiz, let me know. I'd take that kindly, since right now, if it's the Ortiz I know, I'd sure like to have a talk with him. You understand?"

Brett nodded, tipped his hat down, and left the marshal's office.

The smell of smoke was still in the air but not as noticeable as it had been. He struck out for a saloon on the opposite side of the roadway. When he got up there, the big old dingy room was full of armed men who seemed to be all speaking at the same time. There was no point in lingering—they were gringos—so he returned to the roadway, watched two gray-headed Mexicans disappear between two buildings, and he followed. The dogtrot was empty.

He passed through and emerged in Mex town, where the agitation may have been just as bad, except that there were very few people around. But there were saddled horses in front of several adobe buildings, and there was also a low but discernible hum of voices whose words were unintelligible to Brett Kandelin. It sounded like the humming of a million bees.

Two Mexican women appeared, stared, and fled among the *jacales*. An old man the color of wet mud, with a full thatch of gray, nearly white hair, laughed from the shadows of a porch. He said, "*B'dias,* vaquero," and patted the seat of the same wooden bench he was sitting on.

Brett went over, sat down, shoved his legs out, and eyed the old man wryly as he said, "Mister, if you can't speak English . . ."

The old man laughed. "Everyone speaks English, señor. Some don't want to, some won't." He shrugged. "I am eighty years old. At that age, a lot of very important things are—very truly—not important at all. You are a human being. I am a human being. *Cojones,* amigo, my days are limited. Your days will be longer, but in the end we both go somewhere else . . . and we will look back and shake our heads. *Comprende,* vaquero?"

CHAPTER 3
No Way Out

Brett introduced himself, watching the old man. The Mexican nodded without offering a hand. "I am Ramon Velarde," he said, and leaned to rise. "Wait. I'll be right back."

As Brett sat under the warped old *ramada* scanning the empty plaza, the racks where horses patiently waited, he couldn't avoid noticing the contrast: here, it seemed, there was less resolution than in gringo town—at least there was less activity. The dusty roads among the houses were empty, people were only infrequently in sight. The ones he saw moved furtively.

The old man returned with two old tin cups full of dark wine. As he sat down, he handed Brett one cup and said nothing until they'd both sipped; then he gestured with a work-roughened hand. "Everyone hides." He pointed to a large, massive adobe structure with a skinny askew cross atop it. "They'll be in there telling their beads, groaning and praying. The women, maybe some children. You see that place where all the horses are tied? That's the cantina. The men will be there."

There was something about the old man that reminded Brett of Marshal Severn—a kind of fatalistic acceptance that was reflected in calmness while everyone around them was in a panic.

He said, "You are a stranger?"

Brett told him about what he'd told Eames and the town marshal. Ramon sipped wine, watched a bob-tailed lizard stop and cock his head at the seated men, then disappear in a tiny puff of dust.

"Ortiz y Duran? *Gil* Ortiz y Duran?"

Brett looked sharply at the old man. He hadn't mentioned the first name. "You know him?"

Velarde barely inclined his head. "I was born here. I've lived here all my life. Yes, I know Gil Ortiz." He put a dead-calm gaze upon the other man. "So he wanted to buy your cattle? Tell me, friend, did Gil Ortiz give you money in advance?"

Brett felt uncomfortable. "We shook on it," he said, and saw the old man's eyes crinkled in wry amusement. "Is Ortiz in town?"

Velarde regarded his tin cup while replying, "I don't know. I don't think anyone who doesn't live here, who doesn't have a store or a family here, hasn't left. You know about the battle at Ciudad Morales?"

"Yes."

The old man drained his cup and put it aside on the bench. "You've seen the panic in Coyotero? They will come. They always come when they are this close to the border, maybe full of mescal or pulque. They came forty years ago and killed my wife and sister. Amigo, forget the cattle and ride hard away from this place." The old man smiled again, eyeing Brett Kandelin. "Unless you don't care. When they come they will yell '*Viva el muerte.*' It means 'Hurray for death.' Well, you can sit with me and wait, if you like. But I don't think you will meet Gil Ortiz." Velarde paused again to gaze at his companion. "I don't think he meant to buy your cattle. You see, amigo, Gil Ortiz is in the service of the *pronunciados,* one of their high officials. Yes, I know him. They always need herds of cattle. If Gil Ortiz met you somewhere and agreed to pay for the cattle when you delivered them down here, he meant for the *pronunciados* to come and take them from you, amigo. Gil Ortiz will be with them. He will have told them how he talked a gringo into delivering fat cattle down here, and they will all laugh. . . . But, while everyone is now wondering *if* they will come, now you and I *know* they will come—for the cattle."

The old man was echoing the hotel proprietor, Jess Eames. Brett left his cup half empty on the bench as he stood up. "Mr. Velarde, I got two men out there with the cattle."

"Take them with you," the old man replied, looking up from very dark eyes, "and ride." Then he shrugged. "The *pronunciados* will get the cattle whether you leave and stay alive—or whether you stay and get killed. Amigo, Gil Ortiz is very *coyote*. Very clever. He and the other officials of the revolution will have something to laugh about for years. They made a fool out of a gringo."

A surprisingly handsome woman, with wings of dove gray at both temples, came soundlessly around the side of the little *jacal* and stopped stone still at the sight of Brett. They regarded each other for a moment, both startled, she by his presence, he by her beauty. Then she ignored Brett to say something to the old man in Spanish. He nodded slightly and stood, looking slightly apologetic as he spoke in English. "My granddaughter. Lillian, this is Señor Kandelin. Amigo, this is Lillian Velarde." His eyes twinkled. "Just one name, like you. But in Mex town she has two names: Velarde y Pacheco."

Brett smiled and nodded, but the handsome woman neither smiled nor acknowledged the introduction. She instead spoke in Spanish again, and stood waiting for her grandfather to move. The old man remained in place, eyeing Brett. Eventually he spoke again.

"Let me tell you, I know how you feel. They came years ago and stole all my sheep and goats. I could never build up another herd. But I was still alive." Velarde smiled as he turned away.

Brett watched them pass from sight around the west side of the little adobe house. He considered his half-empty cup, drained it in two swallows, and strode back up through the narrow opening between two buildings. Brett emerged into the other world, where people were constantly moving, talking, cursing, raising dust in the roadway, and crowding in front of the marshal's office.

Two riders on lathered horses loped into town from the south, gray with dust, and slid to the ground in front of the jailhouse. They shouldered through the crowd and disappeared inside.

Brett entered the general store. It was also crowded—with what impressed Brett as a multitude of frightened, leaderless, and confused chickens, not customers.

He caught a harried clerk, told him what he wanted, and leaned on a counter as the clerk gathered his supplies. Out the store window Brett could see Marshal Severn across the road southward, talking to the pair of haggard horsemen who had arrived on spent horses.

When the clerk piled the supplies on the counter, Brett told him to sack them and put them behind the counter, that he'd be back from them directly. Then he walked briskly up to the saloon for two bottles of whiskey.

Up there the noise was less, there were fewer customers along the bar, and the proprietor, who wore elegant pink sleeve garters above both elbows, eyed Brett as the money was changing hands. The man said, "Ain't no escape in them bottles, friend."

Brett nodded but did not respond, and returned to the roadway on his way to get his sack before heading toward the livery barn for his horse.

As he was tying the sack behind his cantle, several men walked down the gloomy runway. One of them was Marshal Severn. He recognized Brett, watched him tie the sack, and said, "Wouldn't mind bein' in your boots right now, Mr. Kandelin."

Brett's reply stopped the lawman's companions. Even the hostler turned from what he was doing. "I'm not running, Marshal. I found out about Ortiz. He promised to buy my cattle if I delivered them down here, and I brought them down, and that son of a bitch is one of the rebels or whatever you call them, an' he's going to come up here to take my cattle. Marshal, you want to sit on your butt, you go right ahead. I'm goin' to find Mr. Ortiz and yank him inside out."

No one said a word until Brett was leading his horse out of the barn. One of Severn's companions, a lean, weathered, and lined older man called up front: "How many men you got?"

Brett turned to answer. "Two."

They all stared at him, but not another word was said as he mounted and turned northward, leaving a town of bedlam behind him.

He made good time by alternately loping and walking. His cattle were full as ticks; a few dozen grazed, but the majority were chewing their cuds in thin shade as he rode past.

Enos and Hale Barlow were standing beside their mounts, watching him approach. He'd been visible to them for more than a mile. He came up, swung off his horse, and without a word untied the bundle behind his cantle. Enos said, "You find him?"

Brett dumped the sack and glared. He told them what Ortiz had done, why he had done it, and that if there was anyone down in Coyotero who still believed the *bandoleros* were not coming, Brett knew a damned sight better.

The youngest man said nothing as he knelt to empty the sack. When he found the bottles, he handed one to the dark man and put the other one aside in favor of a tin of peaches.

Enos did not open the bottle but held it while gazing at Brett Kandelin. After a while Enos asked, "You want to head them back? Maybe we could make it. Where are them Messicans? How far down there?"

Brett had no idea where the Mexican revolutionaries were, but he told them what he did know. If they turned north and stampeded the cattle, sure as hell the *pronunciados* would find them. The animals were one of their objectives in riding north of the border.

Enos's next question was: "How many are there?"

Brett sank to the ground to eat as he replied, "A whole damned army of them."

Enos also sat down. For a while they ate in silence. Eventually Hale asked what Brett thought should be done—and got an answer that made his eyes pop wide open.

"You two forget the cattle and head north. If they don't see you, you'll get away. I don't think they'll care a hell of a lot even if they see you. They want the cattle. . . . Me, I'm going back down there. We rode dang near the full length of this damned territory to get down here, and we did it in good faith. I'm going to find Ortiz. He's going to keep his word, pay me for the cattle, or I'm going to make him wish he'd never seen me."

Enos and Hale ate in silence. The sun moved, and more heat beat down on them. A pink-and-dark-striped Gila monster came waddling along, seemingly either unaware of the seated men or indifferent to them, and when it was close enough, Hale kicked dirt over it. The Gila monster sucked back, made a threatening hiss, and waddled more quickly in a different direction.

Hale saw Enos watching him. The younger man said, "Ugly damned thing."

Enos agreed. "Yeah, he is. An' if he'd bit you, you'd be dead by tomorrow."

Hale chewed a moment, squinted in the direction of the sun, swallowed, and said, "What the hell makes anyone want to live in such a country? Lizards are poisonous, rattlers under dang near every rock. Spiders with hair on 'em as big as a man's fist—and them damned Mex brigands."

He did not get an answer.

Enos was stuffing supplies into a capacious pair of army saddlebags when he said, "It bothers the hell out of me to leave these cattle for some renegades to get." He was buckling straps and continued, "I done rode my cheeks sore, got stormed on, missed eatin' a few times, an' covered two-thirds as much hostile countryside as a man had ought to have to cover. For nothing. So some son-of-a-bitching revolutionaries, or whatever they're called, can come up an' take the cattle—an' for all I know maybe my horse an' outfit, too."

Neither Brett nor Hale spoke.

Enos finished with the saddlebags, then resumed his seated position. Facing them, he lifted his old forage cap, reset it, and scowled at Kandelin. "I figure Mr. Ortiz owes me, too."

Brett raised his eyes. "You'll get your wages."

The dark man glowered. "Wages? I know I'll get my wages. You think that's what's troublin' me? No, sir, it ain't. I didn't say anythin' about wages, an' I wasn't thinkin' of them. When a man's been put out like that Messican done to me, I take it personal."

Brett hadn't shifted his gaze from the dark man's face. He seemed almost ready to grin. "Listen to me," he said to Enos. "You and Hale go back. Get out of this damned country. Just turn north and—"

Enos bristled again. "Wait a minute. You're better 'n me, is that it?"

They exchanged a long look before Kandelin suddenly laughed. This had happened between them before. Every time Enos wanted to win an argument, he said that. Brett knew why he said it now, and he laughed.

"No, I don't think that. And I know what you're doing. Take Hale and get away from here. Wait a minute—let me finish. We're going to lose the cattle. I know in my bones that's going to happen. Enos, it's my herd, my loss, and I'm the feller who wants a settlement. You and Hale—"

"Hale ain't a child that's got to be mothered, an' maybe you own the cattle, but I've had to stare at their rear ends so long on this drive I can dang near call 'em by name from behind. You think you're better 'n me, so you're goin' after this double-crossing Messican all by yourself—like I ain't got a right to a piece of his hide, too."

Brett picked up the opened bottle, swallowed twice, passed it to the dark man who also drank. Then Brett threw his head back and laughed. Enos watched him for a while, then grinned, fished for his plug of Kentucky twist, and winked at Hale as he said, "You got to go back by yourself."

Hale did not quite understand what had just transpired, but after listening to Enos's passionate anger, he was roused enough to scowl back at the dark man as he said, "Go back hell. I wouldn't go all the way back up that trail again for a hatful of silver dollars."

Enos made a gesture toward Brett. "Just where is this Messican?"

Brett had already explained about Ortiz's association with the *bandoleros*. That was all he knew. "Somewhere down yonder, Enos. Maybe on his way up here with his damned route-army."

"An' we're goin' to ride through the army, find Ortiz and . . . There's got to be a plan, Brett."

There couldn't be a plan until they knew more. He eyed the dark man and the youngest man and sadly shook his head. "This won't be like getting treed by an old mammy cow with a new calf. I don't know about Messicans, but I know about skirmishes with Indians. You can double the size of the biggest war party you ever heard of, and that's about what's on its way up here to take the cattle, kill folks, maybe burn the town, and play some game they call *ley fuga*."

Hale scowled. "What's that?"

"They stand in the road with their rifles, tell folks to run for it, and shoot 'em in the back."

Neither Hale nor Enos took their eyes off Kandelin's face for a long moment. Then Enos spat, and Hale Barlow blew out a ragged breath before speaking quietly. "Everybody?"

Brett thought so. "That's the idea I got. Everybody. Women, children, old people. Everybody."

Hale stared at his scuffed old boots for a while before speaking again. "You figure you're going to lose the cattle anyway, Brett?"

"Yes."

"Well, suppose you traded them to the revolutionaries if they'd leave the town alone."

Enos scowled but said nothing because Brett spoke first. "Hale, they're going to get both. They don't have to trade. They most likely wouldn't trade, anyway. They got no reason to."

Hale looked around for the bottle. It had already been stowed inside Enos's saddlebags. He looked at the position of the sun, then around the countryside, where dozing cattle were lying in thin shade. The older men could see in his dawning expression that he finally and fully understood their predicament.

Hale surprised both the older men. He stood up, beat dust off, and said, "If we're goin' to buy into this mess . . . If them Messicans is close, they might could get between us an' the town, then we could lose more'n the cattle. Let's go."

Enos and Brett exchanged a brief look as they got to their feet. It did not take long to get back in the saddle. Hale took one last look back at the sleek, resting, totally unsuspecting cattle. His companions could not bear to do the same.

For half the distance to Coyotero not a word was said. Brett and Enos rode like men in a black trance. Hale's alertness pulled them back to reality when he raised a gloved hand and said, "What's that?"

It was a straggling train of wagons piled with household goods, children, even crates of chickens and pigs, being accompanied by older children and a few mounted people driving bands of noisy sheep and goats.

Brett thought the fleeing people should have left a day earlier. He passed to the east of them, with no one on either side raising a hand.

Enos was half a mile past when he said, "Better not to have children and womanfolk down there if there's goin' to be a fight."

Neither of his companions agreed or disagreed. They slouched along, as silent as rocks, watching rooftops against the horizon.

The departing people were a long, thin line, without order, without conversation, a great many on foot, some burdened with small children.

Enos was probably right; these kinds of people would certainly be in the way if there was a fight. It was still unpleasant to watch them moving with their backs to their homes, businesses, relatives, their lifetime accumulations of personal treasures left behind in abandoned *jacales*.

The sun had passed its meridian. Brett squinted at it, then returned his gaze to the dusty town as he did some mental arithmetic. If the Mex town where the battle had been fought was something like fifteen miles below Coyotero, and if Coyotero itself was no more than six miles from the border, the Mexicans, whichever side they belonged to, surely had had enough time to be approaching Coyotero. They would probably be in sight within another hour or less, depending on when they'd finished murdering and looting at Ciudad Morales.

CHAPTER 4

Waning Day

When Brett reached Coyotero in the afternoon, the changes were particularly noticeable. He wondered if they hadn't had something to do with whatever those two haggard riders on spent horses had told Marshal Severn.

Main Street was alive with armed men. There were a few women out there, too. Merchants had boarded up their windows. Some had padlocked their doors, but the saloon man hadn't. He was standing out front, pink sleeve garters, respectable paunch, and all, with a shotgun cradled in his arms as he and several townsmen engaged in what appeared to be a heated discussion.

The liveryman greeted Brett with his broad, false smile and wagged his head. "Just barely can get you fellers in. Folks been arrivin' from the countryside all day. Mostly Messicans that got little cactus ranches hereabouts." His smiling eyes fastened on Enos, then slid back to Brett. "Thought you was quittin' the country. . . . Most likely you should have. The story that's goin' around is that some red flaggers joined the *bandoleros*."

They handed the man their reins and returned to the roadway. Hale Barlow was wide-eyed. He'd seen trouble, had in fact been born into an era of trouble, but he'd never before seen it on this scale.

They went over to the cafe, which wasn't as crowded as Brett expected, and got seats at the counter. When the sweating proprietor came paddling along, he looked stonily at Enos Lee until Brett said, "Supper, friend. For three of us. What's the latest on the *bandoleros*?"

The cafe man blew out a breath. "You can hear whatever you want to hear, mister. Latest thing I heard was that they got artillery along, are maybe a thousand strong, an' have already raided every ranch between us an' the border. Killed everythin' they couldn't eat." The cafe man swung a sidelong glance at Enos again before finishing. "They ain't far off."

"Mr. Severn got scouts out, has he?" Brett asked.

"I expect so. What we need is the army."

Brett nodded about that. "Three suppers, friend," he said again. "And we could use the coffee right now."

This time the cafe man did not look at the dark man as he moved away. Coyotero was noisy even this late in the day, or perhaps because defenses were being pushed. Men came and went during the meal. If they noticed the dark man they gave no indication of it, and Enos leaned to speak knowledgeably about that. "You ever notice it don't matter who a man is if folks are in trouble?"

Brett grinned. "Never noticed. This stew taste like burro meat to you?"

Enos nodded. "At least it don't have red peppers in it." That had been the first thing the dark man had taken a dislike to once they'd gotten into the south desert. Hell, even breakfast was flavored with red peppers!

The burly man from the hotel barged in from out front and then halted to stare at Brett Kandelin's back before approaching the counter. He leaned in to say, "If you don't figure to use that room . . ." He stopped in midsentence because he had just noticed the man sitting north of Kandelin. Then he completed his remark. "I could've rented it a dozen times. Town's fillin' up with folks from out yonder."

Brett smiled. "I figure to use it, Mr. Eames. We'd like two more rooms if you got them. For my friends here."

Again the burly man's gaze jumped to Enos Lee. He hadn't noticed Hale. When he replied, he told the truth. "I don't even have a cot left to rent out."

Brett continued to smile. "I'd like to borrow your hammer, Mr. Eames."

The burly man's brows dropped a notch. "My hammer?"

"To yank the nails out of that back-wall window."

The burly man stepped back, refused to even look at Brett, and called to the cafe man: "Jake, the clerk at the store sent me to tell you if you need anything from down there you'd better hurry up an' get it. They're goin' to bar the place tight pretty soon."

Jess Eames did not await an answer. He walked out of the cafe without a glance or another word.

The cafe man brought three platters, put them down, and scowled in the direction Eames had taken. "How in the hell am I supposed to go down to the general store to stock up when I can't leave my kitchen for ten minutes?"

Hale asked if the cafe man had enough grub and got back an irritable response. "How the hell do I know? Not if they all get hungry at the same time."

Enos was wiping his mouth with a soiled cuff as he said, "You tell me what you want an' I'll fetch it back for you."

The cafe man's gaze settled on the dark man's face. He seemed to want to accept the offer, but stood in dogged silence until Brett told him all three of them would fetch back what he'd need. That finally got the cafe man's tongue pried loose from the roof of his mouth. "Anything they got that's in cans, an' sugar, flour, bakin' soda, salt bacon, an' beef. Anythin' else that looks like it can be made up into cooked grub." The cave man paused. "I've seen you before. You was ridin' north, out of town."

Brett nodded. "Came back."

"You're crazy," the cafe man stated. "Ain't you heard what's goin' to happen?"

Brett nodded and stood up, dumping silver on the counter. The three of them were at the roadway door when the cafe man called, "Go out back an' down the alley. Come along, I'll show you. They got the front door barred an' locked an' the winders boarded over."

Out back, where dust lay thick, the cafe man pointed to

the rear of a large building. "Beat on the door. Tell 'em Jake sent you."

The door they approached had been made to withstand a siege. It was a double thickness of oak, a variety of wood that did not grow within a hundred miles of the south desert. It was Brett's opinion that whoever had made the door, most likely back during the Indians wars, had probably done so as a result of bitter experience some time in his life.

Brett struck the door several times with the butt of his six-gun before the noise of someone lifting down bars was audible. When the door swung inward, a wispy older man peered out at them. He recognized Brett and asked what they wanted. He eyed the dark man with trepidation but allowed them all to enter. The clerk guided them through a rabbit warren of small storerooms to the darkened front of the store as Brett told him what the cafe man needed. The clerk got busy piling things atop the counter. He was nervous enough to keep a running, somewhat disjointed conversation going as he worked.

They could tell him nothing, and what he told them seemed for the most part to be farfetched. Particularly the story that the *bandoleros* and *federales* had joined forces to attack Coyotero, massacre its inhabitants, take everything they could carry, and torch the town.

They loaded up what the clerk had provided and let him precede them back the way they had come. When they were in the alley, they could hear him returning the *trancas* to their steel hangers.

Three heavily armed Mexicans appeared in the fading afternoon sunlight. Brett's arms were full, but the Mexicans nodded and walked on past. Enos was looking backward when he said, "How is anyone supposed to know the good ones from the bad ones? They all look alike."

Brett kicked open the cafe man's alley door, led the way to the cooking area, and put down his load. He could hear loud talk from the eating area and paid no attention to it until Enos and Hale had put down their loads. He thought one of those voices, deep, resonant, and unruffled, might belong to Marshal Severn, so he jerked his head and emerged from the cooking area to see five heavily armed men and the cafe man in the conversation, cups of coffee in their hands.

The big, older man saw them emerge, recognized Brett, and stared. Over the other noise, he said, "Thought you'd be ten miles away by now, Mr. Kandelin."

Enos answered, "Should be."

Marshal Severn studied the dark man, nodded, and said, "Anyone with a lick of sense would be for a fact," as he returned his attention to Kandelin. "Where are your cattle?"

"Up yonder. Three of us couldn't make much of a dent in an army."

With a slight nod, Severn accepted that, too. "You're not goin' to find Ortiz here," he said, retrieving his cup of java.

Brett's reply was curt. "I'll wait." He directed his next words to the cafe man. "Everything's on your worktable."

Before the cafe man could speak, Marshal Severn said, "Won't be much of a wait, Mr. Kandelin. They're coming. Finished wiping out Ciudad Morales this morning an' are on their way. I got a string of vedettes southward, with couriers to bring back the news." Severn drained the cup, set it aside, and moved clear of his companions. He jerked his head for the three drovers to follow him out into the roadway.

Marshal Severn was calm in the increasing anxiety around him. He watched the turmoil briefly before facing the drovers. "Any of you ever been in a fight like's comin' our way?"

Only two of them, Enos and Brett, had even been in skirmishes with Indians. Hale Barlow had never even been in one of those brief, limited confrontations. Brett's reply was short. "No, and I expect darned few other folks down here have. Unless they're old enough to have been in the Civil War."

Marshal Severn faced the roadway, where two men with lariats were dragging a small, ugly bronze cannon through the turmoil of Main Street. People cheered even as they had to get well clear of the center of the road because the little cannon, on its sled, did not follow the riders as much as it crab-walked from side to side.

Hale said, "That ought to make a difference."

Marshal Severn looked around before speaking. "Depends on what the *bandoleros* got. Early settlers took that from a Mex expedition years ago an' hid it until the Messicans left the country."

Brett watched the little gun's uneven progress as he asked if the cannon had been fired lately.

Marshal Severn said dryly, "Not since I been here. That's close to fourteen years. But we got powder, an' some of the lads are breakin' up iron to load the thing with. We got a gunner, feller named Hawkens, who was an artilleryman in the army."

A pair of dark Mexicans approached. They had holstered six-guns, big knives on the same shell belts, and were carrying carbines. Both of them were in their middle years, both looked tough and capable. They walked forward, looking curiously at the dark man. Then they ignored him to address Marshal Severn in Spanish.

Not until he had replied in the same language and the Mexicans had departed, did Enos repeat his earlier question. "How do you tell them apart?"

Big Bill Severn turned slowly to gaze at the dark man, turned away without saying a word. Ever since he'd been a child, he'd heard the same question asked about black people.

A band of armed men, walking in some kind of loose order, followed down the center of the road, and Bill Severn faintly smiled as he said, "The short one out front was in the army six years. I been told his highest rank was sergeant. He calls himself 'Colonel' Daggett. He's the town carpenter." Severn's faint smile lingered as he watched the marchers pass along. "Far as I know, he's likely the only feller in town who'll make money out of this mess. He's also the local coffin maker."

A hatless youth, shockle-headed and pale, rushed up, gesturing southward. "That feller you set atop the roof of the general store called down that he can see dust and horsemen. Hell of a lot of 'em, Mr. Severn."

"Go find out if he can see 'em draggin' cannon, Jamie."

The youth ran southward, and Marshal Severn spoke thoughtfully. "By my calculations, those lads we sent east to the army post had ought to have got there last night—unless someone caught them first. An' if they got there, by now there'd ought to be soldiers coming." He paused to look each of the three drovers in the face. "Unless, of course, the army's out patrolling in some other direction.

A large woman was herding two youngsters northward with a willow stick. Each time they'd turn to gawk, she'd give them a cut from behind. Brett smiled, and the marshal chuckled. "That's the blacksmith's wife. She can lift a barrel of flour off the ground."

A Mexican woman approached from the blind side. None of them noticed her until she held out a piece of paper and Marshal Severn turned to accept it. Brett recognized her immediately. She was Lillian, granddaughter of old Ramon Velarde. She did not take her eyes off the big lawman until he nodded and said, "Thank you." Then, as she turned to depart, she looked directly at Brett Kandelin. He smiled. She did as she'd done before when he'd smiled at her—she ignored him.

He was watching her leave when the big lawman said, "The Messicans made a contact southeast. She's the granddaughter of the local Mex alcalde, old Mex named Ramon Velarde." The big man put the crumpled note into his pocket. "They've been scoutin' since yesterday. They can get closer'n we can. Old Ramon's been through these attacks before. While the fight was still goin' on down at Morales, I went over to talk to him. It was his idea that they might not come up from the south all in one big group. He told me they may have no discipline, but they've been doin' this a long time. They know how to go out an' around so's when the front column hits us, they can come in from both sides."

Marshal Severn paused before continuing. "The folks over in Mex town figure to go out a ways, dig in, and set up a bushwhack." He paused again. "I got men doin' the same thing west of town, where the brush is thicker. . . . Gents, I got to tell you—when I was younger, my paw ran a string of trade wagons down into Mexico. He took me along so's I'd learn the business an' take it over, and right now I wish I had."

Hale had been making calculations while watching the town's anxiety increase as rumors spread. He asked how far the army post was from Coyotero, and when he got an answer it seemed to him that the army could reach Coyotero before nightfall. He said nothing about this, because Marshal Severn had already taken a different view—and at twenty, having your suggestions scorned was the worst kind of humiliation.

Two men, one wearing a sword, came up to take Marshal Severn away with them. The man with the sword eyed the drovers suspiciously. When he and the lawman were beyond earshot, Brett could see the sword bearer jerking his thumb backward and talking fast.

The sun was acquiring its late-day coppery shades, and shadows were beginning to appear on the sheltered sides of buildings. Brett led the way southward as far as the livery barn, where he and his men looked in on their horses. They met no one the full length of the runway, and went out into the back alley to consider the empty land.

Hale thought he could see dust, and perhaps he did see it, because at twenty his sight was better than the sight of older eyes, but neither Brett nor Enos saw anything.

Coyotero was getting quieter, the atmosphere of brisk preparation was less noticeable. There were fewer people on the plank walks, and there were no wagons, buggies, or even saddle animals the full length of Main Street.

For a while the three drovers remained out in the alley. The only noise they heard was from the town, the only dust came from a network of old pole corrals north of the barn, where horses milled restlessly.

Enos stopped in the shade to examine his six-gun. He had a cud in his left cheek. Hale was staring southward, still convinced the army could arrive in time. Brett rolled and lighted a smoke, also gazing southward.

"It's the waiting," he said half to himself.

Enos's reply was pragmatic. "We got to do it. Nothin' else to do. But they even got men atop the roofs around town. Looks to me like breakin' in might be mighty hard on these *bandoleros*."

Hale abruptly threw up an arm. Both older men stood perfectly still, looking southward. They still saw nothing. Hale hadn't, either. When he dropped his arm he explained. "Trumpets. Sounded like maybe six or eight."

Elsewhere others must have heard, them, too, because up in the direction of the north end of town a man's ringing shout from atop a building declared that he heard bugles. Now, finally, he could see a dust banner against the late-day sky, in the direction of the border.

CHAPTER 5

Dusk

Marshal Severn arrived in the vicinity of the barn with a group of men. He was detailing them for the defense when he encountered the three watchers in the alley. He seemed to want to incorporate them into his deployed defense force, but did not mention it, perhaps because when he'd finished placing his riflemen, the three drovers were strolling back up toward the main thoroughfare. He followed them until they all met out front. Brett said, "Looks like you're doing a good job, Marshal," and smiled a little. "If they charge in here, it's likely to cost them."

"It'll cost *us*," Severn said, "an' that worries me. We've got women an' kids and old folks. If you boys figure to stay, we can sure use you."

Brett nodded. "We'll stay. We work good together, but not so good split up."

"You could go over to Mex town. That's where folks think we got a weak link. I don't think so, but most folks do."

"They think the Mexicans'll side with the *bandoleros*?"

"Some of them do, yes."

"And you want us to go over there and maybe stand behind them?"

"Well, maybe . . . But go hunt up the old alcalde. He can tell you what's goin' on over there. Like I said, I don't think they'll be treacherous. All the same . . ."

Brett understood. "All right. Any other gringos over there?"

Bill Severn shook his head. "Not unless they went on their own. I sure haven't sent anyone over there. You boys be careful. If you need me, I'll be somewhere around." He was starting away in response to a shout from northward when he said, "Obliged, gents. If I come across Gil Ortiz, I'll keep him for you."

Brett watched the large man walk away, wondering why when they'd first talked, Marshal Severn had not wanted to admit knowing Gil Ortiz.

Enos cut into his thoughts. He was turning back toward the barn when he said, "We better get our Winchesters."

The liveryman was sitting in his dingy harness room when Enos led the way inside. The liveryman no longer showed his fixed smile. He looked a little green as he watched the drovers get their booted saddle guns and turn to leave. He said, "Fightin' em, maybe hurtin' a few of 'em, is goin' to make it so's the town can't surrender."

Hale Barlow's eyes got perfectly round. "Surrender?" he exclaimed. "From what we've heard, they don't give no quarter, mister. Makes me think folks might just as well die where they're standin', like they done at the Alamo back in Texas, because they're goin' to die, anyway."

The liveryman's eyes went to the far wall and remained there, even after the three men with Winchesters had departed.

Back out front, Hale said, "How many like him they got here?"

Brett replied dryly, "Not many, I hope."

Shadows were thickening as they walked along the east plank walk to the dogtrot Brett had used before. There were a few early lights showing, feeble yet because it was not quite dark. The town seemed to have entered a period of quiet. There were very few people in the roadway, where earlier there had been dozens. Northward, on the outskirts, an overloaded wagon listed perilously to one side with shattered spokes and a broken axle. The animal that had been pulling it had been removed from the shafts.

The exodus had dwindled until it had finally stopped altogether. The people still in Coyotero, less visible as the afternoon waned, intended to resist, probably hoping to hang on until the army arrived. They wanted to try their utmost to defend what was theirs.

In Mex town it was the same; people only infrequently appeared; the plaza, like the dusty streets among the mud houses, was silent and empty, as though Mex town had been abandoned.

In fact, when they emerged from the dogtrot, Hale said, "Ain't nobody here."

Brett led the way to the old man's three-room mud house, ducked under the overhang, and rattled the door with a fist. It was opened almost immediately by the handsome woman with gray at the temples. Brett asked for her grandfather. He was not at home, she told them, and made a gesture. "Some men came back. He went to the cantina to hear what they say." She stepped out, leaned, and pointed toward the distant building where Brett had seen many tethered horses on his first excursion into Mex town. "There," she told them, and stepped back to close the door.

As they trooped in the direction of the cantina, Hale wagged his head. "Not real friendly, was she?"

Neither of the older men replied.

Now there were no horses at the cantina's tie rack at all, and no loafers lounging outside. Inside, it was dingy and smoky. There were quite a number of men, all armed, most smoking dark little cigarillos, some with cups of liquor at hand. When the gringos entered, every head turned.

The alcalde recognized Brett and motioned for him to be seated at a large old table, where he and a number of other older men sat.

A thin man with rumpled black hair and very light skin sipped *cerveza* and waited. Ramon Velarde explained in Spanish who Brett was and why he had come to the south desert. The thin, fair man said something in Spanish most of the other men nodded about.

Velarde looked at Enos Lee as he asked in English who the dark man was. After Brett had introduced both his riders, the Mexicans continued to impassively regard Enos.

He wasn't uncomfortable. He'd endured stares like that most of his life. Sometimes, depending on his mood, he was annoyed. This was not one of those times.

A fat Mexican, wearing oversized sandals, flapped forward with a tray and placed three glasses of beer in front of the newcomers, then smiled broadly. Enos raised his glass and said, "*Salud,* amigo," and while both Brett and Hale stared at him, most of the room's other occupants raised their glasses, and some even smiled.

Finally, the fair Mexican picked up where the arrival of the strangers had interrupted him, switching to English as he said, "No more than about fifty." He shrugged. "Scouts. Maybe to steal horses or to come into Mex town after dark and scare us into joining them. But no more than about fifty. I got a million sand fleas before they rode away and I could dig out and stand up."

For a while there was no comment. Men gravely sipped from tin cups and trickled smoke. A large, pock-faced man broke the silence with a question in Spanish: "These strangers are here for why?"

Old Ramon answered, but in English. He explained about the cattle. He also named Gil Ortiz and told the others what he suspected was the reason for the cattle being down here—because the *pronunciados* had planned for them to be.

When he'd finished, the pock-faced man eyed Brett and smiled. In English, he said, "Everyone is in the same boat, eh?"

Brett smiled back, but addressed the thin man. "How long ago did you scout them up?"

A shrug accompanied the answer. "An hour. Maybe a little longer."

"Where?"

The thin man gestured. "East, and maybe a little south. I knew they were coming." His English was almost totally without accent. "One of them left the others and walked his horse very close to where I was buried. He was wearing a caballero's suit, but he was no caballero. He was a peon, dirty and unshaved, with a scarred chin. To me, in the shadows he looked like Señor *Satán. Muy matador.* You know what that means? A killer.''

The thin man's lips faintly lifted. ''I was afraid. I would have wet my pants—except that I hadn't had a drink of water all afternoon!''

The room sounded with laughter, which the thin man accepted as his due, and when it had subsided he addressed Brett again. ''They will be out there. Maybe more will join them. They will wait for darkness. I think, amigo, they will rest a few miles away, maybe eat and drink whatever they've brought along. . . . There will be a signal, maybe a gun in the dark, then they will come. Maybe more will hear the gunshot and come into town from the west.''

As the thin man stopped speaking, old Ramon, trickling smoke up his face, spoke next. ''Someone has to go tell the marshal.'' He waited for a volunteer, and when no one stood up, he shook his head. ''Listen to me, all of you. We can't do this alone. Neither can the gringos. This is our place. Coyotero belongs to all of us.'' The old man stopped, looked at Enos, pointed at him, and said, ''You see? This will be everyone's fight.''

Enos was regarding the old Mexican with an odd look, but he kept silent as a man stood up, nodded, and walked out of the cantina.

The other men shifted, drank, looked at one another, and seemed to be about to leave. Brett stopped the movement when he said, ''How many of you can ride tonight? If you wait until they charge in here, it'll be too late. How many?''

A long silence ensured. Men looked at one another, at Brett and his companions, at old Ramon the alcalde. It was the fair, thin man who finally spoke. ''Ride where, amigo? He knew where when he asked the question.

''Out where those *bandoleros* are.''

''Señor, I saw fifty. By now there could be a hundred. How many of us can ride tonight? Twenty, maybe thirty, but that has to include some old men, some very old men.''

Brett replied shortly to the thin man, ''Do you want to sit here and get shot, or maybe have your throat cut, or maybe run for *ley fuga*?'' During the unpleasant silence that settled in the smoky, dingy room, a younger man, who was dark and graceful, stood up holding his beer glass. "The *gachupín* is right. There are not enough of us," he said. "Maybe they would sneak around behind us. We would all be killed. Señor, bring some gringos from the other town. The alcalde said we can't do it alone, and he is right."

As the young man sat down, Enos growled into the silence, "I never been around Messicans very much." He glowered around the room. "Do they always talk a lot, like you're doing'? Because if they do, an' them fellers from below the border don't—what you just heard is goin' to come true. While you're settin' and arguin', them gents is goin' to sneak in here and slit your damned gullets."

Enos stood up. The room was utterly still. He gave them a contemptuous look and started for the door. Brett and Hale were starting to rise and follow when a Mexican rose from one of the little tables to bar Enos's departure. He had a fierce mustache and a very large knife shoved into his shell belt on the left side.

He was as tall as Enos and broader. He waited until the distance between them was less than eight feet, then he said, "*Mi conoce?*" and Enos stopped and stared.

"Mister, I only know English. What did you say?"

The Mexican switched. "Do you know me, black man? I know you."

Enos's scowl returned. "I never saw you before in my life."

The Mexican's black eyes did not waver or blink. "I was in El Paso one time and you robbed me there. You hit me over the head."

Enos looked around. Every eye in the saloon was on him. "Mister," he said quietly, facing the Mexican. "I never been in El Paso."

The Mexican's eyes shone in the gloom. "Liar! It was you!" One hand moved to the hilt of the belted knife.

Enos didn't wait. He lashed out, struck the Mexican in the chest, and as the man staggered back, the knife appeared. Enos did not hesitate. He tried for the knife wrist, missed, felt his shirtsleeve part as the slash came a hairbreadth from cutting his arm from elbow to wrist. Enos twisted sideways until the Mexican shifted to meet the threat from this new direction. He whirled back to strike the Mexican in the soft parts.

The Mexican grimaced and doubled forward. Enos caught him by the shirt, jerked his shoulder around. The sound of bone grating over bone could be heard as far as the bar.

The knife's fall was muted by the earthen floor, but its owner struck two chairs on his way down. One of the chairs was occupied. As the seated man went over backward with the other man atop him, he cried out, then kicked and pushed until he was clear, and swore in two languages.

Enos leaned over, lifted the astonished and furious Mexican to his feet, and held him at arm's length. He plucked away the man's six-gun and tossed it aside as he said, "Set down, amigo, an' shut up!"

The Mexican retrieved his chair, sat down, and felt his chest. He made no move to rise as Enos picked up the unconscious man's knife, shoved it into his waistband, and spoke into the deathly silence.

"You're a bunch of damned fools. You want to fight? Follow me out of here, any one of you or two at a time." He paused, but no one moved. He examined his torn shirt. "I'm goin' to sell this son of a bitch's knife to buy a new shirt, an' if I don't get enough from the knife to do that, I'm comin' back and an' break his neck."

He left the cantina, stopped out in the cool, fragrant evening until Brett and Hale joined him. Then he said, "I never saw that man before in my life, an' that's the gospel truth."

Brett asked if Enos was all right, and after getting an affirmative reply, he said, "Remember what you said—they all look alike to you?"

Enos's eyes widened. "That's what it was all about?"

Brett jerked his head and struck out back toward the dogtrot. They didn't quite make it. They were in front of the alcalde's house when the old man and two other Mexicans overtook them. Enos whirled with a snarl, but the alcalde held up a hand. "It was a mistake," he exclaimed. "The light was not good in the saloon. He thought he knew you."

Enos blew out a ragged big breath. "It was a mistake, all right. *His* mistake." He considered the old man for a moment. "How about you, mister?"

Old Velarde considered his reply carefully and smiled. "In my eighty years, señor, I've seen no more than six, maybe eight black men."

Enos looked at Brett and Hale. Brett made a little shrug, and the dark man wagged his head. "Well, maybe he thought I was the feller who hit him over the head. . . . He's goin' to have a bellyache for a few days."

The alcalde gestured toward his nearby porch and led the way. The Mexicans who had accompanied him from the cantina turned back to tell their story among the men at the saloon.

Enos sat in silence, massaging his knuckles. The man he'd knocked senseless had been wearing a shell belt with a large two-pronged steel buckle.

Velarde excused himself, and when Hale squirmed on his bench, Brett said. "He's gone after some wine." Hale was slightly mollified, but like Enos, he knew practically nothing about Mexicans. After what had just happened at the saloon, being among them made him apprehensive.

The old man returned with a tray holding four tin cups. Behind him, there was a light in the house. When he closed the door after himself it was no longer visible. He passed out the cups, seated himself, and offered salve for Enos's sore fist. The dark man shook his head, half drained his tin cup, and within moments had settled back on the bench, eyeing the old man.

Velarde got the conversation away from the recent fight by returning to the more serious problem. What the *gachupín* had said, he told them, was correct. In Mex town there were no more than probably thirty men to fight off the *bandoleros,* and before one of the others could ask what in hell a *gachupín* was, Brett put the question to the old man, and Velarde explained.

"A Spaniard. It means someone who wears spurs. Before

independence, only Spaniards were allowed to wear spurs. Since the revolution, anyone can wear spurs. Now it's not a compliment. Now it is a derision. But . . . time passes, eh?"

Hale rolled his eyes, met Enos's gaze, and both of them wagged their heads.

The alcalde, who had been through his share of attacks from below the border, made one more attempt to get the conversation back where he wanted it, without more diverting interruptions.

He said, "We were talking about the other times when you walked into the cantina. Some of the other old men were recalling things."

Enos grunted, but said nothing. He'd already told them they talked too much and did too little.

Velarde ignored the grunt. "Twice when the *bandoleros* came it was midsummer and we piled dry greasewood around in the night and fired it when they tried to ride into town." He gave Brett a mournful look. "But this is springtime. There is no dry greasewood."

Brett lowered the tin cup to ask what happened those times when the greasewood had burned. Velarde smiled in recollection. "Some horses got singed legs. They bucked and took bits in their teeth and ran way. A few men came back, but too few. We were waiting with guns." The old man shrugged.

Brett was interested. "Both times?"

"*Sí.* Yes, both times. But there isn't even enough dry stove wood now to—"

Brett jackknifed to his feet, put the empty cup aside, and said, "Thanks. Enos, Hale, let's go."

He did not speak again until they were back up in gringo town, with its brooding, bleak stillness, its very few lights showing, and its armed men in recessed doorways, and on rooftops, watching from dozens of hidden places.

One bright light was down at the jailhouse office, which is where Brett led his companions. This time there were no armed men milling out front. The lawman, inside at his desk, was alone when the three cattlemen walked in.

He looked up and rocked back as he said, "I thought you boys was goin' to keep an eye on things in Mex town."

Brett sat down, tipped his hat back, and asked how much gunpowder they had for that little ugly cannon he'd seen earlier.

Marshal Severn sat gazing at Kandelin for a long time before answering. "Enough. Why?"

"Is there a blasting-powder dump in Coyotero, Marshal?"

Again he got that long, quiet stare before being answered. "Not in town. City ordinance won't allow it."

"Beyond town, then?"

"Yes. Out near the graveyard, maybe a half mile from town. Why?"

Again Brett ignored the question to ask one of his own. "How much powder is out there?"

Severn pursed his lips before replying. "Last I heard, must be maybe five barrels. It belongs to the storekeeper. He sells it now an' then to folks who want to open up a water fissure, or blow rocks out of the way. There's a few gold hunters around. They use it for blasting holes in the ground. . . . Mr. Kandelin, just what the hell do you need all this information for?"

"The alcalde told me that years ago they turned back a couple of *bandolero* raids by piling greasewood around Coyotero and firing it when the town was attacked."

"I've heard that story. What of it?"

"If there's enough powder, we could make a couple of trails of it around the town a ways out . . . and when the *bandoleros* charge—fire it."

"Why two trails?"

"Maybe fifty yards apart, Marshal. The second trail to catch the horsemen who get through the first one . . . and by the light, your armed townsmen had ought to be able to aim pretty well."

Marshal Severn sat in silence for a long time. Hale was fidgeting before the lawman finally spoke. "We got to get hold of the storekeeper and find out how much powder he's got. An' if he's got enough, we got to organize details to go out yonder with buckets and string the stuff around the town, farther out an' closer in." Marshal Severn paused, again for a long time, before continuing. "I got men just beyond town, all around, watchin' an' waitin'. They got to be told there'll be men farther out making a dynamite rope around or someone's goin' to get shot."

The big man heaved to his feet with more agility than he'd shown in weeks. "It might work. It's sure as hell worth trying. Let's go roust up the storekeeper."

Brett rose. "You roust out the storekeeper, we'll go see how much powder there is."

Severn said, "The door's locked."

Brett smiled. "That's all right. We'll meet you back here directly. Where is the cemetery?"

"Go east. You can't miss it. The headboards show up good even in the dark. There's a little stone house on the north side—that's it."

CHAPTER 6

The Raiders

The marshal was correct; they could make out headboards and stone grave markers even without moonlight. By the time they could see the powderhouse, they could also sense that they were not alone.

Enos halted a short distance from the powderhouse, tapped Brett's shoulder, and jutted his chin without saying a word.

Moments later, Brett heard men speaking Spanish softly and sank to one knee. Enos and Hale did the same. The voices were in the vicinity of the stone building, but the speakers were invisible until they came around from behind it. There were two men, one with crossed cartridge belts on his upper body, one wearing what seemed to be a short jacket and some kind of visored hat, crouched at the powderhouse door.

The sound of a lock being opened was clearly audible. More men appeared, nearly all with the distinctive crossed shell belts, from which their name of *bandoleros* was derived. Several were leading what looked like horses, but in fact they were pack mules.

Brett turned toward his companions. "They beat us to it."

Hale commented on something the older men had also noticed. Hale said, "They had a key."

Enos grunted in a whisper, "Messicans!"

Brett turned back to listen. If he had gotten out here thirty minutes earlier . . . But he hadn't. Now the bigger question was how to prevent the raiders from carrying off the blasting powder and whatever it was they stoked the little cannon with, which was probably a very poor quality of gunpowder, colloquially called "Mexican coal dust."

The distant wraiths moved swiftly and soundlessly as they entered the powderhouse and emerged carrying small wooden casks that apparently were heavier than they looked. The carriers staggered to the place where other raiders were holding the pack mules.

Without a word, Hale slowly raised his Winchester and snugged it back. As his head was hunching down, Brett reached with a firm hand and forced the barrel down. "You'll blow us up along with them."

Hale scowled. "Dynamite don't go off without a fuse or a fire."

Brett continued to force the gun barrel down. "If there's just one fuse in there—"

"No one in his right mind ever stores fuses an' powder in the same place," Hale argued.

Enos whispered, "Maybe the storekeeper ain't in his right mind. Put the damned gun down."

A wiry Mexican almost fell under his load, and two other Mexicans caught him, steadied him, and muttered prayers aloud in Spanish. The raider in the short, tight artilleryman's jacket emerged from the house and swore at the wiry man.

The other *bandoleros* seemed to become more alert, more careful, and Brett wondered if the officer, or whatever he was, had discovered dynamite caps in the stone structure. He'd certainly acted like it when he'd sworn at the carrier.

The watching men counted nine casks and heard someone call for more animals. Brett turned to whisper to Hale Barlow, "You ever use dynamite?"

The answer was short. "Sure. Blowin' rocks and stumps up in Wyoming."

"Is there some way to detonate it without primers of some kind?"

Hale was scowling at the distant wraiths when he replied,

"Yes, but not from back here. A man'd have to cave in the top of one of them little kegs, lay a trail and fire it, then run like hell."

Enos looked at his companions and wagged his head. There were too many Mexicans over there, armed to the gills and alert. "Any other way?" he asked Hale Barlow.

"I told you—not from back here," was the bitter reply.

The Mexicans worked swiftly. They had emptied the stone house and were lashing kegs of powder to the mules—they were also getting a little louder, probably feeling safe as well as triumphant, until the man in the short jacket swore them into silence.

Brett felt helpless. Enos, too, was exasperated. He spat amber and leaned on his Winchester, silent, brooding, and worried. "If they got cannons along—" he muttered, but did not complete the sentence because one of the Mexicans swore loudly when a mule tried to bite him and the officer knocked him flat.

For seconds all activity stopped over in front of the powder magazine. Two raiders helped the dazed man to his feet as the officer cocked his six-gun, put it to the dazed man's temple, and hissed a deadly promise in Spanish.

After that there was not a word, not even when the kegs had been balanced, one on each side of a mule, and the chief *arriero* was turning to lead the first mule away. He looked at the officer, who nodded; the *arriero* nodded back and started walking.

Brett swore under his breath and stood up. He might have risked getting blown up if there hadn't been so many raiders. Too many for Brett and his companions to approach without being seen, and probably shot, before they could get close.

As the last mule disappeared behind the stone house where, no doubt, there were saddle horses, Brett wagged his head. Enos said, "We can stalk 'em," but Brett growled that it would not get back the little kegs and would only lead them into the arms of other *bandoleros* who, obviously, were all around in the night.

He turned back toward town.

They were on the outskirts when an abrupt rattle of furious gunfire sounded from the direction of Mex town. It stopped as suddenly as it had started. As they resumed their hike, Enos said, "They're like Apaches, sneak in after dark." They began watching on all sides, particularly when they got among the buildings.

Marshal Severn stepped out of a dark recessed doorway as they were passing and cocked an eyebrow. Brett explained, "They beat us to it. A mob of them were already out there loading the kegs."

"Broke the lock?" Severn asked, and received three negative head shakes as Brett replied. "One of them had a key."

Marshal Severn looked straight at Brett for a long moment before saying, "Son of a bitch."

Enos made a sarcastic statement. "You don't expect they brought that key with them, do you, Marshal?"

Severn swung his attention to the dark man without replying. He looked up and down the empty road when two more gunshots sounded, then faced back to say, "All right. Nothin' we can do about that. It was a good idea. You boys better get out of the roadway. They got a camp out yonder. I been waitin' for 'em to light a cookin' fire. If there's enough of 'em, they won't worry about us seein' their fire. But they got up here too late. I figure they'll mostly likely hit us come dawn. There'll be a few broncos sneakin' into town tonight. There's always a few skulkers."

Marshal Severn returned to his dark doorway, which happened to belong to the local saddle and harness maker. Like every other shop in town, it was dark.

Brett led his companions over to the cafe, but the door was locked from the inside, the interior black. They decided to turn up in the direction of the saloon, and had barely reached the site of a dogtrot, when a gunshot sounded from an overhead rooftop. It was answered by a hidden raider on the opposite side of the wide roadway, and Brett ducked down through the dogtrot.

When they emerged in Mex town, there was a faint scent of burned gunpowder in the still air. Hale Barlow made an astute observation. "They'll sure as hell feel easier about infiltratin' over here where everyone's the same color."

Enos made a death-head smile at the younger man. "They all look alike," he murmured, and under different circumstances Brett would have laughed. Now, he led off by keeping to the backs of buildings whose fronts faced Gringo town, using every shadowy advantage to reach the Velarde house. They drew no gunfire. In fact, a breathless silence lingered after the most recent exchange of gunfire.

Then a dog began to bark furiously, his position impossible to determine among the closely spaced mud structures. The barking ended as suddenly as it had erupted. Evidently someone, possibly the dog's owner, had taken quick, positive action.

They were among the *jacales* when several darkly flitting shadows appeared, disappeared, and reappeared as they glided among the adobes. Brett held up a hand to watch. The shadows were several yards ahead, obviously on a predetermined course.

Enos learned toward him to whisper, "The old man's house."

He was correct. As the wraiths progressed, they began moving closer to one another, converging the closer they got to the Velarde *jacal*.

Brett moved against a rough, dark mud wall and eased along it, nearly indistinguishable from his background except when he moved, which he did in fits and starts.

Enos and Hale followed his example until someone opened a door and pushed his head out. The doorway was between the dark man and the youngest one. The householder could see Enos's back because he was peering southward. The gun barrel that dropped the stranger like a stone came from the opposite direction. Hale stepped over the inert figure and tiptoed along.

He did not glance back, or he'd have seen the man he'd knocked senseless, facedown, arms extended, moving backward into the house as a stout woman pulled at his ankles while bitterly cursing him for having been overcome by curiosity.

Hale looked back when the door was closed. There was no sign of the man he'd struck.

Brett stopped to watch the dark shadows converge close by the alcalde's house, then move away as though they'd confirmed some earlier plan.

The house had a rear door and a front door. It was safe to assume that the people forted up in there had dropped *trancas* behind both doors.

Brett waited until two of the wraiths approached the rear door before fisting his handgun. If the door was stout, and the *tranca* firmly in its hangers, the skulkers wouldn't be able to get inside without a lot of trouble and noise.

Brett waited, watching as the door was suddenly pushed inward. He saw one Mexican lean back to sheath a thin-bladed knife. It finally dawned on him that a *tranca* could be very easily lifted from the outside if the person on the outside had a knife whose blade was long enough, and providing the door did not fit tightly to its frame, which no doors did in Mex town.

He grunted to Enos, who was directly behind him, and moved swiftly. One Mexican heard them and whirled, but his companion jumped inside into pitch darkness and froze in place, motionless and not making a sound.

The Mexican facing Brett and Enos had bared teeth and a wicked-looking knife in his fist. He wore a shell belt and holstered Colt, but he seemed willing to rely entirely on the knife . . . at least until his two attackers separated, with several feet between them. Then he hurled the knife at Brett and lunged for his six-gun.

Enos shot him from a distance of no more than six or seven feet. The muzzle blast shattered the night's long moment of silence. The Mexican was punched hard against the *jacal's* back wall and slid to the ground.

Brett picked up the knife and flung it into the house. A gunshot lanced in the direction where the knife fell. Brett leaned around the door to use the muzzle blast as his target, but did not react quickly enough.

The room was as black as the inside of a well. Brett and Enos exchanged a look from opposite sides of the door.

Brett took a chance that the uninjured assassin understood English, and without raising his voice told the man to toss out his weapons and come out, arms shoulder high, pointing in front.

The silence returned. The raider inside the house did not understand English. There was no reason why he should. Below the border, there was no English spoken, except in such cosmopolitan areas as Mexico City, and even there it was not widely used.

Around front, an attacker did not bother using a knife to get inside. He fired three times and blew the door open when impact tore the hangers from the adobe wall, allowing the *tranca* to fall to the floor.

This time gunshot echoes chased each other into the dark distance, making terrified people cringe in their houses. They also caused other gunshots to rattle in different places over in Gringo town. For a while a hot fight continued before silence returned.

Brett held up a hand, meaning for Enos to stay in place. He moved swiftly through the doorway, hugged a wall, and waited. He could see the man Enos had shot very clearly. Dark as the inside was, Brett's eyes, already accustomed to the night, made out objects; a narrow doorway led from the kitchen, where he was standing, to what he assumed would be the sitting room.

He wondered about Lillian and her grandfather—until the men in the outer room brought his attention back to the present very swiftly. They were looting, and they were not being very quiet about it.

Brett thought there had to be no more than three of them. He leaned out, beckoned for Enos to join him inside, and was already sidling silently along the wall when the dark man entered and took immediate advantage of the gloom.

It would have helped if either of the men in the kitchen had understood Spanish, because one of the raiders in the outer room suddenly exclaimed excitedly. His companions rushed to him and also spoke loudly and rapidly.

After that, the rummaging increased in haste and destructiveness. Brett used this period of obvious concentration among the raiders to reach the edge of the doorless opening. He ran the sweaty palm of his right hand down his trouser leg and regripped the six-gun. Behind him, Enos was sidling along the opposite wall. There was no sign of Hale Barlow.

One of the looters laughed and spoke. One word was distinguishable in the kitchen: "Whiskey."

Brett waited, crouched, until he thought they would be sharing the bottle, then he stepped into the opening. One Mexican was raising the bottle when he saw him in the doorway. He froze, his eyes bulged, he could not swallow and made a choking sound as Brett nearly deafened everyone in the house by firing point-blank. The range was too close for a miss. The man was knocked backward, almost to the far wall. The bottle broke on the floor and the other Mexicans were whirling to shoot back when another gun opened on them from the kitchen, this one over and above the crouched figure in the doorway.

It was a wild gun battle in darkness, with the disadvantage belonging to the looting raiders who were nowhere near the front door. Afterward, it made no sense to Brett that they hadn't fled after Enos's gunshot out back should have warned them. The only reason he could imagine why they hadn't been alarmed was because they probably had believed it was one of their companions firing.

Whatever their reasoning, with both Brett and Enos spraying lead, the raiders were more concerned with getting out of the house than in trying to be accurate as they fired at the men in the kitchen doorway.

One man made it. His companion was close when a bullet broke him in the middle. He fell facedown without moving.

Inside, the air was foul with gunsmoke. Outside, where people cringed inside their *jacales* and over in Gringo town, where other people listened intently, trying to decide whether the town was under a general attack, the sudden long silence permitted a slight easing of tension. Then there was one final gunshot.

That last shot had come from the corner of the Velarde house, where Hale Barlow had watched a man escape from the house. Hale shot him through the body as he was fleeing.

It was finished.

Brett and Enos went out the back way, the same way they'd entered, stopped to blink stinging eyes and regard each other. Enos leaned on the wall to punch out casings and reload from his shell belt. When he'd finished, he looked up with a wan smile. "I told you," he said. "They all look alike."

CHAPTER 7

"Do it!"

Men were stealthily infiltrating from Gringo town, led by Marshal Severn, to whom it had seemed a genuine attack was taking place in force. After a long lull of silence occurred, the lawman held up an arm to halt his companions. He selected one man and sent him to scout.

Enos and Brett found a wounded man. The others were dead. They carried him outside, put him flat down, and when he groaned something in Spanish they looked helplessly at each other. Brett knew no Spanish; Enos only knew two words of Spanish.

Hale came around to look at the wounded raider, then wagged his head as he straightened up. ''He ain't goin' to make it.''

Brett's head abruptly came up. He hissed his companions into silence. Moments later they all heard it, the sound of something as soft as moccasins approaching from the west. All three of them abandoned the wounded man and retreated back into the house to wait.

It was one of those incidents where a human presence could be ''felt'' without being seen or head—until the quiet stalker was directly behind the house. The stranger must have heard the wounded Mexican groan and, after a long pause, moved toward him.

Brett was near the east kitchen wall, where he had a slanting view of the wounded man. The newcomer was larger and thicker and stood gazing at the groaning Mexican. Then he sank to one knee, murmuring softly in Spanish, to which the wounded man replied in the same language.

Enos raised his six-gun, but he and Hale were against the opposite kitchen wall. They could not see the back of the house. Brett shook his head at the dark man and lowered his handgun.

Beyond, the newcomer and the wounded man spoke through intervals of silence, and Brett was convinced of one thing: Whoever the stranger was, he had not been born speaking Spanish.

Brett placed one foot ahead of the other, easing his weight down very gradually and repeating the process until he could see both men along the outside wall more clearly. He waited for one of their lulls to cock his six-gun, and at the same time to warn the kneeling stranger not to move.

The stranger obeyed, except that he turned his head and spoke in an almost aggrieved tone of voice. "It's Jess Eames. What'n 'ell are you doin' inside the old man's house?"

Eames had evidently recognized Kandelin. Brett waited a long moment before easing the hammer down as he let his breath out slowly. He said, "Come inside . . . and be awful damned careful, Mr. Eames."

The hotel proprietor rose and moved to the doorway, peering into the darkness. He saw two more of them in the kitchen and wagged his head as he stepped inside. His first question was: "Where's the alcalde an' his girl?"

Brett had no idea where they were. He countered Jess Eames's question with one of his own. "You alone?"

"No. Bill Severn's back there with a dozen men. Was it you three started the ruckus over here?"

Hale replied tartly, "Yeah, it was us. Where was the rest of you? Them bastards is sneakin' around all over the place."

Eames considered what he could see of the pale, youthful face. He then ignored Hale to turn back toward Brett—and made the only pertinent comment thus far: "Ain't no coordination. Darned wonder we aren't shootin' each other. You fellers better come back with me."

Hale asked another question, this time with a hint of steel in his voice. "What did the Messican tell you out yonder?"

Again Eames regarded the youthful face, which looked even younger in the gloom. "He said they was after the crucifix." At the blank look this statement got, he also said, "The alcalde keeps it until Sunday, then takes it over to that old mud church. He brings it back with him after sundown. Once, some In'ians stole it. They got it back and, ever since, one of them keeps it close an' guards it."

Brett abruptly turned to leave the kitchen. They heard him in the sitting room. When he returned, he was holding a large, beautiful old crucifix of heavy, solid gold.

Enos said, "That's what they got all excited about. They'd found it."

Brett shoved the crucifix inside his shirt as he addressed the hotelman. "You go on back. The old man an' his granddaughter may be hurt."

Eames stood a moment looking at them, then shrugged, and went soundlessly back out into the night. The stars, aided by a stingy old scimitar moon, gave very little light, and a slight chill was noticeable. It indicated that the blackest part of night was beginning to pass and dawn was only a few hours away.

Now, finally, there was silence, until Brett spoke to his companions. "How'd they know the crucifix was here?"

Enos answered dourly, "The same way they knew where to get a key to that damned dynamite house."

Hale looked from one of them to the other, then swore. "Sure as hell. Couldn't be no other way. They got a spy right here in Coyotero."

Enos repeated something he'd begun to say often in a tone of contempt: "Messicans!"

A night bird sounded outside somewhere. All three men in the house became quiet and alert. The night bird sounded again, and Brett shook his head. He doubted that it could be a bird after all the gunfire, but his knowledge of birds was very limited, and it certainly was a perfect imitation.

Hale whispered in the darkness, "I wish I'd stayed in Wyoming."

Neither of his companions whispered back.

The night bird called again. This time Brett moved toward the doorway to peek out and around. There was not a sound or any movement outside.

He was beginning to lean back when a quiet voice said, "Over here."

He recognized the voice, leaned to look out again, and saw her standing alone in a clear space northeast of the *jacal*. She was looking in his direction. When he appeared, she spoke again.

"They're gone. I'll walk over . . . if you tell your friends not to shoot."

He didn't have to tell them; they, too, had heard her voice, and without recognizing it, knew there was a woman out there instead of a *bandolero*. Hale whispered, "Who's she?"

Brett answered, without looking around, "She lives here with her grandfather. Her name is Lillian."

"Where the hell did she come from?"

Brett ignored the question and told the handsome woman she would be safe. As she started forward, Enos wagged his head. He, too, was baffled by her abrupt appearance. It was as though she'd come up out of the earth.

When she entered the house, the men stepped back. Like Hale Barlow, she looked younger in the gloom. She did not greet them or smile. She saw a dead Mexican and moved around him to enter the sitting room. The men followed. In the sitting room, she had her back to them as she stood staring at a small broken door in the wall. Brett said, "Was the crucifix in there?"

Instead of replying to the question, she said, "They got it," and turned to face the three men. "We heard them talking. They knew it was here and came to steal it."

Enos looked puzzled. "You heard 'em? Where were you?"

She was looking at Brett and did not respond to the question. "My grandfather has guarded it since it was stolen years ago by Indians. His father guarded it before him. It is a sacred image to the people in Mex town. It's very old. The first Spaniards who came here brought it with them. It was always kept in the mission, until the Indians stole it." She saw another dead Mexican near the front door and seemed dispassionately unconcerned. "This time we may never recover it."

Brett fished inside his shirt, brought forth the heavy relic, and held it out to her. For a moment she did not appear to be breathing, but she took it in both hands and raised her eyes to his face. He told her about the dying Mexican out back and his conversation with the hotel proprietor. "They had it," he said, "but the fight started. They must have dropped it. I found it on the floor."

Enos interrupted with a short question. "How did they know it was here?"

The beautiful woman held the relic to her chest. "Everyone knew my grandfather was the keeper."

"But they're from down in Mexico," Enos exclaimed.

Her reply was totally plausible. "People from here have relatives and friends down there. They go back and forth, have gone back and forth for years."

Hale Barlow, who was the least impressed, asked her where her grandfather was, and she turned to go back the way she had come. She led them out of the house on a northeasterly course and stopped where everything looked normal—except for what appeared to be a large round wooden object propped up off the ground. She leaned over to say something in Spanish, and Ramon Velarde crawled up out of the uncovered hole.

She showed the relic to him as he straightened up. His haggard face brightened immediately. She explained in Spanish how the relic had been saved, and the old man gave Brett a strong *abrazo,* which not only startled Brett, but made the eyebrows of Hale and Enos climb straight up.

Grown men did not hug grown men, they shook hands.

Enos stepped past and leaned over to look into the hole. Ramon was clutching the crucifix when he said, "My father made it many years ago. There were many of them for people to hide in when Indians attacked. In those days it was all we had. It was forbidden by Mexican law for people like us, *colonistas*, to own firearms."

The dark man turned slowly to stare. "How did you protect yourselves?"

Old Ramon shrugged. "With bows and arrows, but we never won. When I was young, every family had graves to kneel beside on days of worship."

Lillian lightly touched Brett's arm and nodded in the direction of the house. They followed her there. Hale and Enos dragged dead *bandoleros* outside, but could do nothing about the unpleasant smell of burned gunpowder.

Marshal Severn loomed in the doorway, gun in hand. Behind him were other men, including the hotel proprietor. Severn gazed at them all in silence. He took his time before speaking, which Brett had come to understand was part of his personality, and said, "If there were others, they've gone. You can light a lamp."

Ramon sat wearily on a bench. "I don't think there were others, *jefe*." He held up the big gold crucifix. "They were after this. They wouldn't tell the others."

Marshal Severn regarded the relic stoically. He'd seen it before, knew its history, and who protected it. He was not a religious individual, but he had no quarrel with those who were. "You better find a better hiding place," he told the alcalde, and faced Brett Kandelin. "It won't be long now. They're quiet out yonder, sleepin' it off, I expect." He was turning to depart when he also said, "I wish to hell you'd got them powder kegs before they did. . . . It's goin' to go hard with Coyotero come daylight."

Lillian lighted two candles, each in a niche in the wall. They failed to yield as much light as a lamp, but a lamp would give off light that would be visible for a considerable distance.

She built a fire in what looked like a mud beehive built into a corner of the kitchen. The men sat and talked without much enthusiasm; they were all tired. Brett watched the handsome woman; she appeared not to be tired at all. Once, when she turned and their eyes met, she almost smiled.

When they finished the meal, Enos yawned hugely and Ramon nodded. There were things that took more out of people than going without sleep. Terror was one, a fierce fight was another. He poured red wine into a tin cup for the dark man as he said, "Now we wait."

Enos drank the wine, nodded his appreciation, and rose to go outside. During his absence, the old man again thanked Brett for rescuing the old crucifix, and finished up by saying, "It is nearly dawn. If any of us are alive by nightfall of this day, it will mean there is gratitude—somewhere—for saving the relic."

Hale watched Brett roll a smoke and go to one of the wall niches to light it. Brett did not return to the table. He inhaled, then exhaled, gazing thoughtfully at the handsome woman. Suddenly he jerked his head at Hale and said, "Let's go."

Outside, Enos was leaning against the wall beside the *bandolero* who was now dead. The wine had done its work. He had been admiring the ageless heavens, no longer tired. When Brett jerked his head, Enos fell in beside Hale without saying a word.

It was still dark, but it would only be another two or three hours until daylight. The chill had increased. As they walked into Gringo town, they could smell smoke, not the tame cooking-stove variety but the wild aroma of greasewood, distinctive from every other smell.

A man came out of a doorway to speak to them. "You can't hardly see it now, but hour or so back you could." He pointed westerly. "Looked to be maybe a mile out. Maybe a little less. Was a big fire, too. Got to be a lot of 'em out there to have a big fire."

They went down to the jailhouse, but it was empty. Brett dropped his smoke and crushed it, moving to a worn old bench, where he sat down and leaned forward to study the sky. Neither of his companions said a word until he rose, jerked his head, and led off southward in the direction of the livery barn.

Down there, with no sign of the proprietor, they rigged out, still in silence, and led their horses up the alley before Brett halted and said, "I got an idea. The old man gave it to me. He's sittin' back there with his relic wondering if he'll be alive this time tomorrow."

Brett swung up across leather. As his companions did the same, the dark man spoke dryly: "You got a relic, partner?"

"No. I got an idea. Let's go."

"Where?"

"We aren't going to have a lot of time, Enos. We can talk later."

The dark man and the youngest one exchanged a look, said nothing, and followed Brett northward out of Coyotero. Once, when they'd dropped back to a walk after a mile or so of loping, Hale leaned over to speak to the dark man. "It's too late to turn the cattle and head north. If that's what we was goin' to do, we should've done it before the raiders got up here."

Enos said nothing.

They picked up the gait again until Brett held his arm up. The place where they halted this time had trampled feed, a powerful smell of cattle, and so much silence there was no room for sound

Enos looped his reins, dug out his lint-encrusted plug, gnawed off a corner, and looked around. He knew where they were. Not by detail, but in general. This was close to where they'd left the cattle.

He didn't believe Brett had rounding everything up and heading north in mind. But he had no idea why else they'd come back here.

When Brett signaled for them to split up, Hale said, "Turn 'em north?"

Brett's retort didn't do much to clear things up. "No. Make a big surround and push 'em all to this spot. Make a roundup. You go east, Hale. Enos'll go west, and I'll go north. If we miss a few it can't be helped. We don't have a hell of a lot of time."

Enos expectorated, his brow wrinkling in thought as he reined away without speaking.

Each man eventually halted to twist in the saddle, free his coat, and shrug into it. Hale told his horse he'd always heard deserts were hot as the hubs of hell. The horse didn't know about that—and wouldn't have care if he *had* known! His attention was on something up ahead that didn't smell like cattle to him.

As he responded to knee pressure, the horse kept his head up, little ears forward, and for a time his rider did not notice the obvious signs. The horse was better at things like this than the man. It ducked its head a couple of times, distended its nostrils, and faintly snorted.

Hale pulled out his Winchester, settled it across his lap, and waited.

It could be a panther out there, he thought, or some other varmint that horses feared. . . . But hell, horses were afraid of just about everything, including their own shadows.

He'd never heard there were panthers in the desert. Or bears, either. But whatever was out there had the full attention of his animal.

He swung off, tied the horse to a big bush, and went ahead on foot. The damned horse wouldn't have gone another hundred yards anyway before it balked. But his real reason for climbing down was that it made him uneasy to be sitting atop a horse like a target if there was trouble ahead.

It was a long walk, during which he startled a dozen cattle out of their bed. But when he'd covered what he estimated as a long country mile, and again encountered cattle, these animals were already standing up. They were also listening intently while facing eastward.

Hale stopped next to a flourishing thornpin bush. The hair on the back of his neck was standing up, but he still had not heard or seen anything.

Not until two Mexicans, recognizable by their huge sombreros and the size of the horns of their saddles—as large as a dinner plate—came very quietly in from the east, talking casually in Spanish, riding on loose reins.

Each of them had crossed bandoleers!

Hale had a moment to wish with his full heart he hadn't come here alone, but he had, and those damned border-jumpers, poking along though they might be, were going to pass within yards of his bush. Worse, very soon now their horses would detect the scent of his animal back yonder.

He very slowly sank to one knee, feeling the stickery bush at his back, and raised his carbine, unable to cock it because the sound would carry, but his thumb lay on the hammer and his finger curved inside the trigger guard.

He heard one of them rattle a long sentence in Spanish and caught one sound: "Ortiz."

The second man sounded scornful when he, too, spoke in Spanish. They were close enough, finally, for Hale to hear the whisper of saddle leather rubbing, the music of rein chains, the soft tread of hooves over dusty soil.

His thumb was ready to ease the hammer back when one of the men laughed and spoke in English. "This one is a fool. He shouldn't have listened to Ortiz. Now, we can't go back because the *federales* are waiting for us, and we can't go forward because the Yanqui army is up ahead. What the hell does he want the cattle for? Better we should scatter and go back one or two at a time."

The reply, also spoken in English, was short. "You know how he is. Always greedy, always looking for valuables to steal. After the battle at Ciudad Morales we should have gone swiftly southward. We could have regrouped. No, he listened to that *pendejo* Gil Ortiz and here we are, to start the cattle back when the others attack the town."

Hale made a wildly rash decision. He did not haul the hammer back until they were less than fifty feet east of him, and even then they probably wouldn't have heard the weapon being cocked because he spoke as he was aiming the Winchester.

"One more goddamn step and we'll blow your guts out past your backbones! Stop! Don't move! Keep your hands on the horn!"

The pair of horsemen stopped and sat stone-still, rolling

their eyes, certain they had ridden into an ambush by a host of enemies.

"Get down . . . slow . . . hands in sight, you bastards!"

The Mexicans obeyed exactly.

"Shed them weapons. Do somethin' silly and you'll be dead before you hit the ground. *Do it!*"

CHAPTER 8

A Long, Dark Night

He hunkered down with his pair of prisoners, eyeing them until one spoke in English. "Where are the others?"

"Ain't no others," Hale replied, the Winchester in both hands pointing at his captives.

One Mexican was fairly large, with a pockmarked face. He was shaggy-headed, coarse-featured, and rumpled. He said his name was Epifanio, and at Hale Barlow's pained expression, he broadly grinned and said, " 'Pifas."

The second Mexican explained that 'Pifas was the nickname of anyone called Epifanio. It advanced Hale's knowledge slightly, but right at this moment he was wondering how he was going to round up cattle and simultaneously keep an eye on these two.

The smaller Mexican was very dark, wiry, and after recovering from his surprise, studied Hale Barlow. He said his name was Francisco and smiled. "Who are you?"

"I'm Hale Barlow. Couple friends and me're roundin' up a herd of cattle."

The man named Francisco looked doubtful. "In the night?"

Hale ignored that as the pock-faced man held up a hand. A rider was approaching. They all listened. The Mexicans scarcely breathed. They had come up here alone, so whoever was approaching was not likely to be anyone who would help them.

Brett Kandelin appeared, stopped in his tracks for a moment—until he saw that the Mexicans had been disarmed and that Hale's Winchester was aimed at them. He swung to the ground and trailed his reins until he was close enough, then halted and asked Hale what had happened.

He listened, while looking directly at the Mexicans. Francisco smiled a little and spoke in nearly accentless English. "Nice to see you again, Mr. Kandelin."

Brett stood hip-shot for a moment, then remembered. These were the two Mexicans who had been with Gil Ortiz up on the northward plains, where Ortiz had contracted for the cattle to be brought down here.

He squatted down. "I thought I knew you two. Where are your friends?"

Francisco held out his hands, palms upward. "We came alone. We left the camp before the others were awake."

"Why?"

"To come up here, find some cattle, and drive them back. The food we brought from Mexico is almost gone. Our *jefe* sent us. Another man told him by now you would have the herd down here."

Brett had heard the word *jefe* before. It seemed to mean a leader. He asked who their *jefe* was, and again the wiry, very dark man replied. "*Coronel* Diego Rivera y Abelardo." The wiry man hesitated, then added a little more. "His aide is *Capitan* Gil Ortiz y Duran." He smiled as he pronounced the name. "You know him."

Brett nodded bleakly. "Yeah, I know him. Where is he?"

"At the camp. At least he was there last night when we were told to go bring back something for the men to eat."

The pockmarked, larger man spoke. "Maybe you don't remember me. My name is Epifanio. They call me 'Pifas." This man's English was excellent, too, but with a strong accent. He smiled at Brett. "You brought the cattle."

Brett's gaze swung to the larger man. "And Ortiz never meant to pay for them, did he?"

'Pifas answered forthrightly, "No," and continued to smile.

Hale stood up to dust himself off as he said, "We're wastin' time."

Brett also stood up. The pair of *bandoleros* rose, too, but slowly, carefully. Brett shook his head. "Tie 'em," he told Hale Barlow. "Tie 'em good enough so they won't get loose for a long time."

Hale casually said, "Shoot 'em. That way they won't never get loose."

The Mexicans looked swiftly at Hale Barlow, then over at Brett Kandelin. They probably had been expecting something like this since Brett had arrived. In Mexico, it was the custom not to be burdened by captives unless they could be ransomed, and even then, more often than not, once the ransom had been collected the prisoners were shot, anyway.

Brett glanced at the horses with the Mexican saddles, back to their owners, and was about to speak when the big man said, "I'll tell you something, *Commandante*. We were not going to go back with any cattle. We were gong to keep riding."

Hale scowled. "Liar," he growled, but the man named Francisco shook his head.

"No. It is the truth. We talked about it all the way up here. If our army retreats back into Mexico, there will be an army waiting. If it stays up here, the Yanqui army will come. *Coronel* Rivera was made a fool of by Gil Ortiz. All Ortiz wanted was to plunder Coyotero, take gold and silver, whatever was valuable. He would then simply ride away. *Commandante*, we are deserters."

As Hale had said, they were wasting time. Somewhere to the west, Enos would be drifting cattle toward the point of rendezvous. Brett made a decision that Hale clearly did not approve of. He said, "Throw those bandoleers away. You can help us round up the herd." He smiled. "If you try to desert us, too, we'll track you to hell—and for two days over the coals. Understand?"

"Where are the cattle, *Commandante*?"

"All around here. I passed some on the way over here."

"And you want to turn them away, turn them northward?"

Brett's smile lingered. "No. We're goin' to drift them southward." At the looks he got for that remark, he also said, "We're going to drift them west of Coyotero, until we see the fires of your friends, then we're goin' to stampede the cattle right over the top of them."

For seconds Hale and the pair of Mexicans stared in silence. Eventually the big man called 'Pifas gazed at his friend. When Francisco smiled, the big man smiled, too. Brett said, "Get on your horses."

Neither of the Mexicans knew the country, but in darkness it wouldn't make much difference. Both had been vaqueros and, most important to them, both were still alive. As for rounding up the cattle to be used against their former comrades, it did not seem to bother them at all.

But none of this was apparent until more than an hour later. With about five hundred cattle milling, Enos rode up beside Brett and jerked a thumb. "Who the hell are those men?" he asked, and listened with a dark look until Brett had explained. Then he rolled his eyes. "I'll take the point," he said. He did not want either 'Pifas or Francisco behind him.

The cold was particularly noticeable as they began the drive, and the sky was still black, which might have puzzled Enos, Hale, and Brett if they'd had time think about it. None of them owned a watch, and except for Brett, never had owned one. They lived their lives and ate their meals according to circumstances, not the hours of the day.

The cattle drove well, although unavoidably some managed to escape and turn back. Once Brett stopped the pockmarked Mexican from charging back to overtake some cutbacks. He told the Mexican it wouldn't be possible to keep all the cattle in sight, and that what mattered most was to get down yonder, not worry about losing a few head. 'Pifas understood, grinned, and turned back.

By the time they'd been on the trail for an hour, the cattle, accustomed to being driven before sunrise, plodded along. They were rested, full of feed, and phlegmatic enough to accept what they could do nothing about.

As they followed the dim figure of Enos up ahead, Brett

and Hale came together in the drag. Hale began to accept the fact that Francisco and his friend were not going to disappear in the night. He even said it made the drive easier having them along. He did not comment about the ease with which the *bandoleros* had changed sides, not even when Brett glanced back where the Mexicans were riding and said, "I got to believe they weren't real happy about bein' up here. But I guess I'd have to know more about Messicans to understand how they could toss in with us."

Hale turned away to hasten a few laggards and did not meet Brett again until shortly before they could smell greasewood smoke. By then the pair of *bandoleros* had already told Brett where the raider encampment was. When he asked how many there were, neither Francisco nor 'Pifas could give a reliable number. All they knew was that while some of the *bandoleros* who had hung back to plunder Ciudad Morales had not come up, it seemed to them that about half the *pronunciado* route-army was on the desert west of Coyotero. When pressed for a count, Francisco shrugged and seemed to pick numbers out of the sky.

"Three hundred, maybe six hundred."

Brett let the subject drop. If his plan was successful, it wasn't going to matter. If it wasn't successful, it probably wouldn't matter, either, because from what he'd seen in Coyotero, there were no more than perhaps a hundred or a hundred and fifty defenders, not enough to turn back five or six hundred.

Hale came out of the gloom wearing a frown. "How far west is Enos takin' us?" he asked Brett.

"The skinny Messican rode down and gave him directions."

That answer did not satisfy the younger man. "Hell, we're goin' to be three, four miles from town when we get down there."

Brett's reply ended the conversation. "Enos'll see their cookin' fires."

He was correct about that, but before Enos, who was at least a half mile from the men in the drag, saw lights, he heard men and animals. The *bandolero* camp was rousing.

He also looked at the sky, where the vaguest hint of dawn light was palely visible on the horizon, but it did not brighten the heavens directly overhead.

Enos thought it had to be close to dawn, and he was right.

He was also hungry. Even his occasional cud of molasses-cured did not entirely alleviate this condition. What drove the thought of food from his mind was men shouting in Spanish. He had no idea what was occurring in the sprawling raider encampment, but he pinpointed the area where most of the shouting was coming from and shifted direction slightly to bear on the noise.

The others eventually also heard the shouting. Hale went over to the pair of *bandoleros* to ask what the shouting was about. 'Pifas replied with a grin. "Some mules got away in the night. They have to pull the cannon sleds by hand. No one wants to help."

Hale's eyes got round. "Cannon? How many?"

"Three cannon, one little howitzer," 'Pifas said, and laughed at the fierce profanity coming from the raider encampment.

A few fires brightened as men rolled out hungry. The few fires became many, and they were still being kindled by the time Brett could discern what was the big, rough circle of the encampment.

He left Hale and the vaqueros and loped up until he found Enos. He considered the direction in which the dark man was leading the drive, and rode stirrup with Enos without either of them saying a word. They listened to the turmoil ahead and watched the little fires brighten to life.

The sky was still dark.

Enos turned up the collar of his old coat, got rid of a cud, and spoke while riding with both gloved hands at rest atop the saddle horn.

"I been tryin' to figure out those two *bandoleros*. They act like this is some kind of a game."

Brett's reply was short. "Maybe it is. I'll tell you one thing, they may have been aides to the son of a bitch who talked me into comin' down here, but they don't like him."

Enos wagged his head. "Can you figure them out?"

Brett couldn't. "It helped havin' them along," he said.

Enos was not ready to abandon the subject. "You reckon they joined us and been stayin' in the drag so's when we bust out the cattle they can shoot us in the back?"

Brett was unable to answer. The shouting in the Mexican camp became louder, but now it sounded like men were cheering, and that, to Brett, meant they were probably moving their guns—some straining to drag the sleds while others cheered them on.

He looked overhead, then ran an exploratory glance along the horizon. He was beginning to frown about the continuing darkness when the cheering stopped and silence settled. The raiders had dragged one of their guns, maybe all three of them, within firing distance of Coyotero.

He stood in his stirrups to estimate the distance to the fire-lighted camp. Someone down there blew a bugle, not very well but well enough. *Bandoleros* turned back to eat before launching their attack. Brett eased down in the saddle. "I don't know much about soldiering," he told the dark man. "But if I was their officer—"

"You wouldn't waste time. Hell, they had all night to maybe surround the town or sneak in among the buildings," Enos exclaimed. "Brett, I'm beginnin' to wonder if they're soldiers at all."

Of course they were not soldiers, at least by most definitions of the term. But among themselves, having beaten an occasional federal army, plundered and destroyed towns, become loaded down with whatever they had taken as prizes of war, they considered themselves soldiers.

When Brett halted and raised his arm for the men in the drag to stop crowding the cattle, Enos leaned on his saddle fork, squinting and listening. There was still noise down there, but not the kind of noise there had been when men were doing the work of mules, pulling cannon sleds by hand.

A man rose up from the ground within pistol range and called to someone named Chato. Another *bandolero* answered some distance off. "*Que?*"

The first man rattled something neither Brett nor Enos

understood, although they both knew the sounds of astonishment. Brett twisted to look back; he could barely make out three riders sitting like statues. As he faced forward, he told Enos sure as hell those men up ahead were sentries and they'd heard the drive. Brett raised his hand to spin aside and told Enos to ride to the West.

The Mexican sentries had come together. Both were probing into the darkness; they could smell cattle, but could not see them. But they failed to shout, to give a warning, perhaps because they thought a band of cattle approaching meant some of their companions had gone up-country to find beef and drive it back. Whatever reason, they did not shout an alarm, and that was a bad mistake.

When Brett was sure Enos was out of the path of the lead cattle, he threw his pistol into the air and fired. From the far side of the herd, Enos also fired, and from far back, Hale fired. All that 'Pifas and Francisco could do was grin. They had no guns.

The stampede started.

The cattle had been bunched a little before reaching this site. Because panic spread like lightning among the cattle, when they started to run toward the campfires, they came on in a broad, dense front.

Men screamed. The first to become pulp beneath hundreds of hooves were the pair of sentries. They had barely time to yell in terror before the cattle charged over them.

Francisco and 'Pifas were riding like Indians, using romals to keep the cattle charging in a mindless rush. Some of their improvident exuberance was contagious. Hale Barlow rode with them, shouting at the top of his voice and firing like a madman.

Finally there was the unnerving bawling of hundreds of mindlessly terrified cattle. Gunfire barely overrode this other sound. Even the screams and curses of *bandoleros* squatting around breakfast fires were barely audible over the bedlam of charging cattle. Here and there little fires sent sparks in every direction, then blinked out as large animals charged through them, bowled over men, upset cooking pots, and trampled those unable to get clear. They reached the remuda, scattering horses and mules, knocking a heavy little cannon on its side, and spreading out in two directions so the more closely packed animals in their wake made an extended front, overrunning everything in their path.

Bandoleros were screaming in the darkness. Some fired into the herd, others dropped everything and ran for their lives. Those who did not try to outrun the cattle but turned away from them had the best chance for surviving.

But panic spread among the border-jumpers as it had among the cattle. Everything had happened too fast, too unexpectedly, and the continuing darkness added to the confusion. Shooting into the herd seemed not to slacken it at all. If it accomplished anything, it was to increase the panic of the animals. By itself it would have caused a stampede.

Where Enos and Brett drew rein on excited horses they were joined by Hale and the pair of Mexicans. The Mexicans seemed to be fascinated by the chaos, the screams and gunshots, the devastation being visited upon their former comrades. They shouted excitedly back and forth in Spanish. For them to stay alive the stampede had to succeed. For the three other spectators the stampede's success was clinical, not personal.

The *bandolero* camp was completely overrun, its inhabitants ground to red gore by dozens of sharp hooves or fleeing in all directions, mostly on foot and mostly running for their lives, even after the stampede began to lose momentum.

Brett eased forward when the onslaught had passed well southward. He saw the two luckless sentries. He also saw the overturned cannon, smelled smashed bottles of mescal and pulque, saw ruined saddlery, torn blankets, broken rifles and carbines, and some bloody, dazed, wandering Mexicans who had miraculously survived.

Where Brett halted near what had once been a soiled old army tent, Hale and the two Mexicans rode up. One of them said, "Headquarters. Maybe the *coronel* is inside under the canvas."

He wasn't. No one had been inside the tent when the cattle had charged over it. Francisco looked, shook his head in disgust, and got back astride, listening to the racket southward. 'Pifas nudged him and laughed. "They will run all night."

The wiry man nodded soberly. "Into the arms of the *federales*. They will invoke the *acordada*."

Hale screwed up his face. "The what?"

"*Acordada*. That's when they crucify and hang people." The wiry man faced Hale and smiled at him. "From every tree still standing down there. From doorways and the roofs of houses."

The noise had passed far southward. There was a comparative silence where the devastated encampment had been . . . until a solitary gunshot ran out and the wiry man named Francisco, but called Frank, wilted a little at a time before sliding down off his horse to the ground.

The pock-faced man's shock lasted only seconds before he whirled his horse and snatched Enos's holstered Colt. He yelled like a Comanche and zigzagged among the debris until the wounded man with two broken legs, who had killed his *compañero*, tried to roll toward cover. The *compañero* fired a wild shot that missed as 'Pifas bore down on him in a furious charge, emptying Enos's six-gun as he rode.

CHAPTER 9

Unexpected Horror

The town was in an uproar, and still the darkness lingered. Lights brightened, there was a distant sound of shouting, and a few gunshots.

The big Mexican rode back at a walk, handed Enos his gun, and without a word, reined off into the gloom. No one called him back.

Brett swung to the ground, trailing his reins. He listened to the distant noise, glanced in the direction of the town, and said, "Maybe the cafe is open. You hungry, Enos?"

"I been hungry since yesterday, but first maybe we ought to ride around out here. . . . Brett, you just went out of the cattle business."

Brett nodded. He'd thought of that as he'd been sitting his horse during the stampede. He got back astride.

They rode at a dead walk over what had been the raider's encampment. There were dazed survivors, otherwise even in darkness the place looked like a hurricane had gone through it.

Hale, mindful of the man with two broken legs who had shot Francisco, kept his handgun in his lap as he rode, but the aimlessly wandering men they encountered scarcely more than glanced at them. They found the tipped-over cannon and the howitzer. Its sled was still in place, with the gun aimed toward the town, a reminder of what could have happened.

Brett turned toward the town, halted on the outskirts, and called ahead. As he led his companions forward, he could see the functional but ugly livery barn. He also saw lights and dark silhouettes of armed men watching as he rode up the middle of the roadway.

Marshal Severn was out in front of his jailhouse with several townsmen, leaning on the tie rack, when Brett halted and said, "Good morning."

The big man was slow to reply, and when he did, he did not return the greeting. "Was that you with the cattle?" he said.

Brett nodded.

Severn again hung fire before speaking. "You did a good lick of business, Mr. Kandelin. I never saw such a mess in my life. You could hear 'em hollerin' for a mile. The town owes you. Who's that Messican with you?"

Brett turned. Enos, farther back, replied to the town marshal. "His name's 'Pifas. We met him up north. He did as much as the rest of us."

Severn and the solemn men around him at the hitch rack eyed the pock-faced Mexican, but Brett, who had not seen 'Pifas rejoin them down by the livery barn, stared longest.

One of the men with the lawman cleared his throat before speaking. "Darn good thing you had them cattle up yonder."

Brett's reply was dry. "I guess it was. Now I'm out of the cattle business."

Severn and his companions said no more, so Brett led off in the direction of the cafe, which was dark, the door barred from the inside. As they were tying up out front, 'Pifas came up beside Brett. "I'll help you get the cattle back," he said.

Brett studied the big man. "Yeah, maybe. I'm sorry about your friend."

The Mexican corrected him. "My brother."

Hale crossed to the cafe door and struck it with the butt of his six-gun. When nothing happened, he struck it hard enough for the noise to be heard as far as the jailhouse. The men with Marshal Severn started across in the direction of the cafe at about the same time someone pushed a rifle barrel through a hole in the front wall. Evidently the gunman's visibility was limited. He pointed the gun straight at the big Mexican.

Hale stepped over, grabbed the barrel, forced it up as far as it would go, and snarled, "Open the damn door!"

The men with Marshal Severn stopped back a ways and let the big lawman step onto the plank walk and call to the man inside holding the Winchester. "Open the door, Jake. It's all right."

Hale was left holding the barrel as the cafe man unbarred his door and looked out. He was unshaven, his hair was askew, and he malevolently eyed them all before settling his stare on the marshal. Then he shrugged, stepped back to shove in his shirttail as he moved aside.

Severn shook his head but said nothing as Brett led his companions inside. South of town someone was yelling indistinguishable words that were followed by a gunshot. The marshal and his townsmen returned to the roadway as the cafe man lighted a lamp, set it on his pie table, and watched the men across his counter sit down. He looked longest at 'Pifas but did not say a word until Brett told him they were hungry.

"Get that Messican out of here."

Enos, who'd earlier felt the cafe man's antagonism, spoke as he leaned on the counter. "If it wasn't for that damned Messican, mister, by now your building would be a pile of sticks. They had cannons aimed this way. You goin' to feed us, or do I have to walk over you and rassle some grub?"

The cafe man wavered before turning abruptly and going to his cooking area, where they heard him slamming pots and pans around.

Enos leaned around Brett to address the pockmarked Mexican. "Real friendly town, ain't it?"

'Pifas's teeth flashed in a smile, but he did not speak.

By the time their food arrived, townspeople were beginning to appear in the roadway, and finally, a little daylight showed through. Brett went to the door to look upward. He returned to the counter. "Rain clouds," he murmured.

The cafe man, who heard that, snorted. "Don't rain down here this time of year. Never has since I been here, an' that's goin' onto twenty years."

No one replied; they were too busy taking the pleats out of their stomachs. The cafe man was not an outstanding cook, but to hungry men he could have been.

People entered the cafe, not to eat but to stare at the men who had saved their town. More people stood outside, peering through the window. One man, burly and disheveled, sat down at the counter and spoke. "That was right clever, Mr. Kandelin. How'n hell did you do it in the dark?"

Brett answered without looking up. "We did it *because* of the dark."

With the ice broken, a surly-looking man put in his bits' worth. "All well an' good, but mark my words, they'll be back."

Brett looked around irritably. "We did our part, now it's up to you."

When they finished eating and returned to the roadway, merchants were uncovering boarded-up windows and an aproned saloon man was sweeping off the duckboards north of the cafe. He did not even glance up when a mob of armed townsmen herded a number of soiled, unarmed *bandoleros* up into town from below the livery barn.

During the day, more *bandoleros* were rounded up. Some energetic teamsters went out with draft horses, tied onto the gun sleds, and dragged them into town, where people could see the artillery that had been aimed at their town.

Some scouts sent out by Marshal Severn returned in late afternoon to report that the *bandoleros* had established a camp a few miles in the direction of the border and were down there licking their wounds. Marshal Severn told Brett he'd also sent men to find the army and hasten it into town.

People eventually understood what had happened. To show their appreciation, they shook hands with Brett and his companions, offered to stand them drinks, buy them supper, even put them up for as long as they wanted to stay on the south desert.

Jess Eames, the hotel proprietor, told Brett his room was still paid for, and if Brett and his riders wanted more rooms, he'd make them available. No charge.

That offer, at least, had strong appeal. None of the drovers had slept in a long time. They left Brett out in front of the jailhouse, went up to the hotel where a sign just inside the door saying no blacks or Mexicans were welcome was visible from the porch. Enos pulled it off the wall, handed it to 'Pifas, and Eames seemed not to notice as he led the way to empty rooms. He told them where the washhouse was out back and left them.

Marshal Severn came out front to sit on a bench and gaze around his town before speaking to Brett. "There's a feelin' it ain't over," he said. "But I think maybe the the worst part of it is." He considered a moment, then faced around. "But there's a Mex army waitin' down over the line, an' I think that means those damned crazy *bandoleros* won't dare go back down there. . . . So maybe it ain't over."

Brett said nothing. He'd lost his cattle. In the lull that followed the wild stampede and the scattering of the border-jumpers, he was not very interested in whatever came next. The lawman continued. "While you was up yonder after the cattle, they raided hell out of Mex town. We went down there, but among all those mud houses and goat corrals and whatnot, the best we could do was run 'em off. They put up a stiff fight, though."

Brett was watching youngsters climbing over the captured artillery when he responded. "Did you see the alcalde?"

"Couldn't find him—or the girl. Them Messicans got hidey-holes. A man could poke around down there for a month and never find 'em."

Brett stood up as more bedraggled *bandoleros* were being driven into town from the direction of the ruined encampment. This time they were carrying wounded men slung on blankets. He asked if there was a doctor in Coyotero and got a dry reply.

"We got some *curanderas* over in Mex town. Otherwise we got a midwife who does some doctoring. The army usually has a pill pusher along. . . . Where you goin'?"

Brett was already stepping off the plank walk when he replied, "To Mex town."

Marshal Severn continued to sit on the bench, watching Brett Kandelin until he disappeared down one of those narrow passageways between buildings.Then he was called by a large, red-faced woman to chase the children off the cannons in the roadway.

The sun came out. Three hours late, but welcome anyway. In Mex town there was less visible activity. In the plaza a few women were drawing water, and at the cantina where Enos had nearly been knifed, some people congregated, but as Brett strode in the direction of the alcalde's house, he could distantly hear voices coming from the direction of the old adobe church.

Ramon Velarde's house was empty. The dead raiders had been taken away. Both doors still stood open, and when he looked inside the sitting room, it remained exactly as it had been the night before. Furniture was overturned, bullet holes pocked the walls, even the acrid scent of burned powder was still noticeable. He walked through, emerged out back, startled an old woman gathering wood who fled at the sight of him, and approached the hidey-hole. The lid was not in place, nor was there anyone down in the hole.

He stood a moment looking around. An old man with hair as white as snow came along using a crooked cane. He said something in Spanish. Brett shook his head to indicate he did not understand. The old man shrugged and shuffled away.

Someone from inside the cantina, speaking loudly in a spirited voice, drew Brett's attention. He started toward that direction.

The room was full of armed men—some were drinking,

some sitting with blank eyes, neither listening nor seeing. The paunchy barman smiled as Brett walked in. Whatever loud discussion had been taking place was replaced by silence.

He asked the barman about the alcalde and the silence deepened as men moved their eyes away from him. Even the affable-seeming barman remained silent as he became busy mopping off his countertop.

Brett walked over and leaned on the bar, no more than two feet from the barman. He asked what had happened. Still, no one spoke. He settled back and faced around. "I want to know," he said to the silent room, and fixed his gaze upon a graying man with a knife scar down the entire side of one cheek. "Do you know?" he asked, and when the knife-scarred man moved uneasily on his stool and shrugged, Brett crossed the room, lifted the man off his seat by the shirtfront, and held him with his toes barely touching the floor.

The scar-faced man looked straight into Brett's eyes without making a sound, but behind him and against the north wall a man said, "Put him down. Listen to me, señor. There was nothing to be done. We were all out trying to catch loose horses."

Brett released the knife-scarred man, turned his back on him, and sought out the man who had spoken. He was very dark, with a thick gray mustache that matched the color of his hair, and looked villainous. He had a rifle leaning against the wall at his back, as well as a big knife in a worn old scabbard on one side of his shell belt and an ivory-stocked handgun in its holster on the opposite side. He was weathered and lined. He looked around the silent room before continuing to speak.

"We were talking about it when you walked in. . . . We fought them hard last night, got them out of town. Then the cattle came, and we heard them screaming. We went out to catch some of the horses they abandoned when they fled from the cattle." The villainous-looking man ran his eyes around the room before continuing. None of the other patrons looked back. "I don't know how it happened. I told you. . . . We fought them away, ran them off, killed six of them. They ran away in the night."

Brett went to the bar, where the barman had set up a glass of red wine for him. He took the glass but did not raise it as he turned to face the graying man. In a very quiet voice, he asked a question: "What happened?"

The speaker looked at his friends again before speaking. "Some of them came back, but like Indians, without using guns or making noise. I don't know how many. Maybe ten, maybe twenty. They caught the alcalde in his house. We were talking about it when you walked in. Why just the alcalde and his granddaughter? Men don't risk their lives for nothing."

Another Mexican growled at the long-winded speaker. "Why don't you tell him, José?"

The villainous-looking man rebuked the man who had interrupted with a searing glare.

Brett put the wineglass back on the counter. "Tell me what?" he demanded.

The man Brett had lifted off his feet, who had the scarred face, spoke next, quietly. "No one knows why, but everyone knows Gil Ortiz was once married to the alcalde's granddaughter. She ran away from him and didn't return to Mex town for two years."

Brett stared at the knife-scarred man. "Gil Ortiz is her husband?"

"*Sí*. He beat her. He even beat the alcalde. She ran away because she told some of the women she was afraid he would kill her."

"Why in the hell," Brett exclaimed, "didn't she just divorce him?"

There was a long silence before the knife-scarred man said, "*Catolica,* señor," and shrugged. "But he would have killed her anyway. So she disappeared." The man shrugged again. "Maybe she thought Ortiz would forget or never return to Coyotero. But he did return. With the *bandoleros*. That's what we were talking about, señor. No one can be sure, except that before one of the raiders died last night—during our fight with them—he said he and his companions had been promised gold if they would find the woman and bring her to him at the encampment west of town.''

Brett's heart stopped for two seconds. There were mangled bodies all over the desert out there.

The barman held out the glass of red wine. ''Drink, señor,'' he said. ''You better sit down.''

The villainous-looking man spoke. ''While we're talking about it, where is the alcalde? Did they take him, too? Why? He is an old man. What good is an old man to the *bandoleros*?''

Brett went to a bench and sat down. ''For the crucifix,'' he murmured in almost a whisper, but it carried around the room. Every man in the cantina stared at him until one, younger than most of the others, slapped a tabletop with his palm and yelled something in Spanish. The knife-scarred man leaned toward Brett to translate. ''He said they all knew Gil Ortiz. They said the *bandoleros* took the old man for the sacred relic. It is solid gold and very heavy. Worth a lot of money even if they melt it down.''

Evidently the suggestion of desecration stopped all the Mexicans from moving, perhaps even from breathing. When Brett rose they watched him start for the door. He had almost reached it when the knife-scarred man called to him.

''Wait, señor. We were talking about searching for the alcalde and his granddaughter. We fought hard last night. We are tired this morning. . . . We didn't know about the relic. Señor, what are you going to do?''

Brett turned back wearing a deadly smile. ''I'm going to find Lillian Velarde. Then I am going to kill Ortiz.''

The knife-scarred man stood up. He was as tall as Brett but thin. ''I caught four horses last night. I'll pick out the best one, señor. I'll wait for you at the south end of town.''

Brett left the cantina for Gringo town scarcely remembering what the scar-faced Mexican had said.

He made no attempt to analyze his feelings toward the lovely woman beyond being indignantly angry that a man had beaten her and had also had her kidnapped along with her grandfather, a man Brett had warmed to at their first meeting.

There was no time to be thoughtful. He'd made up his mind to kill Gil Ortiz on sight long before he'd heard about the abductions. That determination had simply been reinforced at the cantina.

CHAPTER 10
A Deadly Ride

Marshal Severn was down at the livery barn when Brett Kandelin walked in, and while the big lawman was not a prime conversationalist, his mind was quick. He nodded at the younger man, made a deliberate study, then said, "You look like you could sleep for a week."

Brett let that pass. "Did you know a band of raiders returned to Mex town last night and carried off the alcalde and his granddaughter?"

It was obvious from Severn's expression that he did not know, but again his reply was slow arriving. "Where'd you hear that?"

"From some local Mexicans at the cantina."

Severn turned that over in his mind. "Why?"

"They tried to get that big old gold crucifix before my friends and I went after the cattle. My guess is that they came back for it. . . . His granddaughter is married to Gil Ortiz."

Severn knew about the marriage and had little difficulty believing the part about the crucifix. He'd seen it and knew for a fact it was worth a lot of money, not as a relic, but because it was large, heavy, and solid gold.

He stood in thought as Brett went down the row of stalls looking for his animal. It wasn't in a stall but out back in a large corral with the other horses Brett and his companions had ridden into town.

He hunted up a lead shank and was ready to open the gate when Bill Severn came up. "You got somethin' in mind?" the marshal asked mildly.

Brett looked at Severn. "Couple of things I got to take care of."

"Goin' to ride out, are you? Mr. Kandelin, it's not safe beyond town, an' I wouldn't be surprised if it wasn't safe in town, either. For a while, anyway."

A lean horseman came up the alley astride a breedy-looking dark horse with a spidery Mexican brand on its left shoulder. The rider saw the men at the corral gate and watched them. He was the color of old leather and had a knife-scarred cheek.

Brett had forgotten about their encounter at the saloon, but remembered as he saw the Mexican. Marshal Severn had one advantage over Kandelin; he knew the lean rider. He turned, eyed him briefly, then nodded. "Juan . . ."

The rider returned the nod and the short greeting. "Marshal . . ."

Severn looked from one of them to the other before speaking again. "I'm gettin' a bad feelin' about this," he told Brett, who was opening the gate to catch his horse. Severn leaned on the corral watching. When Brett was leading the animal out, the marshal said, "Whatever you're up to, Mr. Kandelin, seems to me you'd ought to postpone until you've rested up. Juan, don't he look dog-tired to you?"

The mounted man shrugged and did not reply.

Severn followed Brett back inside the barn and waited until the other man was rigging out his horse to speak again. Then all he said was, "If you got some notion of goin' after the woman an' the old man . . . They're stirred up. They'll be mean as snakes after what happened to 'em last night. An' they'll have spies out all over the country down there. There's a Mex federal army below the line waitin' for them. More'n likely there'll be red flaggers down there, too, and those lads aren't nowhere nearly as skittish about crossing the line as the Mex army is."

Brett finished rigging out, picked up his reins, and led the horse out of the barn before mounting. Bill Severn followed him to make a final suggestion. "Wait a few hours. The U.S. Army'll be along by then. I got word of that a while back."

Brett swung up over leather and was straightening his reins when he spoke. "Did you look over the corpses out yonder?"

Severn nodded.

"Was Ortiz among them?"

Severn shook his head, and this time he also spoke. "Their colonel was. Diego Rivera. He used to be a brigand chieftain down yonder." Severn paused. "The stampede didn't kill him, a bullet did. From behind. Through the head. Mr. Kandelin, just get down an' wait. I've known Gil Ortiz for several years. He's one of those fellers a man don't like to talk about. Him an' Rivera was like two peas in a pod. It wouldn't surprise me one damned bit to find out Ortiz shot Rivera."

Brett gazed at the large older man for a moment. "You knew Lillian Velarde was his wife."

"Yes. Everyone knew that."

"And that he beat her?"

Marshal Severn stroked his jaw with a thick hand. "Folks in Gringo town don't get involved with things down in Mex town. We like it what way, so do the Messicans. Isn't that right, Juan?"

The lean Mexican was still sitting his saddle. He'd followed Brett up the runway and out to the roadway. As before, he shrugged but did not speak.

Brett gazed at the older man for a long moment, then jerked his head at Juan and rode away southward toward the lower end of town, where a number of shacks marked Coyotero's limits.

He and the man with the scarred face had barely cleared the last of the shacks before Marshal Severn strode in the direction of the hotel.

The clouds were thinning out, but it was still partially overcast, so the day was neither chilly nor hot. For a while Brett rode along studying the sky. He'd had an uncomfortable feeling about it in the wee hours. When dawn should have arrived, it hadn't, and from what he'd heard about the south desert, where it rarely rained even when it was supposed to, that prolonged darkness had him puzzled. He turned to study his companion.

Juan was one of those men who wore his booted Winchester slung forward, the butt plate tipped upwards. It was not entirely for a quick draw but because if weapons in a saddle boot were slung the conventional way, the butt could interfere with a horse's neck when it had to be turned quickly.

Juan rarely spoke unless he was spoken to. When their eyes met, he smiled, made a gesture over the countryside, and shrugged.

Brett thought he understood; they were beginning what could be their last ride. He asked if Juan knew the country and got an amused look back.

"As well as anyone. Better than most. I was born here. I've trapped wild horses, herded cattle and sheep all over the south desert. Where we are heading, there will be watchers on every little low rise in the land."

Brett was puzzled. "Then why did you come along?"

"The señora is a *curandera*. Six years ago, I was bucked off a horse into a scorpion nest. I don't know how many, but when I got back to town and fell off the horse, I had been stung four times. One time will make you sick. Two times very sick, and maybe you will die. Four times . . ." Juan rolled his eyes heavenward before completing what he had to say. "She took me into their house. I was out of my head. Later, the alcalde told me she stayed with me five days, making poultices to draw out the poison. Eleven chickens and *curandera* medicine. She is a fine woman. When she ran away, it was like my own sister had run off. When she came back because the old man was sick, I heard that Gil Ortiz had beaten her. I wanted to kill him." Juan smiled. "I still want to."

Brett continued to regard the lean man for a few moments, then faced forward.

Although the area around Coyotero, because of the underground water, was pleasantly green the farther south they rode, the more desolate the land looked. The only sign of habitation they encountered was about three miles below Coyotero, where someone, without good sense, had erected a square, one-roomed *jacal* with walls of packed earth three feet thick. Too thick for a bullet to penetrate. Then he, whoever he had been, put a roof of faggot thatch overhead—and when Apaches or border-jumpers up out of Mexico came along, they didn't have to try to shoot through the walls. They simply had to wait until nightfall and toss burning wood on the roof.

Juan gazed at the four sturdy walls with the sky for a roof and shook his head. "A priest," he told Brett. "A *gachupín* priest from Mexico. He built the *jacal* to live in while he built a church." Juan's dark eyes went from the ruin to the man he was riding with. He swung his arm in an all-encompassing gesture. "There was no one down here. No one has ever stayed very long between the border and Coyotero. He wouldn't have had a congregation."

Juan's clear conviction that the priest had been a fool showed in every word he said and every gesture he made.

Brett asked how long ago that had been, and his companion slouched along in thought before replying, "When my father was a young man."

The sun finally broke through the diminishing clouds, and within moments the riders could feel its welcome warmth. Juan tipped down his old hat against sunlight that bounced upward from millions of mica particles in the soil. He drew rein in the lacy shade of a large paloverde, eased his weight in the saddle, and while studying the onward country through slitted eyes, made a dry remark.

"By now they have seen us." He did not sound particularly worried. In fact, he wore a faint smile as he continued to watch for movement, for sunlight bouncing off metal.

Brett also scanned the land. It not only looked empty, it even felt empty. "They'll need water," he said, and the lean man nodded.

"Miles west there is a place called Tanque Verde. It has a good spring. It runs this time of year, but in a couple of months it will dry up."

"No other water?"

"No. They could have their camp at Tanque Verde, *compadre*, but what you did last night was like kicking an anthill. They will be all around. A few, maybe alone, maybe in squads." Juan's steady gaze went to Brett and remained there. "If we keep on like this, they will catch us."

Brett had been learning things about the man with the scarred face since they'd left Coyotero, but one thing he never could figure out was how Juan could let himself be led into deadly danger without protesting.

"If they've seen us," Brett said, "what are they waiting for?"

"Maybe for us to die in an ambush. Maybe for night. Drunk, they would charge us in broad daylight. Sober, they don't throw away their lives."

Brett swung to the ground. "So we wait for nightfall, too?"

"Yes. But not here." Juan dismounted, stood in the shade, and continued to watch for some movements. "I think we should stop here. Maybe for a couple of hours. They'll have sent back word. Others will come. Señor, it is cat and mouse from now on." He smiled. "When it is right to do so, we will tie the horses. No one but a crazy person leaves his horse in this country. Leave the horses and go west on foot. They can't see us very well in the underbrush if we're on foot. After dark they can't see us or track us. Señor, do you know what the odds are?"

Brett knew. Perhaps half of the original force of border-jumpers was still around. He nodded at the Mexican. "The odds are about even, Juan. Couple hundred *bandoleros* against you'n me."

The Mexican laughed, rolled his eyes heavenward, and shrugged.

The horses dozed, stamped occasionally, or swung their tails. The day remained pleasantly warm, and the land was steeped in endless silence, with no sign of life until a greenish-looking rattlesnake about the size of a man's wrist eased out of his shady place among some nearby dusty old bushes and flicked his tongue. His lidless eyes were tan-tawny and seemingly motionless. With nothing else to do, Juan and Brett watched the snake. It wasn't very long, a little more than a couple of feet, but it was thick. Brett knew about rattlers, though he'd never seen one colored like this, but a rattlesnake was still a rattlesnake, wherever one encountered him.

Juan stood perfectly still. The horses had evidently neither seen the snake nor scented him. They probably wouldn't have detected the scent anyway, unless he had just emerged from shedding his skin, at which time even people could smell rattlesnakes.

A reckless lizard dashed for shade. The snake's lunge was too quick for the eye. The lizard scrambled, twisted, and raced away without his tail.

Neither of the men moved until the snake, satisfied peril was not imminent, began slithering across a patch of open ground, its course directly in front of the two motionless men.

Unless it detected them, it was not a danger. Brett rested his hand on the butt of his holstered Colt as the reptile came steadily toward him. Once, it stopped to lift its head and twist to look back. Brett had not heard or seen anything, but clearly something had caught the reptile's attention.

While it was facing away, Juan twisted a forked limb from a bush and held it at his side without moving. When the snake turned back to continue on its way, which would take it close to Juan's feet, the Mexican would be armed with the little forked stick held a few inches off the ground at his side.

The snake halted again, this time clearly alarmed, probably by the scent or "feel" of men close by. It went into a coil less than a yard from Brett's feet. It did not rattle, though, it simply maintained its striking coil. Neither man seemed to be breathing. Eventually the snake came out of its coil, stretched to its full length, and slithered close enough to Juan's booted feet to almost brush them. The Mexican jammed his forked stick down very hard.

The rattler was pinioned to the ground inches behind its flat head. The head barely moved, but the thick body whipped and twisted, strained and lashed furiously.

Juan waited before slowly sinking to one knee, easing his hand up the reptile's back until his fingers were poised against the stick to grip hard when the stick was removed.

Brett clutched his gunhandle, ready to draw and fire if the snake got loose, but it didn't. Even after Juan had flung the twig aside and slowly rose with the rattler coiling fiercely around his arm, Brett remained motionless. He'd seen some damned fool things in his life, but this one took the cake.

The snake had its mouth open wide, both fangs locked into striking position. A single drop of transparent venom showed on one fang.

Brett spoke very quietly. "Throw the damned thing as far as you can."

Juan neither spoke nor moved. He was looking steadily at the reptile and wearing a faint smile. He said something in Spanish, raised his arm should high, twisted from the waist, and hurled the reptile into the thick underbrush.

Its body twisted and writhed as it sailed high into the air and began to descend quite a distance from where the men were watching.

When it came down and was lost to sight, Juan was turning to say something when a scream of raw terror came out of the distant underbrush.

Both men lunged ahead at the same time. Juan had been right, but it hadn't seemed likely a raider could have gotten that close to their paloverde tree in the length of time they had been standing in its shade.

He hadn't. He'd already been hiding there, watching Brett and his companion coming down country.

When they broke into the tiny clearing, they saw a Mexican trying to club the rattlesnake with his six-gun. The man was oblivious to everything except the terror that gripped him—and the cause of it, which was trying desperately to crawl as fast as it could in among the spiny lower limbs of a big bush.

He repeatedly struck at the reptile. Each time the snake felt the ground shake nearby, it changed course and increased its speed.

The *bandolero* was set to jump up and pursue the snake

when he turned his head. He clearly hadn't heard Brett and Juan crash through the bush because his eyes bulged and his body froze in a crouched position. When Brett cocked his six-gun, the Mexican's mouth contorted as though he would cry out. But no sound came.

Juan told him in Spanish to let the gun fall. The raider obeyed but still did not straighten up. His fear had been transferred from the snake, which had escaped, to the pair of men.

Brett went over, roughly searched him, found a knife and a little belly gun, flung them away, and knocked the man to the ground.

Juan knelt beside the raider, whose soiled, half-ragged shirt was darkening with sweat. He asked if the man spoke English. He shook his head, so Juan spoke to him in Spanish.

He asked how long the Mexican had been watching them, and translated the reply to Brett. "Two hours." Juan also asked where the *bandolero* camp was, and this time Juan did not have to translate. Their terrified prisoner pointed westward. When Juan said, "Tanque Verde?" the Mexican bobbed his head.

Juan continued to kneel for a moment, studying their prisoner. Then Juan reached to pick up the discarded knife and put the tip of the blade into the Mexican's ear. This time, when the man spoke in Spanish, Brett recognized the sound of raw terror without understanding a single word their captive said.

CHAPTER 11

In The Enemy's Heartland

They learned something from their captive. Since disaster struck the previous night and the raiders finally came together at Tanque Verde, less than two hundred men remained, and while two beeves were being barbecued, another ten or fifteen had straggled in.

The captive spoke in Spanish. "The *commandante* was killed. They told us they saw his body. They said there were many bodies, but about a third of us were still alive." The captive rolled his eyes toward Brett, then back to the man with the scarred face. "In the night, the others, maybe as many as three hundred, deserted. So there were only a couple hundred of us left."

Juan translated, and while he was doing so, their captive's dark eyes moved slyly. When Juan turned back, the captive told him something else. "The *commandante*'s aide became our leader."

Juan cocked his head slightly. "His name is what?"

"General Ortiz y Duran," the Mexican said, and at the look on his interrogator's face, the captive shrugged eloquently. "He was a colonel, but as new commander, he has to be a general, no?"

The captive, no longer terrified, was a narrow-faced individual, very dark, with close-set black eyes and a cruel, sly cast to his features. In a very matter-of-fact tone of voice, he said, "They know you are down here. They will be closing in.'' The raider thinly, menacingly, smiled. ''This whole territory down here has men wandering everywhere. Since we've been talking, there will be men creeping up . . . señores, surrender to me. I'll take you to the camp . . . and keep the others from shooting you.''

Juan and Brett gazed at the Mexican from expressionless faces. Brett asked if Gil Ortiz had a woman with him. After this had been interpreted, the Mexican's sly eyes lingered on Brett, laughing at him. The man said, ''Yes. I saw them bring her in. Also an old man. I think he was hurt. Two men rode, one on each side of the old man.''

''Are they still at the camp?'' Juan asked, and got back the ambiguous shrug. They had been at the camp when the captive had joined dozens of other raiders in fanning out over the desert south of Coyotero and north of the border.

When Juan rose to dust off, the captive eyed him craftily. All his terror was gone. He repeated his offer to accept their surrender and take them safely to the general, and was maliciously smiling when Juan killed him with the man's own knife.

It happened too fast for Brett to intervene, and afterward there was no point in protesting, so he turned his back on the body as Juan shot a glance at the sky. He cursed under his breath because the sun was still high and, with only a jerk of his head, he and Brett struck out on a zigzagging course toward Tanque Verde.

They did not stop until a man's raised voice came down the distance to them. The sound was northward, and quite far away.

Brett tapped Juan's shoulder. ''Right smack-dab in the middle of 'em,'' he said.

Juan nodded. ''You want to go back? We can maybe make it—unless they've found our horses.''

The Mexican back yonder with the knife sticking in him had been right. The farther Brett and his companion penetrated the thorny, flourishing, and closely spaced stands of thornpin, the more they detected sounds. Many were on horseback, but some of the Mexicans were walking through the thicket as they wove their way eastward. They were probably responding to the dead raider's earlier shout when the rattlesnake had landed on him out of the sky. They were on foot. The horsemen remained out where the thornpin was less impenetrable.

Juan never faltered. But once, after they had traversed more than a mile, he looked over his shoulder and rolled his eyes in response to some raiders catcalling back and forth to keep track of one another as they moved through the underbrush. Brett's impression was of a great many aimlessly wandering men perhaps testing the limits of their safety, restless and fearful. They certainly knew a Mexican federal army was waiting for them to try and slip back into Mexico, and they had lost their *commandante*. But the longer they remained where they were, the more they realized that after what had happened at Coyotero, retribution would also be waiting for them from the north.

When they finally halted, Juan said, "Did you know a rattlesnake is blind when it sheds its skin?"

Brett nodded.

"Blind rattlesnakes will strike at any sound, any movement of the ground." Juan gestured. "So will two hundred leaderless *bandoleros* caught between enemies to the south and more enemies up north somewhere. From here on, we have to move very slowly—and wait for darkness. I can tell you something about these men . . . they will shoot first. They will kill one another. Anything that makes a noise."

Brett nodded. "And they will desert. Sneak away one or two at a time. Sneak back down over the line if they can."

Juan smiled sardonically. "The red flaggers will be waiting like Indians, watching miles of the border." Juan shrugged. "For every five who try to sneak back, even in darkness, maybe one will make it. Señor, down there they behave the same; they will shoot at anything that moves in daylight or that makes a noise in the dark."

Brett could feel other men around him in the underbrush. A couple of times he heard men talking together in Spanish. Whenever they could hear other men, Juan changed course. He had an uncanny, almost unbelievable way of avoiding confrontations. Once, after a very narrow escape, he grinned, whispering, "I am sweating. Are you?"

Brett nodded. From this point on, he did not even think about abandoning their manhunt—womanhunt, too—but he began to seriously doubt that they would ever reach Tanque Verde.

Several horsemen appeared to the south, out where the underbrush was less impenetrable. Brett could see their heads and shoulders as they worked their way along. One of them swore in Spanish when his horse inadvertently scraped its rider's leg against a thornpin bush.

Juan faded abruptly, pressing his back into a thicket, unmindful of the thorns as three loosely moving men wearing crossed bandoleers, traveling in single file, like Indians, passed by within ten feet. They were dirty, sweaty, and obviously either tired or coming off a drunk because they looked haggard, but they moved swiftly along, carrying Winchesters.

Brett and Juan were working their way very slowly, avoiding contact with the undergrowth to avoid the sound of disturbed brush, when not very far ahead a rustling noise pulled them down to a dead stop. The sound persisted. Juan pushed into the nearest underbrush, with Brett beside him. He turned, and whispered, "He's coming straight toward us."

Brett lifted out his Colt and waited. If he and his companion moved, the man dead ahead would hear them. The invisible *bandolero* was still making noise pushing through the undergrowth when Juan, too, brought his gun to hand. He and Brett were scarcely breathing as they waited for the inevitable confrontation. Then it happened.

From *behind* them, a voice that sounded thin and high spoke first in Spanish, then in English. "Hey, *stupidos*. . . . Don't move. Not even your eyes."

Someone had been tracking them for more than a mile. It was impossible in a country of hardpan—*caliche*—soil covered with at least an inch of ancient dust, not to leave tracks. Their capture was accomplished, not from in front, the direction they'd been concentrating their full attention on, but from in back.

"Drop the guns, *pelados*!"

The voice wasn't loud or angry; it was contemptuous. They dropped their weapons.

There were two of them. One, short, bandy-legged, with straight black hair and a moon face the color of wet dirt, had restless, animallike, small dark eyes. He was an Indian—not of any tribe Brett had ever seen—some kind of Mexican Indian. His companion, who had done the talking, was taller, lighter-colored, but with the same black eyes. He was holding a six-gun in his right fist. The Indian hadn't drawn his holstered sidearm; he had what appeared to be a three-sided rifle bayonet in his hand. It had been shortened by at least a foot and honed on all three edges.

The lighter man walked a little closer while studying his prisoners. He was of an indeterminate age, perhaps somewhere between thirty and forty. His crossed bandoleers had wide gaps between their cartridge loops. His trousers and blouse were dirty, and the shirt had been caught by thorns in several places. The Indian was without shoes. His companion was wearing huaraches with a heel strap, but what Brett and Juan particularly noticed was his handgun. It was a U.S.-issue cavalry weapon, old, without a trace of its original bluing, fully charged, with no front sight.

The taller man halted in front of Brett and Juan, slowly cocked his six-gun, and waited—perhaps for them to beg for mercy. When neither of them moved nor spoke, but looked steadily back, the raider addressed Juan in Spanish. "Who are you? Who is this *norteamericano*? What are you doing down here?"

Juan answered truthfully. "Looking for someone."

The light-complexioned Mexican said, "Who?" and spoke again before Juan could reply. "There is a dead man with a knife in him down your back trail." The raider's black eyes glowed with irony. "He fell on his knife, no? But, of course, that's easy to do when the knife is sticking out of his chest, isn't it?"

Juan was silent . . . until the raider pointed his handgun straight at him and said, "Who are you looking for?"

"Friends. They're somewhere down here. Maybe over at the watering place."

"Where are you from?"

"Up north."

The Indian, tired of the conversation, growled and made threatening gestures with his knife. "I never saw that one before, and the gringo couldn't have been with us, so they came from the town. Manuel, they killed that man back there."

The taller *bandolero* did not reply. He seemed to be thinking. Eventually he told the Indian in Spanish to pick up their weapons and to put up his knife. The Indian obeyed without hesitation, which both the prisoners noticed. He then switched back to English as he stared at Brett.

"What is your name?"

"Brett Kandelin."

"Did you knife that man where your tracks met his?"

Two lives were at stake. "He was dead when we passed by."

The Indian clearly did not believe this. His companion may not have, either, but he did not really care about the dead man. He gestured with his six-gun. "Walk ahead. One behind the other." He turned aside to briefly order the Indian to walk up ahead and if he encountered other raiders to call out who they were and that they had two prisoners.

Brett's deduction was that the lighter-complexioned man, Manuel, would have killed them on the spot, or might have stood watching as the Indian did it, except that live hostages were bargaining points and dead ones were not.

As they worked their way through the underbrush, the taller raider asked if they had come to the border country alone. When they told him the truth, he asked another question: "Are there people from the town looking for us?"

Again the reply he got was the truth. Brett said, "We don't know. It was early when we rode out." He paused before adding a little more. "I'd guess they are." He didn't mention the army on its way to Coyotero and neither did their captor.

Juan finally risked asking a question. "Why are you still

here? Why haven't you scattered in all directions? The longer you stay, the more danger you are in."

The *bandolero* did not deny the peril when he replied to the question. "We are leaving. That is the *commandante*'s plan. But slowly, a trickle at a time. We can't go back and we can't go north. And large numbers of us can't be seen. If what happened at Coyotero hasn't already spread over the countryside, it still would be dangerous for bands of us to be seen."

Encouraged by the raider's candor, Brett entered the conversation. "You should have gone south after Ciudad Morales, not north."

Their captor shrugged. "We routed the army down there. How do you convince hundreds of drunken plunderers what they should do? I was told by everyone I talked to that if we routed a Mexican army four times our size, we could much more easily go over the line and attack some towns, carry away everything, and race down over the border."

Brett looked back, met the tall Mexican's gaze, and said nothing. But the *bandolero* understood the look. "Now everyone knows better. Now they are saying whoever stampeded a big herd of cattle through our camp did something no one could expect." The Mexican smiled bitterly. "Now we have lost our leader. The one in his place is not interested in the revolution, only in plunder and, some say, for vengeance against a woman. We lost eleven men so she could be captured and brought to him." Manuel paused to swear.

Brett let the conversation lag, because up ahead the bandy-legged Indian was down on one knee with his head cocked. He turned, ignored the prisoners, and made a slashing motion with one hand. Manuel stood like a stone for a moment before signaling back.

Brett had heard nothing. He and Juan followed the Indian's example of sinking to one knee, but the man behind them remained standing.

It was a long wait, during which Brett noticed that the sun was lower than it had been the last time he'd looked. He probably should have followed Juan's suggestion to wait until nightfall. Hindsight was a splendid gift.

The Indian rose, walked back, whispered to the taller raider, and gestured southward. Manuel listened, nodded, and motioned for the Indian to return to his lead position. When they were moving again, Manuel said, "That was a band of riders with men along on foot going eastward. We are close to the camp. They will kill you no matter what I say. They are angry and want revenge for what happened up at that town. . . ."

Brett looked back. "How are you going to keep some drunk from shooting us anyway?"

Manuel smiled bleakly. "Maybe I can't," he replied, and gestured for Brett to keep moving.

When they eventually came to the edge of the thick underbrush, there was a tantalizing aroma of cooking. There was also a very rare sight, which would grow even rarer as the years passed: a sprawling, noisy, unkempt encampment where hundreds of men wandered, or ate, or drank, or slept amid incredible squalor.

The wounded had been placed side by side like cordwood, with no shelter from the sun and with only a few attendants among them.

There were several horses, nowhere nearly as many as would be required by the number of men in the camp, and someone had set up a scrap of soiled old canvas in a circular clearing. Manuel walked up beside Brett and jutted his jaw. "There. *Commandante* Ortiz." Manuel paused, eyeing the disorganized, unkempt camp. "If we can get over there before someone knows you are a gringo, it will be better."

Juan had the solution to that. He pointed to the sun as he said, "Wait here an hour, until dusk arrives."

Manuel seemed to be considering this when the Indian suddenly jerked upright as six mounted border-jumpers, riding along the front of the thicket, saw them, saw the *norteamericano* with them, and reined to a startled halt.

Manuel walked ahead, and as he passed, the Indian growled something to him without breaking stride as he approached the startled riders. He held up a hand and called out in Spanish.

The palaver was prolonged. By the time Manuel walked back, Brett was waiting. "What did you tell them?"

"That we captured you, that you are a gun-running *Comanchero*. We are taking you to the *commandante* and need their help getting you through the camp without someone shooting you." Manuel smiled. "They agreed."

The Indian did not smile or look relieved. He clearly did not care whether the prisoners were delivered to the *commandante* or not. If they got shot in the back, he had no objection. In fact, if trouble started, he would shoot them himself.

Manuel waited until the riders were fairly close, then ordered the Indian to lead off.

The horsemen were bronzed, lean, ragged men with carbines and pistols, and although their mounts looked very much the worse for wear, the men themselves appeared anything but demoralized. They rode along, three to a side, passing through camps where routed men cursed and shook fists at them. They ignored the dark looks until they were close enough to the clearing where the old tarp had been erected, then stopped to allow Manuel and the Indian to proceed toward the tent. The riders sat at moment, watching, then turned back.

From where Brett stood, the encampment, for all its disorganization and squalor, looked no worse than the encampment he had run his cattle over, except that there were nowhere nearly as many men. His rough estimate was perhaps two hundred, perhaps a hundred and a half. Instinct told him that without being encouraged to slip away a few at a time and try to get back home, desertion would have accomplished the same end.

CHAPTER 12

The Black Hole

In front of the propped-up tarpaulin there were two sullen armed men who eyed Juan and Brett without curiosity, but rather with malevolent stares. When Juan enquired about the *commandante*, one of the slouching sentries made an indifferent gesture, and spoke in Spanish.

"He is somewhere else."

No further conversation was offered or solicited as Juan turned and warned Brett in English, "Don't even cough." He then searched the surrounding area and jutted his jaw. "There. Where the meat is cooking. The man with the sword."

Brett had difficulty locating Ortiz because of the smoke, but there was only one man wearing a sword, and his back was to Brett.

One of the menacing Mexicans, a man whose hairline almost met his eyebrows, pushed upright to lean on a rifle and ask in Spanish who they were and what they wanted.

Juan looked the man straight in the eye and repeated what their light-complexioned captor had told the mounted *bandoleros*. "We have many guns. Our trade is selling them."

The Mexican's lips curled. *"Comancheros?"*

"*Sí.*"

The Mexican's black eyes looked cruelly amused. "We don't need your guns," he stated in Spanish. "Friend, what we need is horses. Where did you come from?"

Juan's reply was curt. "Up north."

The second sentry's face brightened. "Coyotero?"

Juan put a slow gaze upon this sentry. "Near there . . . and when we passed, there was a large band of armed men with two guns on sleds leaving town."

"Going which way, *señor*?"

Juan put a disgusted look on the sentry. "South."

"How many?"

Juan shrugged. "We were a mile out. Maybe fifty, maybe a hundred."

The two sentries exchanged a look before one left his rifle behind and started toward the crowd of men down where the meat was being cooked. Brett and Juan watched him. When he got up beside the man wearing the sword, there was a brief conversation and, as the sentry turned back, the man with the sword turned back with him.

Brett recognized the sword bearer as the same man who had promised to pay him for his herd when it had been delivered down near Coytero. Gil Ortiz.

He looked unshaven, soiled, ridiculous wearing the sword. When Ortiz was close enough to recognize Brett, he faltered in his stride, recovered, and continued on. His face was expressionless, except for the strange look in his hazel eyes. He stopped, motioned the sentries away, and let go a long breath as he wagged his head at Brett Kandelin. "If I'd prayed for this meeting, it couldn't have been better. You had the only cattle down here. My men cursed you all night without having any idea who you were, and I didn't tell them. But I knew, and one reason I'm still down here is because I sent ten men back up there to find you and bring you back to me—alive."

Brett stared. Ortiz was risking the lives of all his men by keeping them with him simply to satisfy a desire for personal vengeance.

As they faced each other, Brett Kandelin's hatred for Ortiz was increasing. He could not resist saying, "You'd risk the lives of all these men just to capture me?"

Ortiz replied with a question. "Now that won't be necessary, will it?"

Brett's gaze was unwavering. "Where is the alcalde and his granddaughter?"

Ortiz's answer shocked both Brett and Juan. "The alcalde is—there." He turned and pointed toward several mounds of fresh earth—graves. He turned back. "Old Ramon couldn't hide this time. He tried to put up a fight. He got hurt."

Brett's glance came back to the other man's face. "And his granddaughter?"

"She's my wife, gringo. It's none of your business where she is."

Brett's gaze returned to the graves. There were at least sixteen of them. Ortiz laughed. "Not out there. Now tell me, where is the U.S. Army?"

Brett gave a slow and delayed reply. "I don't know."

"You know," stated the Mexican. "They reached Coyotero, didn't they?"

"Not that I know of. They hadn't when Juan and I left."

"You're lying, gringo!"

Juan spoke. "He's telling the truth."

Ortiz looked at Juan for a moment before addressing Brett again. "They have to be there. My spy in Coyotero told us Marshal Severn sent riders to bring them back."

Brett shook his head. "Your spy was right about someone going to find the army, but when Juan and I left there were no soldiers. A lot of people were mad about them not showing up, but they weren't there . . . and I don't know where they are." Brett cocked his head slightly. "Your spy . . . He gave you that key to the powderhouse?"

Ortiz took his time answering, and when he finally did, it was with contempt in his voice. "Find a coward," he said, "and tell him he is going to be killed unless he helps."

Brett had an intuitive flash. He had met one frightened individual in Coyotero. The man who had whined about surrendering the town. Brett nodded at Ortiz. "The liveryman."

Ortiz shrugged. It did not matter to him if the betrayer of Coyotero was hanged by his own townsmen. He said, "A coward, Mr. Kandelin,'' and swung the conversation back to the army. ''I have scouts all around. When I've finished with you, whether they find soldiers or armed townsmen or not, we will leave the country. I've already told most of the men to leave, especially the wounded and the ones who have lost the heart to make war.''

Brett considered the other man coldly. ''If the army came, or the townsmen, you would get men killed—for what? Simply because you've made up your mind to get back at me?''

Ortiz's answer was proof to those who heard it that Ortiz was completely disinterested in what happened to his followers. ''I am going to make you scream about how sorry you are that you stampeded those cattle over my soldiers. Whether they all leave or get killed, I'm going to work on you until you beg me to let you die.''

Juan made a gentle sigh as he stood looking at the man with the sword, but he remained silent and more or less expressionless.

The light-complexioned Mexican, Manuel, who had made the capture, came up with his old hat in his hands. ''General,'' he said in English, shooting Brett a quick glance. ''Gringo soldiers are up north. Three of our horsemen saw them.''

''Where up north?''

''Making a camp a mile or so below Coyotero.''

Ortiz looked incredulous, then suspicious. ''Making a camp while there's still daylight?''

''I only know what the scouts reported, General. They said the horses looked tired and the soldiers don't look any better. It will be dark before long. They couldn't get down here soon enough.''

Ortiz's face cleared. Whether the soldiers were tired or not, it was true they could not get down this close to the border before nightfall. He nodded to the light-complexioned man. ''They will come in the morning,'' he said, and paused to consider a stray idea. ''Supposing,'' he said, musing aloud, ''supposing we slipped up there in the dark and attacked them?''

Manuel's face froze in an expression of disbelief. "But, General, we have to get away. Besides, I don't think the men will do that. . . . General, every hour we stay in this camp—"

Ortiz interrupted. "Don't tell anyone about the soldiers. You understand?"

Manuel understood, but as he was turning away and Ortiz could not see his face, he looked at Brett and rolled his eyes heavenward.

Brett caught Ortiz was off-balance and strove to keep him that way. "You'll never get away now, even if you use darkness for cover."

Ortiz leaned on the big old sword. "We will be gone in the morning. Right now I want to show you something." He motioned for Brett and Juan to precede him inside the tarpaulin shelter.

There was jumbled saddlery and small sacks among the scraps of uneaten food and rumpled personal attire. One area contained two heavy ammunition boxes side by side. Ortiz gestured for Juan to move the boxes, which he did, and exposed a dark hole. Brett could not see the bottom, which probably had less to do with the depth of the hole than its dark interior.

He'd seen one of these holes before. Ortiz did not get close to either of his prisoners as he called out: "A friend of yours is here, Lillian. He's coming down to see you."

There was no answer.

Ortiz called again. "Lillian, this friend of yours—can you guess how stupid he is? He came down here with only one man to rescue you. Lillian? Speak to me! I'm going to put him down there with you . . . after I've broken his arms and put out his eyes and cut open his belly so you two can talk while he is bleeding to death. *Answer me!*"

The voice from the depths of the dark hole sounded faint, either ill or completely demoralized. "Let him go, Gil. He's not my friend. I hardly know him. He was the alcalde's friend."

Ortiz made a high-pitched laugh. "I know better, Lillian. A man doesn't risk his life to help a woman he barely knows. . . . And a woman doesn't beg for the life of a man she barely knows. How do you feel now, Lillian?"

This time the reply was almost too faint to be heard. "I don't feel well. . . . Gil, let him go."

"I can't do that, Lillian, after the hard work I did getting Diego Rivera to come up here. Did you know—no, of course, you didn't—Rivera, that peacock of a man, wanted to stay at Ciudad Morales, where we'd beaten the federal army. He wanted to fortify Morales and make it our revolutionary stronghold. The damned idiot. I had to tell him about your grandfather's sacred relic, such heavy gold a man had to use both hands to lift it. Finally I had to get him half drunk—and promise him more loot than he could imagine—before he agreed to lead the men up here. . . . Do you know what your friend here with me did? He stampeded a whole big herd of cattle over our encampment in the night. He scattered the men in all directions, ruined the camp. And do you know what happened to *Commandante* Rivera? The cattle trampled him to death."

Brett and Juan exchanged a glance, and Brett turned slowly to face the man with the sword. "What happened to her, Ortiz?"

The Mexican raised his shoulders and let them drop. "She had an accident. She would have been all right, but when she stood up, she had the same accident again." Ortiz pointed to the hole. "Get down in there. Both of you." He looked steadily at them, and when neither of them moved, he pointed with a rigid arm. "Get down in there!"

Juan spoke quietly to Brett. "I'll go first."

As Juan was testing for depth, Ortiz spoke to Brett. "I'll be back for you. I'll bring a rope and some men to help you climb out."

Juan let himself down slowly, but the hole, while it was not shallow, was not as deep as its darkness made it appear to be.

When he moved clear of the wall and looked up, he could not see Ortiz, just Brett. He held up a hand to gesture. "Let yourself down with your fingers, then drop."

Brett turned for a long look at Gil Ortiz. They exchanged stares, with neither of them saying a word before Brett went down, easing his body over the edge. He waited until Juan steadied him before dropping. The hole was no more than twelve feet deep.

It was too dark for either of the men to see how wide it was, and when Ortiz wrestled the ammunition boxes back into place to cover the opening, it was too dark for either man to see the other until their eyes adjusted, and even then visibility was limited to little more than near blindness.

The hole was about ten feet wide at the bottom. They found Lillian slumped against the cool earthen wall and sank down beside her. When Brett put out a hand, her fingers closed weakly around it. She said, "My grandfather told me you would come."

Brett gently felt her face. It was badly swollen and bloody. She pushed his hand away. "If I could have died last night I would have. . . . My grandfather tried to fight them off. They knew where the hiding place was in the wall. When he pushed at them, one of them struck him in the side with a gun barrel. . . . I didn't think he would last until we got down here. He was spitting blood. . . ."

"He died then?" Juan asked softly.

"No. Not then. But I think he would have. Gil told some men who were melting lead to make bullets to pour a ladle of the melted lead into his ear. . . ."

Juan breathed half a prayer. "*Madre de Dios*!"

Brett changed the subject, but when he asked questions, the handsome woman sat dumbly, in an agony of silence.

Juan tapped his arm in the darkness, moved away, and stopped where he could dimly discern the metal-bound bottoms of the ammunition boxes. "If I get down on all fours," he said, "and you stand on my back . . ." He peered inquiringly at Brett, who had no chance to speak; above them, two men grumbled in Spanish. Evidently the sullen sentries had returned and been instructed to watch the hole.

Juan threw up his hands, a gesture Brett could barely discern in the darkness.

They returned to the injured woman and sat down, with their backs against the cool earth.

Eventually Juan said, "If the army attacks in the morning, unless Ortiz is killed soon, I think he will come back and spray bullets into the hole. You know what I think, *Commandante?* I think he is crazy. *Loco en cabeza.*"

Brett said nothing. He felt for the woman's fingers, which were cold, and closed his hand around them. Her response was feeble, but at least she tried to squeeze his hand.

Juan made a rattling sigh and relaxed. He was quiet for a long time and finally rousing when the sentries above mentioned food and shuffled back out, at least as far as the front of the makeshift *bandolero* headquarters. He nudged Brett in the darkness. "Now we could try," he said.

They tried, but although Brett could reach the bottom of the heavy boxes, he had to extend his arms almost straight upward—and in this position he lacked the strength to do more than barely slide one box. The reason he stopped straining was because he could suddenly see dying daylight from one end of the box. The thing wasn't moving sideways, it was moving forward. One more grunting push and it would fall down into the hole.

He stepped down off Juan's back and shook his head. The Mexican rose, mopped sweat off his scarred face while peering upward, and heard the sentries returning. One of them spoke sharply in Spanish at the sight of the moved box. It required both of them to put the box back into place, and after accomplishing this, one of them called to the men below.

Juan didn't bother do interpret. Being threatened with death had lost its ability to cause terror.

They groped back beside the woman and sank down. Brett listened, nudged his companion, and whispered, "She's asleep."

Juan whispered back, "Good. I would trade ten years off my life to be able to get close to Gil Ortiz for just two minutes." He held up two strong hands, pretended to close them slowly around a human neck, and smiled.

Brett had learned one thing about his gentle-seeming companion. When his mind was made up that an evil human being was taking up space a more responsible human being required, he had no compunction about committing murder.

Someone came inside the tarp tent and spoke in Spanish to the sentries. Juan listened, then sat up a little straighter as the conversation Brett did not understand continued.

When the visitor departed and the pair of sentries discussed what he had said, Juan leaned to whisper, "Maybe Manuel, but someone, anyway, has been telling the *bandoleros* the Yanqui army is on its way. What the man told the sentries was that he was going to wait until midnight, then take one of the horses and leave, and if they had any sense they would leave with him. He told them there is a lot of murmuring among the men. They don't want to fight anymore, and they don't want to stay here just because Gil Ortiz wants to."

Brett wasn't very encouraged about the prospect of a wholesale desertion. It wasn't the peon raiders he feared, it was Gil Ortiz, and if he kept his word about torturing and murdering his captives, it was not going to matter whether his "army" would still be there or not.

As Juan had said, Ortiz was probably about equal parts crazy and eaten alive with a bloody desire for revenge. With that kind of a person, nothing was going to matter but the fulfillment of his goal. Brett had seen Indians face certain death, blind to any chance of avoiding it, because of their motivation. Among Indians, such souls were called "Bloody Hands."

He went over to look up at the bottom of the heavy boxes, convinced that if he, Juan, and Lillian were down there when Ortiz returned, if Ortiz did not have time to torture them, he would spray them with gunfire like cornered rats.

The sentries were carrying on a desultory, growling conversation, of which Brett did not understand one word, until the word "gringos" was mentioned several times. He hissed for Juan to listen.

When Juan stood, head raised, the conversation dwindled—until one of the sentries made an ugly chuckle and said something that made Juan wince.

He turned toward Brett. "They want her. They are going to sneak away with their friend about midnight. They are going to take Lillian with them."

CHAPTER 13

The Face of Death

Sounds did not penetrate the earth very well. It was not possible for the prisoners in the hole to hear anything except occasional snatches of talk directly above them and the infrequent arrival of someone on horseback. Ortiz did not return.

Eventually the sentries were replaced, but the second pair seemed to be no different from the others. Except for warning the people in the hole that they would be shot if they tried to climb out, the guards ignored them.

Lillian needed water. Her attempt to stifle small whimpering sounds of agony made Brett stand directly beneath the ammunition boxes and call to the sentries. The first couple of calls were ignored; when he persisted, he got a reply, surprisingly, in English. "If you don't shut up, I'll shoot you in both legs."

Brett did not shut up. "There is a very sick woman down here—"

"What do we care about a sick woman," the raider stated.

"I will give you fifteen gringo dollars for a canteen of water."

There was not a sound from above. The offer had caught both the sentries unprepared. One called back, "Where is the money?"

"In my pocket."

One of the ammunition boxes was abruptly lifted away. The sentries were young men, ragged, unwashed, and predatory. One said, "Show us."

Brett held up some greenbacks. The Mexicans exchanged a look, and one of them abruptly turned away. His companion hunkered down and grinned at Brett. "All right. One canteen of water . . . Gringo, how much more money do you have?"

Brett's mind raced. Was this an opportunity to be freed from the hole? "Some," he admitted, looking straight up until his neck hurt. "Did you know the American army is coming?"

"*Sí*, everyone knows that, but we will be gone by the time they get down here."

Brett's reply wiped the grin off the sentry's face. "No, you won't. They aren't coming straight south. They have a plan to spread out, to surround you, cut you off from the border and all other directions."

The younger man looked hard at Brett. "How do you know this? You came here alone, and have been in this hole ever since."

Brett elaborated on his prevarication. "I know because I heard the officers talking before Juan and I started south."

The sentry bearing the canteen returned. His companion said nothing until he'd handed down the canteen and had pulled back with the money, then he told his companion what Brett had said. The second sentry's reaction was to scoff as he counted the money, divided it, and handed half to his friend. "We will be gone by then," he said, sounding cheerful as he stuffed greenbacks into a ragged pocket.

His friend sounded enormously relieved as he said, "We will? It is the *commandante*'s order?"

"The *commandante*," spat out his companion in a derisive voice. "It's because of the *commandante*. We should have been gone long ago. Hernan', no one pays attention to the *commandante*. He let everyone go until now we couldn't fight anyone anymore. But he keeps the rest of us here. For no reason anyone knows of, except that maybe he's crazy.

"Do you know Manuel Vargas, the one who was supposed to aim the cannon? Well, he was the one who captured those men in the hole. He told me he thought the *commandante* was crazy in the head. He told me Gil Ortiz found that big sword somewhere and thinks it belonged to Santa Anna and that it will protect him, allow him to beat any army sent against him." The speaker paused, then also said, "The woman in the hole . . . she is his wife."

Brett was holding the canteen for Lillian as the sentries talked. He hadn't abandoned the idea of trying to bribe their way out of the hole, but there was one difficulty. When he'd handed up the fifteen dollars, it left him with less than ten more dollars.

He and Juan pooled their money. The total amount was less than twenty dollars. Juan shrugged and said, "Twenty is better than none, and peons from Mexico think twenty greenbacks is a fortune." He shrugged again. "We can only try."

Lillian wet both hands and held them to her feverish face. The water revived her somewhat. She thanked Brett and leaned her head on his shoulder. He could hear her breathing, which was deep and steady, and felt her face again, using hands cooled by moisture. One eye was nearly closed. It was swollen out of all proportion to the rest of her features. Her lower lip had been split, and there was a thin gash beneath one eye, down across her cheekbone. He used his bandanna soaked in water to cool her face as he soothed her.

There was very little he could truthfully say about their situation. She knew their danger as well as he did. She simply rested against him until he whispered to her about the possibility of bribing the sentries; then she sat up a little, moved in the darkness, and eventually felt for one of his hands. She turned it palm upward and placed something inside.

As she was lowering her head to his shoulder again, she said, "Sixty dollars."

Juan and Brett stared.

The sentries were silent now. Beyond their position the camp was restless; men who should have been sleeping were wandering. Others sat hunched beneath blankets talking and smoking. Gil Ortiz was with some horsemen whose animals were dull-eyed racks of bone.

A number of glowing little fires were dying because there was no one to tend them.

Stars shone brilliantly, as dazzling as only stars can be on a south desert night. The aroma of cooking lingered, although most of two beeves had been consumed hours earlier, and tendrils of smoke lay everywhere.

Men passed the improvised tent. Occasionally they hesitated briefly to talk with the sentries. While Brett was very gently easing the sleeping woman off his shoulder, Juan whispered to him.

"Ortiz has passed an order; no one is to leave. No more men can be spared." Juan leaned over to see his companion's face and grinned. "That order put the fear of God in those who remain. They think he means to march north and attack the Yanqui army. They are sneaking away in droves."

Brett patted the Mexican on the shoulder and went to stand directly beneath the ammunition boxes as he quietly called, "You up there, can you hear me?"

They heard him, but did no more than acknowledge that.

"Listen closely. We put all our money together. You can have it by helping us out of here and looking the other way so we can escape."

One of the sentries snorted, "You can't escape. No one is asleep out there. You wouldn't get a hundred yards."

"You can have the money to let us try."

Juan called softly upward in Spanish. "Listen to me, friends. Help us out of here. For that you can have sixty American dollars between you. If you are smart, you will then take the two horses and leave like others are doing, like the men who guarded us before you plan to do at midnight. Señores, unless you leave this place, you are dead men. You must know that."

There was no reply from above until after some horsemen rattled past, heading east. Then one sentry said to the other the *commandante* must have sent them in that direction to find the gringos, otherwise they should have been riding in the opposite direction.

His companion barely heeded the horsemen. In Spanish, he said, "Thirty dollars for each of us. Do you know how much I have gotten so far in plunder? Three gold coins—and someone stole them from me in my sleep! Hernan'?"

One of the sentries rose from the front of the improved tent and went back to kneel above the ammunition boxes. He spoke in English.

"All right. But the only way for you to make it is if Gavilan and I go with you. We know where the horses are. You understand?"

Brett understood perfectly; their guards did not care whether they escaped or not, they only cared that they could use the captives as shields and hostages for their own escape. He said, "Move the boxes."

The sentry struggled alone until his friend came back to help. Between them they got the boxes away from the hole and looked down. Brett said, "A rope, something we can use to climb out."

One of the guards rummaged for a rope and returned with it. He was nervous and told his companion to go out front and watch for anyone approaching the tent. When he was alone, this man lowered the rope. Brett was too heavy for the guard to help, so Juan stepped forward. This time the guard had less trouble because Juan was a lithe, lean individual.

Lifting Lillian up took time. The watcher out front was also getting nervous and hissed for them to hasten.

When she was out of the hole, Juan had to lend a hand getting Brett up. When all three of them were out of the hole, their guard raised a handgun and cocked it. Without a word, Brett handed over sixty dollars.

The man out front swore and stepped back under the tarp, where the darkness was deeper. Someone was approaching, he warned, and palmed his handgun as he crouched.

A thick, heavy *bandolero* with a stubbly beard came to

the front of the tent to look into the darkness as he said, "Hernando?"

The slighter of the guards answered, "Pepe, what is it?"

"It is Ortiz."

"What about him?"

"He has gone wild."

"Why?"

"Because everyone is leaving. He tried to kill a man with his sword. The man knocked him down and threw the sword away, and if I hadn't stopped him he would have shot Ortiz. Hernan', I am leaving. Come with me. I think we can get home if we are careful."

The slight man's reply was slow arriving. "You go ahead, Pepe. Gavilan and I will find you. If not on the trail then later, in the village."

The burly man considered this for a moment before speaking again. "If you don't come soon, the gringos will get you."

Hernan' replied in a reassuring way. "No, they won't even get down here until after daylight. Go. We'll catch up."

The burly man grumbled as he turned away, but he hadn't gone very far when the sentry called Gavilan spoke to his friend from the darkness. "Maybe we should go with him."

Hernando's reply to that was brusque. "No! We have to take the prisoners, too. If they come after us, we can let them have the prisoners—someone is coming."

Brett led Lillian to a pile of horse equipment, whispered for her to lie flat, and found a holstered Colt in the tangle of horsemen's leather. He shoved the weapon into the back of his waistband.

This time the noise of someone approaching was louder. It sounded like two or three men, and one of them was cursing. Brett recognized the voice of Gil Ortiz. He crouched beside the woman, reached around, and palmed the six-gun. He hadn't checked it for loads. It was too dark to see them, so he ran the tip of one finger over the cylinder, feeling for rounded heads. The gun was ready to fire.

Juan whispered, "Ortiz!"

Brett did not reply, but up near the front of the tent the heavier of their guards also whispered, this time in Spanish, to the slightly built guard, "They'll come inside. Hernando!"

The way the name was said made it sound like a plea. But the slight man showed no fear when he whispered back, "Wait! Don't shoot, or it will bring others. Wait! Maybe nothing will happen."

Brett thought that was wishful thinking and tightened his grip on the gun he was holding.

The approaching men halted east of the tent, out of the sight of the desperate people who waited inside.

The unmistakable voice of Gil Ortiz snarled at someone who answered back in Spanish, his voice full of deference. Brett had no time to look at Juan for an interpretation. Ortiz stormed right up to the entrance of the tent and halted to give an order in Spanish.

There were three men with him, not two. He had told one of them to bring his saddle out front. The man was hatless. He wore two guns and looked formidable as he started ahead into the darkness.

Brett had no hope of this man not seeing them if he got close enough, and he did. He walked over to the very pile of horse equipment Lillian was hiding behind, with Brett Kandelin crouching nearby.

But even as Brett was bringing his gun hand up, someone yelled up front, sounding surprised, and the next moment scarlet muzzle blasts ripped the darkness apart. Ortiz whirled away. His three companions stood their ground, firing into the tent. Two guns blasted back from the darkness. One *bandolero* went down like a pole-axed steer, and another one screamed in pain as a bullet shattered his knee. He, too, went down, but he writhed and groaned. The other downed man did not move.

Farther out men shouted; the entire camp came alive. Someone kept yelling, "Gringos! Gringos!" Panic ensued, but in the pandemonium the remaining Mexican out front fired to his right before Brett and one of the guards killed him.

The slight man sprang up, yelling for everyone to run. His companion did not respond. He was dead behind a mound of cast asides.

Brett got Lillian to her feet, gripped her around the waist, and followed Juan, who went around the gaping hole and out the back of the improvised tent. Most of the shouting came from the opposite direction, but Juan and Brett could both make out more raiders converging on the tent from the north, too. Not many, but enough.

Juan turned abruptly eastward and ran like a deer toward the nearest underbrush. Brett could not make as good time, even though Lillian courageously tried not to slow him.

Juan turned with brush at his back, watching for pursuit. There was none. Not right away. Men were shouting, running in all directions; some even fired at nonexistent attackers.

The escapees got into the thicket. Juan did not stop until they'd penetrated the thorny shelter for several hundred yards. When he finally did halt, Lillian slumped in Brett's arms and a distant voice, made louder by rage, called an offer in Spanish of one thousand American dollars to anyone who found the people who had escaped from the hole. He wanted them alive.

"Ortiz," Juan said. "They will comb the brush. We have to keep moving."

Lillian traveled on nothing but spirit. Brett remained with her until Juan halted again, this time close to the place where he'd killed the first Mexican.

Brett waited for sounds of furious raiders beating the brush behind them. He heard nothing until they were moving again, and this time there was no question about it—they were being hunted.

Juan bemoaned his lack of a weapon as he set an unerring course in the direction of the horses they had left tied in the underbrush up ahead. If the animals had been found and taken, he could do no more than continue to try and stay ahead of their pursuit. Once, he looked around where Brett was half carrying the exhausted woman. Juan shook his head. "From the cooking pot into the fire," he observed, and widened his stride.

What finally halted them was the clearly audible sound of loping horsemen to the south of them. They were riding eastward. Juan threw up his hands. He was sweating despite the late-night chill. "They will be ahead of us," he told Brett. "If the horses are still there, they will find them. Partner, I think it will soon be over."

Brett eased the handsome woman to the ground, counted the slugs remaining in his handgun, and swore under his breath. The gun held only three unfired cartridges. Juan knew that it would not make any difference whether Brett had a full charge or no charge at all. It was not going to alter the outcome of their difficultly by more than a few minutes.

A man shouted from behind them and was answered by another man southward. A third man called out. He sounded gleeful. "I can smell them," he said in Spanish. "Just a little farther, friends. And remember—a thousand Yanqui dollars."

It seemed to Brett that the brush beaters were on both sides of them as well as to the rear. He felt the woman's fingers reaching for him. He leaned over to grip her hand and smile downward. She had tears streaming down both cheeks, but she cried silently.

He leaned over farther, kissed her cheek, and whispered, "I want to say something to you. . . . The first time I saw you, I thought you were the prettiest woman I'd ever seen. I still think so."

Her shoulders convulsed, she freed his hand to cover her face as she cried, but she still did not make a sound.

Juan had wrenched a wrist-thick dead limb from a bush and was holding it like a club as the infiltrating raiders pushed their relentless search. For them, the purpose was one thousand U.S. dollars. The fleeing people meant nothing to them, whether they took them alive or dead—except that Ortiz had told them he wanted the prisoners brought back alive. A thousand U.S. dollars was a fortune, more than most of them could acquire through either legal or illegal methods.

Juan tried a ruse. He yelled in Spanish that the fugitives had turned northward through the underbrush. He repeated that twice, and it seemed to cause hesitation.

Juan wiped away sweat as he listened. He knew that although his ruse might work temporarily, the end was going to be the same.

Brett would have helped Lillian to her feet, but Juan gestured. "No need," he told the older man. "They are in front of us, too." He looked sadly at the injured woman. "I'm sorry," he told her in Spanish, and joined Brett in watching her as she brought forth the old relic of Mission Coyotero and bowed her head above it.

Both men had thought Gil Ortiz had stolen the crucifix. Obviously he hadn't, but that was not going to make any difference, either. Nevertheless, Juan pulled off his hat as the handsome woman prayed.

CHAPTER 14
Toward Dawn

There was a thin streak of light along the horizon and the chill was more noticeable than ever. So was the racket from the *bandolero* encampment. Normally this was the time of early morning when men slept best. Not now on the south desert.

The little fires were down to coals that occasionally sparked in a fitful way. There seemed to be a great many of them. What was puzzling to Enos was that the yelling and commotion seemed to be moving eastward, away from the encampment.

He turned to the disheveled, pock-faced Mexican and cocked an eyebrow. 'Pifas ignored the expectant look for a while. He tried to analyze the sounds, and once, hearing an outcry about a thousand gringo dollars, he finally figured out what was occurring southward, down through the thicket about a hundred yards south of where he, the dark man, and the youngest man were standing, trailing their reins and listening.

"They are hunting someone in the underbrush. There is a big reward for the fugitives. A thousand dollars." 'Pifas turned his head slowly, met the dark man's stare, then slowly faced southward again, where the sound of men was now louder. He said one more thing: "Whoever it is, why don't they shoot?"

Hale Barlow answered. "Because they ain't got no guns."

Enos said, "Hell, yes. Prisoners don't have guns. Sure as hell it's—Leave the horses. Fetch your carbines an' let's go."

Enos plunged through underbrush, most of it taller than he was, until his shirt hung in shreds. Behind him the big Mexican broke trail for Hale Barlow. None of them reached the site of all the noise uninjured. Some of the thorns were nearly two inches long.

It was Hale, sidling around a threatening bush, who nearly collided with a startled Mexican wearing crossed bandoleers and using his rifle to fend off the undergrowth. The Mexican had been hurrying eastward, probably with some idea of getting in front of the fugitives.

When Hale came around, into the Mexican's sight, the *bandolero* froze, eyes wide, his mouth slack from breathing hard.

Hale raised his Winchester, aimed and cocked it. The raider's eyes bulged, while around them the shouting, cursing, and catcalling continued. Hale said, "Drop the gun," and made a downward gesture with his own weapon in case the Mexican did not understand English. A man did not have to understand any language under these circumstances. The Mexican let the rifle fall.

Hale walked toward him, finger crooked inside his trigger guard. The Mexican was too petrified to even speak. Hale turned him by the shoulder and struck him over the head with the Winchester's barrel.

He turned back to catch up with his companions.

Enos and the pock-faced Mexican were standing like stones when Hale reached them. He turned to follow their line of vision and saw what appeared to be a kneeling woman through the scraggly limbs of a large thicket. As they stared, a *bandolero* appeared in the clearing, yelling he had found them, and 'Pifas shot him through the chest. Other raiders, probably believing the man who had shouted so exultantly was beginning the slaughter, raised their voices as they converged on the tiny clearing. Enos, 'Pifas, and Hale Barlow plunged forward, finally seeing Brett and his companions. But this time, hastening *ban-*

doleros were coming from all directions, some shouting, some cursing the thorns, others simply pushing ahead for the kill.

Four ragged, breathless raiders appeared simultaneously from the west, using rifles to push ahead into the little clearing.

Enos, 'Pifas, and Hale Barlow opened up on them from a distance of no more than two hundred feet. Other raiders, hearing the massed gunfire, rushed ahead. One of them came through the underbrush, almost directly in front of 'Pifas, who held off until the man saw him, then fired.

The gunfire was brisk, too brisk to be coming from the fugitives, but the raiders still charged ahead. Someone yelled in Spanish it was the gringo army, and that stopped most of the shouting, even though it did not immediately slacken the rush of the attackers. After a number of *bandoleros* had been shot in the confusion, the Mexicans began to scramble back the way they had come, which was fortunate because the firing trio had just about shot out their weapons and needed time to reload.

One large *bandolero* emerged at the south side of the small clearing, gun lifting as he saw Brett, Juan, and the kneeling woman. His features had been wiped clean of every expression except one. He had not completely raised his Colt when he fired. The bullet made Juan flinch. As the man was pulling back the hammer for another shot, a withering blast of gunfire knocked him back into a large bush, where he hung impaled like a large insect.

Brett was holding an empty six-gun when 'Pifas, Hale, and Enos pushed through.

In the distance, horsemen were approaching at a dead run. There was no time for talk. Brett retrieved the large Mexican's weapon and was yanking his shell belt off when 'Pifas yelled for everyone to hide—and set the example by pushing into the underbrush on the south side of the opening.

Brett flung the shell belt over one shoulder, shoved the six-gun into his waistband, went over to Lillian, and pulled her upright. He grabbed her around the middle and hastened after the others.

The oncoming horsemen were shouting to the *bandoleros* who had been routed. With no one to interpret, Brett had to assume the horsemen were cursing the men on foot for allowing themselves to be chased away, but there was too much shouting on both ides to make any kind of an accurate guess about what was being said.

Brett ignored the noise to concentrate on the horse sounds. They reached the southernmost edge of the dense thicket before stopping, and this time, as 'Pifas said loudly in English, there were too many, and they weren't peons. He looked around for Juan, who was lying flat on the ground with his Winchester in front of him, and reverted to Spanish. "*Los caballos, compañero, los caballos!*"

Juan raised his head but otherwise gave no indication that he had heard or had understood that 'Pifas was urging them to get the horses the dismounted Mexicans had left.

The pock-faced man had no chance to cry out again. The *bandoleros* were firing as they advanced. With nothing to aim at, and shooting waist high, bullets cut through the underbrush without coming close to the fugitives.

The dark man got to one knee, snugged back his weapon, and waited until he could dimly discern a man pushing through the brush toward him. He fired once, the *bandolero* disappeared, and the firing on both sides brisked up as Enos dropped flat.

As happened before, the gunfire from those invisible people near the small clearing was too fierce and prolonged; the dismounted horsemen began withdrawing back toward their horses.

'Pifas looked around for Juan again, but this time he said nothing. Hale Barlow came up beside the big Mexican. "If them bastards get back to their horses . . ."

'Pifas made a death-head grin and jerked his head. He was pushing forward when he said, "We need the horses worse than they do."

Brett watched 'Pifas and Hale disappear through the underbrush and moved toward Juan, where he stopped, looked, and was about to speak when he saw the blood. For the moment, there was nothing he could do. He turned toward the handsome woman and pointed downward, and continued on an easterly course until he, too, was hidden by underbrush.

He heard someone speaking in rapid and angry Spanish, fixed the location of that voice, and began moving toward it when a growly, quiet voice said, "Ain't no such thing as a one-man army."

Neither Brett nor Enos had any idea what the argument had been about, but both men slackened their advance and became doubly alert. Whoever had been angry was not very far ahead and was slightly west of where Brett and Enos would emerge.

Back in the direction of the encampment, someone fired a rifle. Just one shot, but the echoes carried easily in the dawn-brightening, cold morning air.

Brett sank down, parted some brush, and looked out. Enos, more to the west, did not have to push brush aside; he could see the *bandoleros* in open country, south of his thicket.

There were six of them, with one man lying flat out on the ground at the feet of a hawk-faced, very dark man with a gun in his fist as he addressed the other *bandoleros*.

He seemed to be challenging them. From his fierce stance and their abject faces, it appeared he was not going to be challenged for knocking one of them unconscious.

Enos brought his carbine to bear in agonizingly slow movement. The horsemen were turning toward their mounts to comply with whatever the fierce man wanted done when Enos squeezed the trigger.

The fierce man, in the act of mounting when the slug hit him between the shoulder blades, was punched forward against the horse. He reached desperately for something to grasp, found nothing, and fell down to the ground while his companions, also about to mount, wasted a precious moment looking back. Brett fired, levered up, and fired again.

Enos's firing was so closely spaced the muzzle blasts sounded almost like one continuous roar.

One *bandolero* took to his heels, threw away his weapon,

and both Enos and Brett, who could have shot him on the wing, lowered their guns as they watched.

Brett pushed through and caught a horse by the reins. Enos, westward a short distance, caught two other horses. Brett tried to catch another one, but the horse whirled and ran. Brett moved more slowly the second time and was able to catch another horse.

'Pifas and Hale Barlow came out of the underbrush and were able to catch another animal. 'Pifas and Hale Barlow, who had started forward first, had been delayed from joining the fight because they had no idea who was shooting from the north.

Brett said it would be easier to bring the woman and Juan out to the horses than to get the horses to crash through the thicket. He and Hale went back. Enos and the big Mexican remained with the animals.

Over where the raider camp was, men were yelling, firing guns, and creating a pandemonium of total confusion. Enos looked in the camp's direction and smiled. "What gringo army?" He laughed derisively while reloading.

'Pifas smiled but neither laughed nor spoke. There was no need to. What had happened was obvious. The *bandolero* who had cried out that the gringos were upon them had started a rout.

After Enos had holstered his gun, he gazed at the big Mexican. "You all right?"

Without replying to the question, 'Pifas smiled. "The next time we have trouble at night, I'll take you along. You're hard to see."

Enos was looking steadily at the pockmarked man as Brett and Hale emerged from the underbrush, shirts nearly in shreds as they brought the battered woman and Juan into sight.

Juan had a clumsy bandage around his upper left leg. Part of his trousers were soaked with blood.

It required some effort to get them both astride. When everyone was mounted, Brett led off westward and did not stop until Enos pointed to an opening in the underbrush and said he was going back for his horse.

Brett said nothing as the dark man and the youngest man swung off and disappeared into the thicket, but when 'Pifas rolled his eyes and muttered something about the world being full of horses but men only had one life, Brett nodded in agreement. He kneed his Mexican mount over beside Lillian and smiled at her.

Until this moment, he had not realized the night was gone: watery dawnlight of a new day was at hand. Before long, the sun would arrive.

Enos and Hale returned astride their own animals. Without a word, Brett led off again in the direction where he and Juan had left their horses the night before.

The animals were still there, fretful, thirsty, and hungry, but still tied.

This time when the ride was resumed Brett and 'Pifas did not abandon the Mexican mounts; they led them along while angling northward.

Reaction eventually set in. They rode slumped and mostly quiet. Juan held to his saddle horn. He was tired, worn out to the point of dull lethargy, and had lost enough blood from his wounded leg to be groggy. Enos rode beside him.

Hale Barlow had acquired a six-gun during the fight and rode along examining it. In semidarkness it had seemed to be a good weapon, but by daylight it showed too many signs of neglect and abuse. He threw it away.

By sunrise they were back up near the roofless adobe where the God-trusting priest had learned, too late, that for whatever reason, he was not supposed to build a church.

Thirst was a problem, more for the animals than for their riders, but there was nothing to be done about that until they got back to Coyotero.

It would have been worse if they'd been riding through midday heat. Dawn chill remained for a couple of hours. Then, as the sunlight increased, they could make out the roofs of Coyotero.

This appeared to have a refreshing effect upon Hale Barlow. He mentioned that first *bandolero* to be shot and sounded proud—until Enos fixed him with dark eyes in a setting of muddy whites.

"Couple things you might want to remember, Hale," he said. "One is that for all them prayers the Messicans make when they get into trouble, God is on the side of the heaviest caliber. The other thing is that in a mess like last night, you only got one instinct, survival."

Silence settled again. Enos tucked a chew into his cheek and kept an eye on Juan, whom he did not know, and Brett rode with the handsome woman whose face looked terrible in daylight. Tired as he was, his blood boiled. He'd been dead set on finding Gil Ortiz and killing him, and all he'd done was find him.

Lillian interrupted his thoughts. "Grandfather was right, wasn't he? He said you'd come."

Brett smiled a little. "I'm very sorry about what happened to him."

She spoke in a way that implied to Brett that she'd thought a lot about this. She said, "He couldn't have survived what we went through. For one thing, his legs weren't strong. He couldn't have run from the tent to the underbrush. What I wish is that he could have died in comfort and could have been buried at the mission." She changed the subject. "Before they came to take us away, he heard that you had gone to find your cattle. He told me he knew you, knew what you were going to do with the cattle. . . . And he prayed. He told me what he prayed for . . . that the darkness would last long enough for you to get down here and the *bandoleros* would not see you."

Brett gazed steadily at the handsome woman.

She spoke again. "Gil Ortiz took the relic from me and beat me with it. It is very heavy."

"How did you get it back?"

"Some men came to the tent to say messengers had arrived from Mexico. He flung it down and left the tent. I put it inside my dress. He didn't come back, but he sent men to throw me into the hole. . . . Would you like to know something else?"

Brett nodded.

"In that little clearing, I watched you count your bullets—and Juan did not have a gun. They were so close I could feel them closing in. . . . I asked the relic to help us."

Brett let go with a long silent breath and looked ahead, where the town seemed to draw nearer. Lillian studied his profile before speaking again. "You don't believe we were helped?"

He rubbed his stubbly jaw before replying, and he also picked his words very carefully. "Well, yes'm, we were helped. Enos and Hale and 'Pifas—"

She smiled at him. "It doesn't matter. You don't have to understand. You are a gringo. Do you know how long we've had the relic in Coyotero? Maybe three hundred years; that's what my grandfather said. In three hundred years the town has been attacked many times, people have been killed, livestock driven away."

He looked at her. She looked back. "For three hundred years we have suffered, have been killed, have gone hungry . . . and we are still here."

He cleared his throat.

Her eyes were calmly quiet as she looked at him, even the one that had been swollen shut. "I won't talk about this anymore. I owe you—and your companions—everything. My life—everything. I don't know the English words to tell you how much I am thankful."

He tipped his hat down because sunlight was being reflected off mica flakes. "You need a doctor," he said, and she gently shook her head at him.

"I know what to do. The cheek will have a small scar, otherwise time will help me."

"I could ride north, find one, and bring him back for you."

"No." She watched the town get closer for a moment. "No. Can I show you?"

"Show me what?"

"That I know the cures. Will you stay in Coyotero for a week so I can show you? Because it will take that long."

He straightened in the saddle to ease his back, looked at her, and said, "I'll stay longer if you'd like me to."

CHAPTER 15

The Long Ride Back

Marshal Severn had gone with the soldiers, Jake the cafe man told them as they waited to be fed at his empty counter. Brett asked where the liveryman was, and Jake shook his head as he was turning away. "Ain't seen him since yes-tiddy. Maybe he went with the soldiers, too."

Brett doubted that, but did not speak again as the cafe man went to his cooking area. He looked at them; they looked filthy, ragged, bruised, and sunken-eyed. Lillian was not with them. She had refused to go to the cafe with them after the horses had been left down at the livery barn in the charge of a scrawny-looking day man. She told Brett she needed to be alone for a while and to sleep. She said she was dead on her feet. She certainly looked it. She would not even allow him to accompany her to the first dogtrot, but he watched until she was no longer in sight, then led the others to the cafe.

When the cafe man brought their platters and got their coffee, he said, "Last night there was a hell of a fight down near the border somewhere. Maybe the Mex army came over the line and caught them raiders."

No one spoke. At this juncture, nothing was more important than food, water, and coffee.

The cafe man was untroubled about being ignored. "About half the able-bodied men rode with the soldiers. Beefed up their strength."

Hale Barlow raised an eye. "How many soldiers was there?"

"Couple companies. Maybe sixty, seventy-five men."

Hale stared. Even with all those draining desertions there still had been about twice that number of raiders down there.

He did not say anything before returning to his meal.

Inevitably, word had spread. Before the hungry men finished breakfast and returned to the roadway, people were beginning to congregate out front, some across the road, some directly in front of the cafe man's grimy window, and a few bold souls came inside, ordered coffee, and smiled at the ragged and haggard-looking diners.

One man asked if they had found the alcalde and his granddaughter. Brett said they had and went on eating. The townsman asked another question: "An' that old cross they set such store by in Mex town. We heard that disappeared, too."

Brett paused to say, "It's been recovered."

The townsman had one more question. "Where are the *bandoleros*?"

This time, Enos answered. "With any luck at all, on their way to hell!" He abruptly rose, tapped Juan, got 'Pifas to help him, and made a chair of their arms to carry the injured man up to the hotel.

Jess Eames was not there. The thick-bodied woman of middle age and middling pleasantness who was minding the place while Eames was gone, eyed their bedraggled appearance and seemed inclined to block the doorway until 'Pifas said, "You forget very fast, señora, who saved you and your town."

The woman held back whatever she might have said as Enos shouldered roughly past her on one side, the pock-faced large man on the other side.

They were still busy with Juan's injury, bathing it, cleansing it, and using the only disinfectant available—carbolic acid—when the sturdy woman returned with a tall, gray, lean woman with a testy look—the local midwife. She elbowed her way to the cot, looked at Juan, put several fingers to the side of his throat, seemed to be listening to something for a moment, then leaned back and inspected the bandaging before she spoke.

"Did you wash his leg good?"

Brett explained the sequence they'd followed. The woman leaned to sniff the bandaging, tried to peek beneath it, then stepped back, looking at the dark-eyed man who was looking up at her. He said, "*B'dias, Tia* Eileen."

The woman leaned closer. "Juan? Juan Escalante? What are you doing here? The last I heard you were tending sheep for the Gonzagas over at Desplobado. How did you get injured?"

Juan's smile was fading as he replied, "*Bandoleros*, señora.

She stood a moment looking downward then abruptly turned and herded them out of the little room, using both arms and a hissing sound. As she leaned in the doorway, she said, "Don't come back. I'll look after him." She rolled her eyes. "I delivered him. I've known him all his life." She closed the door, and the sturdy woman who was managing the hotel in Eames's absence flapped her arms.

"If anyone can look after him, Eileen O'Grady can."

She stood in place as the men crowded past, entered the room Brett had been using, and closed the door. The woman rolled her eyes. When Mr. Eames got back and found out she'd let two Messicans and a black man bed down in his hotel, he'd raise hell and prop it up.

Brett slept until midafternoon before going out back to the washhouse, bathing, shaving, and trooping back for his only change of clothing. None of the others stirred. He might not have, either, if some troublesome thoughts had not arrived to haunt him.

Over in Mex town it was still siesta time. Except for some wandering chickens and a couple of sleeping sprawled dogs who raised their heads to watch him pass, then to drop their heads back down and close their eyes, there was almost no activity. Brett came upon a grizzled, lined old man with bright eyes and two teeth that showed, who was shuffling along with the aid of a stick whittled from a red-barked manzanita bush. They had met once before in the identical manner.

The old man stopped, eyed Kandelin, and at this meeting he did not smile. He simply said, "The alcalde is dead."

Brett halted and nodded. "I'm very sorry."

The old man continued to study Kandelin. "Well, now he knows something we don't know, eh?"

"I reckon he does. I'm glad to see you came through the fighting."

The old man pointed with his manzanita cane. "Some of us went to the secret cellar at the mission. But we heard things. They searched for the crucifix." The old man lowered his stick to lean on as he shook his head. "This is the third time. It was recovered the other two times. This time"—he shrugged thin shoulders—"this time they will melt it down."

Brett smiled. "Lillian Velarde brought it back with her."

The old man's eyes widened. "But she . . . wasn't killed, then?"

"No. She has the cross." Before the old man could speak, Brett asked him a question. "The alcalde's name was Velarde?"

"*Sí.* Yes."

"And his granddaughter's name is Velarde?"

The old man's gaze plainly said gringos were pretty dense at times. "It should have been. The man who was her father was also named Velarde."

Brett decided that someday, when he had the time, he was going to have to look into how these people used names. He gave the old man a gentle slap on the back and was preparing to move on, but the old man wanted to know what had become of the soldiers.

Brett explained. He also said men from Gringo town had ridden with the soldiers. The old man replied that so had most of the men from Mex town. Except for one man, and no one had been able to find him. A man named Juan Escalante.

Brett told the old man where Juan was and what had happened to him. The old man rolled his eyes. "Señor

Eames will throw him out," he said, and at Brett's mildly enquiring expression, the old man also said, "He won't have Mexicans in his hotel."

"This time he will," replied the younger man as he gave *el viejo* a light slap on the shoulder and continued on his way to the Velarde adobe.

The day was flawless, pleasantly cool and soft-scented from the springtime desert. When he reached the *jacal*, he sat down on the bench out front.

Some children, in their wonderful innocence, appeared over near the walled water well to play in the dust. A vaquero entered town from the south, nodded at Brett as he rode past, and disappeared among the crooked little narrow streets.

An Indian, old as the dust underfoot, came through, leading a burro laden with faggots painstakingly gathered on the desert for sale as cooking fuel. He was very dark, with a low hairline, a thick upper body, and spindly legs, and neither nodded nor spoke as he saw the gringo watching him.

A buxom, handsome older woman appeared, hands on ample hips, frowning in the direction of the shaded bench. Brett smiled and nodded. She said, "Why don't you knock on the door, vaquero?"

"She's sleeping. She's been through what no human being should even see in a nightmare. I'll wait."

The buxom woman eyed the door, the shade where Brett sat beneath the rickety old *ramada*, sighed, and said, "I know who you are, señor." She flaunted her head in the direction of the doorway. "Go ahead. Knock." When Brett did not move, the woman rolled her eyes in exasperation. "You are a cattleman? And you know horses? Maybe even dogs? . . . But nothing about women!"

She stepped into the shade, struck the door several times with a powerful fist, and ignored the man watching from her left side until the door opened. She said something sharp in Spanish, turned, and marched back the way she had come.

Lillian looked out. Brett rose. She still showed clear evidence of abuse, but her swollen eye was partially open and her gashed cheek had been cared for until only the thin line itself remained. She smiled at him as she stepped aside for him to enter.

"I was uncomfortable," he told her. "It's peaceful on the bench. Did you sleep?"

She had. She had also eaten, and wondered if he had. He told her he'd eaten like a horse, but he was now thirsty.

Someone had put the overturned furniture back where it belonged, had cleaned the sitting room and kitchen, but had been unable to scrub out the bloodstains. In fact, they would never be fully removed no matter how much scrubbing was done. But they could be hidden by small rugs. Of the bullet holes, they were a small consideration in an adobe house. Eventually someone would simply go over near the hidey-hole with a small pail, sift stones out of the dirt, mix in water, perhaps some horse manure or straw, and plaster over the holes.

She got him a dipperful of cold water and watched him drink it. She offered to cook a meal. When he declined, she brought forth the bottle of red wine he'd last seen when he and the alcalde had shared it. She put in on the table, went around to the opposite side to sit down, and waited until he sat across from her before she asked about Juan.

He explained all that had been done. He also mentioned the witchlike midwife, and she smiled. She knew Eileen O'Grady very well. "If anyone can help him, she can."

He filled a small glass with wine, set it in front of her, and filled one for himself as he gazed over at her . . . and remembered something he'd told her last night, or very early this morning.

His color started rising. What he'd said last night, or this morning, he'd said because he'd been sure none of them would survive.

Lilian put her head slightly to one side as she watched him. "Are you sure you're not hungry?" she said. "Because after only a few swallows of the wine your face is getting red."

He asked about the crucifix, turning her attention elsewhere. "It's back in its little niche. . . . There has to be another alcalde. It will be his responsibility." Her smile faded as she picked up her wineglass.

She asked about the army. There was nothing he could tell her, except that men from both Gringo town and Mex town had ridden south with the soldiers.

"And," she said softly, "Gil Ortiz?"

He knew nothing about Ortiz, either. The last time he'd seen the man had been while they had been hiding inside the improvised tent.

She looked into her wineglass. "Maybe he will be foolish enough to try and sneak back into Mexico. Maybe he will get a good horse and ride west, or maybe even north, where he's not known. Maybe he'll ride a long way." She stopped to meet his eyes across the table. "But what I think, señor, is that he will come back, maybe in the night, and cut my throat."

Brett drained the little glass and leaned on the table. He did not deny the possibility. Before all the trouble, he'd only met Ortiz up on the northern plains as someone who wanted to buy cattle. Since those days, he'd encountered an altogether different Gil Ortiz.

He changed the subject again. "What will you do? Will you stay here?"

Her large, liquid dark eyes widened at the question. "Yes. This is where I was born. Someday, when I can afford it, I want to have my grandfather brought to the mission and buried there."

"You're not afraid he will return?"

"Gil Ortiz?" She shrugged. "Yes, I am afraid, but once I ran away and stayed away until my grandfather was ill, then I came back. But I wanted to return long before that. Do you understand?"

He nodded, although, in fact, he had never had a home.

She said, "Can you recover your cattle?"

He didn't think so. "Maybe some, but with the people below the line—as well as the *bandoleros* and whoever else is hungry down here—I'd be lucky to get back half, or maybe less than half."

She was solicitous. "But the town should pay you for them. The cattle did what the townsmen couldn't have done—they routed the raiders."

He smiled wryly. "*Should* and *will* are two different words. Already folks seem to be forgetting. In a month or two it'll most likely be history. We'll make out, Lillian. Enos, Hale, and I were picking up a few head here and there before we got down this far. We can do it again."

He rose. "I'm glad you're feeling better. That was something to remember, wasn't it? Someday you can tell your grandchildren . . . and they won't believe you!"

She rose, smiling. "Will you do something for me, señor?"

"My name is Brett, Brett Kandelin. And yes, I'll do something for you."

"Will you come back tonight for supper?"

He looked steadily at her while replying. "There's nothing I'd rather do. What time?"

She shrugged. "Sundown?"

He went through to the front door, stood with his hands held out until she gripped them, then he said, "You thought that wine was getting to me?"

"You were getting red in the face."

"Probably was, but it wasn't the wine. I remembered what I told you when I thought we were one breath away from getting killed."

She looked away. "Sundown?"

He squeezed her fingers, turned, and walked up in the direction of the nearest dogtrot.

There was a tired horse standing hip-shot over in front of the jailhouse. Brett walked over to the building, pushed on in, and saw Marshal Severn doing what he'd been doing once before when Brett had walked in—getting a cup of hot coffee at the little iron stove.

The marshal looked tired, dirty, and rumpled. He nodded, went around behind his table, and sat down before speaking. "Help yourself. It's a fresh pot. We got different stories down there. They said you'd been killed, or had escaped, or had snuck away with the alcalde's granddaughter, ridin' west.'' Marshal Severn tasted his coffee while Brett sat down near the door. Brett told him all he could remember, and the older man leaned forward, hands clasped, listening. When it was his turn, he drained the cup before beginning, made a rueful face.

''The army had some notion of gettin' around 'em, between them an' the border. Trouble was, they wasn't all in their camp. Hell, we commenced runnin' into 'em, one and two at a time, before we even got close. Deserters all over the desert. The army rounded 'em up, put 'em under guard, and the lieutenant changed plans. He strung his men out from east to west, and started a full-length advance.

''They fought. They didn't have no choice. It was us, or the red flaggers and regulars waitin' south of the border.

''It was a pretty hot little squabble for a while, but there wasn't enough of 'em that stood and fought. . . . We took a passel of prisoners. The army struck out for home, takin' the prisoners along.''

''Gil Ortiz?''

''Nope. The lieutenant personally went through 'em, and like before, every man he questioned said somethin' different.'' Marshal Severn dismissed Gil Ortiz. ''We got more damn plunder, horses, and whatnot than the army could pack away. A lot of Mex money, useless except for the gold. A lot of gold, too, mostly stolen from churches down there, and ranches.'' Marshall Severn wagged his head. ''When the lieutenant said he was goin' to strike out for home, I asked him what the hell I was supposed to do with a jailhouse full of *bandoleros*! You know what he said? He said, 'Take 'em down to the border, whistle up the Mex army, and run the damned prisoners over the line to them.' ''

Brett's brows raised a little. ''What's wrong with that?''

''Nothing,'' stated the lawman, ''except that, what with that same damned thicket and thornpin country, half of 'em'd disappear in there. I'm not sure I can get up a posse to help herd 'em. Folks did their share, the town was saved. Now they want to get back to business.''

''All right. Then what are you going to do with them?''

Severn leaned back, eyeing Brett. "You got any ideas, amigo?"

"Don't take 'em south. The soldiers can't be very far off. Herd 'em along until you find the army, leave 'em, turn around, and ride back."

Marshal Severn took one of his long delays before speaking again. "Maybe. Folks aren't happy about us being left with 'em. All right, in the morning I'll see who I can round up to ride with me. . . . I saw the alcalde's grave."

Brett didn't comment about that. "You should have seen his granddaughter. Ortiz beat her in the face with that big heavy old crucifix."

The marshal's next remark was even longer coming. "Is that a fact? I kind of figured after you'n Juan left town, if I got your black friend and the other one started out soon enough, they'd find you and maybe stop you from gettin' yourself killed. To be downright truthful, Mr. Kandelin, I would have bet my wages for a year I'd never see you again—or her. . . . Now that she's home, how does she feel?"

"Better, but it'll be a while. Tell me something, Marshal. Where do you think Ortiz went?"

Severn spread both hands palms upward. "Your guess is as good as mine. Most likely as far as he can get."

CHAPTER 16

The Hang Rope's Shadow

As life in Coyotero began to get back to normal, there were a number of annoying and lingering aftershocks. One of them was the prisoners, many of whom had to be put under armed guard at the adobe that doubled for the firehouse and the Masonic lodge.

The townsmen were reluctant to leave their businesses to go with Marshal Severn in pursuit of the army, herding the prisoners along. When the lawman finally had everyone lined up in the roadway in front of the firehouse, there was grumbling among the posse men, even a few threats. But Marshal Severn got the procession moving and, except for bitter-faced onlookers, nothing more was said.

Another problem left over from the rout west of town was the plunder. Not including the artillery pieces, every day someone was finding loose horses, many still saddled, to bring to the public corral.

The liveryman complained. Because there was no place else to put them, he had Mexican horses and mules in his private corrals. If Marshal Severn had still been in town, he could have held a legal auction. He was not in town, so over the span of a week, the number of animals noticeably diminished, the result of something rather like the customary wartime Midnight Remount Requisition Service. Others were bought outright from the liveryman, who said he was accumulating boarding and feeding charges and under the law he was entitled to take animals to satisfy his claims against them.

The Mexican horse equipment was by and large ignored in Gringo town, but in Mex town the best of it was snapped up. Eventually the field pieces were dragged over behind the jailhouse and left there for some future disposal. Getting them out of sight pretty well guaranteed they'd still be there when golden trumpets signaled the arrival of the Second Coming.

By the early part of the second week following the rout and skirmishing, physical aspects of the memorable raid had been fairly well disposed of. Now, in the inevitable recapitulating, mostly at the saloon in Gringo town and the cantina in Mex town, troubling questions surfaced. One of them, of equal interest in both parts of Coyotero, had to do with Kandelin's raid on the powderhouse.

Enos and Juan Escalante, the latter able to sit out front on the hotel porch, told Jess Eames, who'd returned from the brush battle down near the border with two buckskin pouches from among the plunder of the *bandolero* camp, each containing a respectably heavy amount of raw gold, said the traitor who'd supplied the *bandoleros* with the key had to be someone over in Mex town.

Enos might have agreed, but Juan Escalante, who'd been a prisoner and had heard the conversation between Gil Ortiz and Brett Kandelin, thought differently. He told them what he'd heard.

Eames, whose segregation policy had gotten lost somewhere during the past couple of weeks, regarded Juan for a moment before saying, "Alex Herman?" and sounded less than incredulous.

Juan shrugged. "Yes. There's no other liveryman, is there?"

Enos was silent. Jess Eames leaned forward in his old chair, frowning at the ground. Nothing was said until he sat up, looking steadily at Juan. He said, "That son of a bitch."

Enos scowled. "You know him well enough to believe that, Mr. Eames?"

"Well, I know I never liked him, an' I know he'd

rather lie than tell the truth, even when the truth'd fit better. As a horse trader he's about as honest as Señor *Satán* himself."

Enos leaned back, gazing southward toward the lower end of town where the livery barn was located in what—so it was said, anyway—had once been a barracks for the Mexican Army when Mexico had owned the south desert.

Enos remembered the events out at the powderhouse and the comments about how the raiders had gotten inside. He did not know the liveryman, had only seen him a few times. Eventually he said, "You got to be sure, Mr. Eames. Otherwise, when folks hear about this, they just damned well might lynch the wrong man."

Eames eyed Enos. Until this moment, he hadn't thought about a lynching. He blew out a loud breath and also stared southward.

Their discussion ended there. Enos and Juan returned to the room where the wounded man now lived, and when they were alone, Enos asked if Juan was sure he'd heard that discussion between Gil Ortiz and Brett Kandelin. Instead of immediately answering, the scar-faced Mexican eased down on the edge of his cot and gazed sardonically at the dark man. "You don't have to take my word for it. Go ask your friend."

Enos was cutting off a chew and did not look at Juan Escalante. "I'll lay you four bits Mr. Eames ain't out there right now."

Juan smiled thinly, because he knew the hotelman better than the dark man did. "You'd win," he said. "He's over at the saloon with everyone listening to him."

Enos snapped his clasp knife closed, stood up to pocket it, and fixed the wounded man with a hard look. "I won't say he don't deserve hanging, but I know how lynchings happen, Juan. There's no sense in a mob of men with a rope. I'm goin' to find Brett."

Escalante's dark eyes kindled. "You know where he'll be?"

The dark man hung fire briefly, then smiled and nodded as he started for the door.

But all Lillian could tell the dark was that Brett would be in Mex town for supper, and as he struck out for Gringo town, she watched his departure with worried eyes. She didn't know the dark man very well, but under some circumstances it wasn't necessary to know a person to understand they were dead serious about something—like trouble, for instance.

When Enos eventually located Brett Kandelin, he was exactly where Enos didn't want him to be—down at the livery barn. He was talking to a scrawny hostler whose eyes watered and whose nose ran as though he were catching a cold, except that the hostler hadn't had a cold in years, and even if it had been the onset of a cold, his hands wouldn't be shaking.

Enos waited until Brett saw him, then jerked his head and went out front to relate what Juan had said and what Jess Eames had thought of it.

Brett listened in thoughtful silence; he'd also been looking for Alex Herman. The drunk of a day man hadn't seen his employer lately. Not since a few days after the disaster on the western desert, when that big herd of wild-eyed cattle had stampeded through the raider encampment.

When Enos had said it all, Brett had to tell him there was no sign of the liveryman. Enos said, "Well, I don't say he don't deserve a lynching, but if he's gone I'd feel better. I know somethin' about lynchings."

When they parted, with the sun beginning to slant away, Enos went up to the saloon and found Hale up there sipping sour mash during a desultory conversation with the barman. There was no sign of Jess Eames, but evidently he'd been there—because Hale Barlow knew of the rumor, and of the hotelman's solution if the liveryman could be found.

Without the candidate for a lynching being present, the story of Alex Herman's treachery spread slowly, but it spread. Later in the afternoon, when the sun was high, a number of townsmen went looking for the liveryman. Brett did not know this because he was over in Mex town, where Lillian had greeted him with a calm, quiet smile and had taken him to the kitchen where she had their supper under way.

Her swollen eye was more presentable than it had been. She had soaked in a tub of hot water, had dressed carefully and had brushed her wealth of dark hair with the gray dove wings on each side until it shone. As Brett sat watching, talking and sipping red wine, she told him in a quiet, grave voice of her marriage to Gil Ortiz, of the treatment that had eventually made her flee in a desperate search for peace, and concluded by facing around to softly smile at him as she said, "But it's not possible to run away, is it?"

He sipped wine, studied her a moment, then said, "I guess not. But it don't do any good to think about those things, either. It's over and done with. You've got a long future ahead." He smiled. "That's what matters."

She softly nodded and turned back to her cooking as she spoke in a lighter tone. "Do you like Mexican food?"

He'd tried it since being on the south desert and couldn't honestly say he felt it would ever replace boiled potatoes and steak, but he said, "When a man's in a place where that's what folks eat, he likes it, I guess."

She laughed at him. "I think you are telling me Mexican food is better than starving. Don't worry, I haven't put much pepper in."

He walked over to peer across her shoulder. "What are those things?"

"*Rellenos.*" She turned; their faces were inches apart, and she quickly faced forward. "Beef inside and—"

"Are they hot?"

She jutted her jaw in the direction of a small sauce dish. "That's hot sauce. You can make them as hot as you like, or don't use the sauce and they're not hot at all."

He remained close behind her. "What do you eat on Christmas?" he asked. "I haven't seen any turkeys down here."

"We have them, but at Christmas we only sometimes eat turkey. Never when I was a child, but now some Mexicans do." She grinned without facing around. "The gringos take charge wherever they go. Would you like a turkey for Christmas dinner?"

He gazed at the *rellenos* in her pan. They resembled something. . . . He remembered what it was: skinned dog ears, maybe a little longer, but just as rounded.

She turned because he hadn't answered. Their eyes met, and without being aware of it, they both reddened. He said, "For Christmas, what would you eat?"

"Tamales."

He'd eaten them; they weren't bad. In fact, he'd rather liked them, mainly because they hadn't been slathered with hot sauce and the filling had been cooked beef. "Well, let's have tamales," he said, looking her straight in her eyes.

She swung away, moved toward the stove to put their supper on plates, and neither spoke again nor looked around as he went to the table and filled two glasses with red wine. As he held the jug, he thought of her grandfather, but wisely kept those thoughts to himself.

As they were sitting down, she asked a question. "Do you know how old I am?"

He didn't know, and the question surprised him. "No."

"Almost forty."

He unconsciously shrugged. "It's a good age to be."

"Not in the villages down here. Forty . . . is an old woman."

He certainly did not agree with that. "Not where I come from." He looked over at her. "I'm almost ten years beyond forty. Is that an old man down here?"

"No. But men don't age as quickly as women do."

He smiled at her, and screwed up his courage to say, "How long do you reckon we'd have until we're really old?"

She had trouble answering, and took refuge in her meal. But after a while, she looked straight across the table at him. "I don't like men," she said, and he accepted that easily because the first few times they'd met he'd gotten that impression from her cold aloofness.

He went right on eating. They might have been discussing the weather. "Men, Lillian, or one man?"

She had trouble with that one, too. He did not allow her the time to form an answer. "How about your grandfather? Did you like your father? Maybe other men, maybe the priest? There's an old man with two teeth who uses a red cane and putters around—"

"That's Abizu Corales. Do you know him?"

"No. I've met him twice."

"He's not a Mexican. Did you know that?"

Brett shook his head while reaching for the wine. He had thought the old man was typically Mexican. "What is he, then?"

"He came from Spain a long time ago. When my grandfather was a young man. But he's not Spanish. He came from somewhere in the mountains. One time when I was small, he showed us on a map. The mountains between Spain and France."

He tipped her glass full, too, as he said, "Do you like him?"

"Yes," she said, before she caught the implication.

He smiled at her. "He's a man."

She ate for a moment in silence between them, and then he stole a look. When she caught his look, she smiled. "Do you know the Spanish word for a lawyer?" she asked.

He shook his head. "I don't know any Spanish words, but lately I've figured out what some of them might mean."

"You should have been a lawyer."

He laughed. "Will you teach me Spanish?"

"Yes."

"I'm a slow learner, Lillian."

He didn't confuse her this time; she was a woman with the instincts of all women. She replied without looking at him. "Time is all I have. I don't know whether or not I would be a good teacher."

They hadn't finished their meal, but now the hunger part of it was gone, which was fortunate because someone out front rolled a hard fist across the door. Lillian's reaction was to grip the edge of the table and give him a wide-eyed look.

He rose, winked at her, and went through to the sitting

room, where Enos and Hale Barlow were standing in the dusk. Neither of them smiled as Enos mentioned the liveryman, the town's lynching mood, and concluded by saying the people in Gringo town had found the liveryman and had dragged him to the jailhouse. He was locked in a cell until they could organize the hanging.

Brett was silent for a long time. Finally, he told them to wait and returned to the kitchen, where Lillian was stiffly standing with one hand pressed to her heart. She had heard.

"I have to leave," he told her. "I'm sorry. Can I come back later?"

She nodded without making a sound.

He reached for her free hand. It was limp until he squeezed, then she squeezed back. He hovered with uncertainty for a moment, then leaned over and kissed her, released her hand, and went back out front. She heard the door close, remained standing for a minute before returning to the table to sit down.

Too many things had occurred within the last couple of hours. External and internal things. She knew Alex Herman, had been avoiding his leer since she'd returned to Coyotero. That people were aroused against Alex Herman, wanted to lynch him, did not scare her, but the bloody violence did.

She rose and began clearing the table. The other thing that had brought her turmoil was what she knew about the handsome cowman, his droll sagacity and his kindness. If he came back later this night, she would not be able to control her own inner fears and needs.

A light knock sounded on the kitchen door. Lillian froze. The knocking was repeated, accompanied by a woman's voice.

Lillian felt weak as she lifted the *tranca*. The buxom, handsome woman who entered was the same person who had literally pushed Lillian and Brett Kandelin together earlier.

She looked around, rolled her eyes, and said, "Where did he go? Lillian . . . Don't let him get away."

They sat at the cleared table, the buxom woman watching

Lillian with the piercing gaze of a hawk. "Didn't he like the meal?"

Lillian explained about the dark man and the younger man coming over from Gringo town with talk of a lynching and that Brett had gone back with them.

That seemed to drive the buxom woman into a deep silence, but not for long. She shrugged. "Let them settle things among themselves." She paused. "Do you know who Epifanio Valdez is?"

Lillian didn't.

"He was the aide to—well, that doesn't matter. He is the *compañero* of Brett Kandelin. They were down there fighting the *bandoleros* together. A large man with pock scars."

"What about him?"

"He knows you. He told me he did. He rode back from down near the border with you and the others."

Lillian's eyes widened. She knew the man who had been described, and had probably heard his name, but until this moment she did not connect the two.

The buxom woman said, "He was to come to my house for supper tonight. He didn't come."

"Why?"

"I don't know, except that maybe it has something to do with why your man went away early. Trouble up there."

"I didn't remember his name, and I didn't know that you knew him."

"I didn't. We met yesterday, by accident. He was very nice. Lillian, I've been a widow seven years."

Lillian remembered the buxom woman's late husband, a meek, diffident, colorless man. It had been said throughout Mex town, partly in humor, that the husband of this formidable woman should have borne the children they'd never had, worn the trousers, and castrated the sheep and goats.

Lillian had some difficulty with this fresh revelation. Over the years, the buxom woman had been one of her closest friends. They had grown to maturity together, had discovered the inequalities and disillusionments all young women encounter sooner or later in a masculine world.

They were very different in temperament, but they had always been close.

But right now, after so much pain and bewilderment, Lillian could only gaze at her old friend and suggest two glasses of red wine.

CHAPTER 17

Another Long Night

Instead of going to the lighted, noisy saloon, the only building in Coyotero showing activity, Brett and his companions went to the jailhouse. They found it was locked from the outside and, as they were trying the door, a shadow firmed up under the warped overhang, cradling a scattergun in his arms.

He recognized them, stood a moment in silence, then said, ''Can't nobody go in there without Jess Eames's permission. He's up at the saloon.''

Three sets of eyes stared at the jailhouse. Brett asked if the guard had the key. He did not, he said. Jess had it, and if the men in front of him had something in mind concerning the prisoner in there, if it didn't have to do with a hanging, they'd best be on their way.

Hale's right hand was moving surreptitiously downward when Brett said, ''Where did you find the liveryman?''

Evidently the guard saw nothing wrong with answering. ''About where we figured he might be—in a shack he's got east of town, where he turns horses out to rest up once in a while.'' The guard relaxed slightly and smiled. ''It was so easy when we got over there and seen candlelight, I figured it might be a trick. But hell, there he was, setting at a table with a bottle of whiskey and a dish of hash.'' The man's smile broadened. ''It was like walkin' in on a schoolboy. He didn't even have a gun on when we kicked the door open.''

Brett considered the guard. He felt confident they could overpower him, but without the key to get inside, it seemed useless. He jerked his head and struck out for the saloon.

The noise was audible as far southward as the general store. Hale said there were a lot of men in there, and from the sounds, they'd been drinking.

Enos's assessment was different and deadly serious. "Brett, we walk in there and ask for the key, they're goin' to come down on us like a ton of rocks. Let me tell you somethin' about men who been drinkin' an' are bent on lynching someone—they's different as night and day from ordinary folks."

Brett halted a few doors south of the saloon and watched three mounted men walk their animals up to the tie rack out front and swing to the ground. They muttered gruffly among themselves as they looped reins and stamped across the plank walk to enter the saloon.

Enos shook his head. "That saloon's a powder keg," he told his companions.

Again, his thoughts differed from those of Hale Barlow, who said, "Hell, let 'em lynch the son of a bitch. It's what he deserves."

Brett leaned on a storefront. Enos was right about one thing: if the three of them walked into the saloon to protest the lynching, they weren't going to help the liveryman—and just damned well might get themselves shot.

He looked at Enos. "Let 'em lynch him?"

The dark man was torn between what he knew of lynchings and his conviction that what the liveryman had done deserved nothing less than what those men were drinking themselves into a frame of mind to do.

He sat down on an old wooden bench bolted to the front of the store behind them. He had to compromise, and that didn't satisfy him, either.

A large man, walking slowly, crossed from the opposite side of the road and spoke before reaching their side. "Vaqueros," he said, teeth showing in the darkness. When he was close enough to see their faces, he said, "What is it?"

Hale explained that the liveryman was at the jailhouse under guard and the men in the saloon were working themselves up to a lynching.

'Pifas looked in the direction of the noise and lights and shrugged. "You don't want to join them?"

The only answer he got was two stares of indecision from Enos and Brett, and one malevolent look from Hale Barlow.

'Pifas shrugged again and told them Juan was making a good recovery. He also said the local midwife was a witch, and smiled as he said it. "But she makes a good *curandera.*"

After a moment of silence, when none of his friends seemed inclined toward unity of action, 'Pifas straightened up. "I have to leave," he told them. Brett's gaze lingered on the large Mexican. 'Pifas seemed uncomfortable under the scrutiny. "I am late for supper over in Mex town."

Enos raised his eyebrows. "You, too?"

'Pifas returned the dark man's look for a moment, then shrugged again, said, "Adios," and left them. He did not quite reach a dogtrot when sounds of horsemen coming into town from the south stopped him in his tracks.

He could not make out much, except that they were riding all in a bunch, without talk and without haste. He turned back in the direction of his friends and started pointing even before he reached them.

"Riders! Coming from the direction of the border," he exclaimed.

Brett, Enos, and Hale Barlow went to the edge of the plank walk and watched the horsemen turn in at the livery barn. Hale said, "Severn and the fellers who went with him."

They started down the plank walk, but 'Pifas disappeared at the first dogtrot and was not among them when they met the tired men emerging from the barn with big Marshal Severn.

The others left, but Marshal Severn remained when he recognized the men coming toward him on an angling course from the far side of the road. He looked around, went to a bench, and sat down to wait. When Brett came up, the marshal said, "Now, what the hell?"

Brett told him, and as with others around town on this

particular night, Bill Severn sat and listened. He eyed Brett and his companions, cleared his pipes, spat aside, and began to methodically pull off his riding gloves as he spoke.

"Well, gents, they aren't goin' to lynch nobody. Who says Alex was in cahoots with the *bandoleros*?"

Brett repeated his conversation with Gil Ortiz about someone in town agreeing to betray the town. He also told Severn that Juan Escalante had overheard their conversation.

The marshal was folding the gloves under his shell belt, gazing at Kandelin when he replied. "Gents, Gil Ortiz would lie to his own priest," and when the other men stood looking down at him, the lawman finally got to his feet and hitched at his sagging belt. He wagged his head and said, "All right. But no lynching. We'll hold court tomorrow—after I've talked to the prisoner."

"Eames has the key," Enos stated, and got a sardonic gaze from the big town marshal.

"He's maybe got one key—an' I'll relieve him of that—but I got my own key. You lads go settle in, leave this to me."

But they didn't "settle in," they remained on the west side of the road while Marshal Severn crossed to the east side and walked purposefully up to the saloon.

There was a bench out in front of the store opposite the saloon. Brett and Enos sat on it. Hale leaned against an upright. Enos carved a chew, pouched it into his cheek, spat once, then settled himself comfortably for the wait that followed.

The noise across the road had stopped. In fact, it was so quiet now that a coyote sounding to the moon from miles out seemed no more distant than the east side of town.

Hale muttered from his leaning post. "That don't make sense, him walkin' in there by himself."

Brett was inclined to agree, but Enos again held a different view from the youngest of them. "It's his town, his folks, an' a man'd want to think twice before crossing Marshal Severn."

Brett sat, waiting and watching. Hale did not take his eyes off the distant spindle doors. A man emerged from the saloon, started southward at a brisk pace with three sets of eyes watching until he stopped in front of the cafe and dug in both trouser pockets for a key.

"That's one," stated Brett.

Hale was unimpressed. "One out of how many? That place sounded like it had the whole U.S. Army in there."

Another man walked out into the night, but this one paused to breathe deeply a few times before also walking away. He had an erect bearing and a strong stride. If he'd been one of the noisy drinkers, he certainly hadn't taken on much of a load.

No one commented on this second man, or three more who left the saloon, one at a time. Not until Hale made another vinegary remark. "The rats is leavin' the sinkin' ship," he said.

No more men emerged past the spindle door. Brett did not look away until Enos nudged him. "I told you. He knows his townfolk."

One moment later, his remark was put into question as two men, locked together, staggered out into the night and down onto the plank walk, where tethered horses instinctively set back a little.

Other men appeared in the doorway. There was almost no sound, except for the straining, scuffling boots of the struggling men, one of whom stepped off the plank walk, which ruined his balance, and they both fell into the dust, still locked together.

Hale spoke sarcastically to Enos. "Yeah. He knows his town and its folks."

Several of the men in the saloon doorway pushed on out. One of them, large and thick and also a little unsteady, started toward the struggling men in the roadway, where dust was rising.

Brett rose off the old bench with Enos beside him. Hale joined them on the walk toward the center of the road. Their approach was seen by the bearlike man with the unsteady gait, as well as by the onlookers up in front of the saloon. The latter said nothing, but the bear-built man squinted and called out:

"Who'n hell are you? Mind your own damned business! Stay out of it! Don't nobody tell folks what they can do an' what they can't. Not even Bill Severn."

Brett, Enos, and Hale continued until they were close to the struggling antagonists. Brett pointed a finger at the bear-built, slightly unsteady man and said, "You step off the plank walk, mister, and you'll regret it."

The warning brought silence, but as Brett leaned forward to grab a handful of long black hair and pull, the bear-built man roared and almost stumbled as he stepped from the sidewalk into the roadway. He was approaching with the fury of an enraged bull.

Someone yelled at him from in front of the saloon, "Harry, you damned fool! There's three of 'em!"

Harry roared a reply. "Three? Looks like five, an' that's the way I like it." He stood above the men straining in the dust at his feet, lifted out a Colt, then leaned to ascertain which head belonged to the lawman, and swung.

Brett and Enos did not reach the man in time, but he missed because the fighters on the ground had rolled.

Enos caught hold of the big man's gun arm, swung it savagely up between his shoulder blades in back, and kept up the pressure until the man's gun fell. Enos turned him, poked a rigid finger into the man's chest, and did not raise his voice. "You get back on them duckboards."

The bear-like man squinted, flexed his painful arm and shoulder, and started a roundhouse swing with the other fist.

It missed, not entirely because Enos got under it, but the large man wasn't capable of good aim or proper coordination. Enos didn't strike back; he jammed a booted foot into the large man's knee, and when he collapsed with a howl of pain, Enos turned toward the wide-eyed onlookers. "Which one of you is his friend? Come get him, because if you don't an' he gets up, I'm going to overhaul his plow real good."

No one came from among the onlookers, whose attention had turned to Brett, who had pulled a man's head so far back by the hair, the man's white, exposed throat showed in the feeble starlight.

The man gasped something unintelligible. Brett raised

him to his feet by the scalp, released him, and gave him a violent push. He fell across the man with the injured knee who had gotten up onto all fours before being knocked flat again by the collision.

Marshal Severn stood up, beat off the dust, and looked around for his hat. He spat dust as he icily regarded the semidrunk and his assailant, both of whom were cursing as they tried to get disentangled.

He did not address those two, but he faced the crowd out in front of the saloon. "What I said stands. Alex'll be tried by a jury, legal an' proper. Anyone who thinks otherwise, better think again." Severn walked over to the pair of men who were finally standing upright. He jerked his head in the direction of the jailhouse, and when the unsteady man glowered and stood fast, Marshal Severn knocked him unconscious with one punch and left him lying there as he herded the other man across the road.

The silent crowd in front of the saloon lost interest and stood like statues looking at the men who had broken up the fight.

One of them eventually said, "Well . . . I left a full glass on the bar," and pushed through to enter the saloon as his companions followed him.

Brett led off in the direction of the jailhouse. There, Marshal Severn called from his cell room, asking who was up in the office. When Brett replied, the lawman finished locking up his prisoner, stepped in front of the cell holding the liveryman, growled something, and returned to the lighted office, venomous-looking, bruised, and rumpled. He glowered at his visitors as he went behind his desk. He dug out a bottle, drank deeply from it, and placed it on the edge of the desk for the use of his visitors before sinking down into a cushioned chair with a loud sigh.

None of the three men in front of the desk touched the bottle. Severn rubbed his eyes, ran bent fingers through his hair, and said, "Thirty miles to catch up with the army. Half-hour argument with the officer about us just leavin' our captured raiders down there and ridin' away, and tired clean through when I got into town—and walked right into this."

He took another short pull from the bottle, capped it, and put it out of sight before continuing. "Well, gents, there won't be no lynching." He nodded slightly to Brett. "Thanks for the help up yonder, but I didn't need it."

Enos rubbed his jaw in doubt. "Looked to me like you needed it," he stated.

Marshal Severn grinned wearily at the dark man. "That's Jim Kuhn. I've whipped his plow half-a-dozen times over the years. He drinks a little, remembers those times, and's got to try it one more time."

Brett asked if they could see the liveryman, and Marshal Severn slowly shook his head. "Not until tomorrow up at the Masonic lodge, where we hold trials. I'm takin' no chances on this one, an' if anyone comes close when I'm herdin' him up center of the roadway in irons, I'll be right behind with a sawed-off shotgun loaded with lead slugs." The marshal was beginning to get life in his cheeks and eyes.

Hale spoke disgustedly. "Who'd want to take that son of a bitch away from you? Everyone around wants him pulled so high birds'll build nests in his hair."

Marshal Severn offered no rebuttal. "It's the law, lad. It works down here on the border like it works most other places. A man gets tried before we hang the son of bitch."

Brett led the way back out into the cooling night. There were no more sounds up at the saloon. Nor were the lamps still burning. What few stragglers were still abroad seemed to move like uneasy wraiths as they saw the three cattlemen walking northward.

Brett paused under the interested gaze of his companions, gave them each a slap on the back, and without a word headed across the roadway in the direction of a dogtrot. Hale stood dumbly watching. By the time he faced the dark man, looking quizzical, Brett had disappeared.

Enos made a gesture that had been foreign to him, too, until he'd come down into the south desert. He shrugged before resuming his stroll in the direction of the hotel.

When he and Hale got up there, they encountered Jess Eames, without his shell belt and Colt, looking uncomfortable and rumpled. Before either of them could growl, Eames said, "All you boys did was put it off for one more day."

Enos did not question that. He simply said, "Mister, I just don't like lynchings."

The hotelman repeated, "One more day, amigos," and turned on his heel to disappear at the lower end of a dingy hall.

Juan was asleep, which surprised Enos and Hale. Hale wagged his head, went to a bunk, and sat down to pull off his boots as he gave the dark man a look.

"How the hell could he sleep through all that racket out front of the saloon?"

Enos also gazed at the sleeping man, but his comment was different. He said, "Don't they all look the same to you? They sure do to me." Then he laughed, leaving Hale Barlow squinting perplexedly at him, holding a boot in his hand. By the time he'd shed the other boot, had tossed his hat aside and removed his shell belt and holstered six-gun, he had another question: "Where's Brett? A man can't go forever without sleep."

Enos was settling into some moth-eaten hotel blankets, tan and wool, probably stolen from the army, when he replied, "You're a nice lad, Hale. Young, but a good hand. Just go to sleep."

"Enos?"

"What?"

"They don't all look the same."

"To me they do. Good night, Hale."

"Enos?"

"What?"

"Where's 'Pifas?"

"Like I said, Hale, you're a good hand . . . but young. Now, *go to sleep!*"

CHAPTER 18

The Verdict

True to his word, Marshal Severn marched Alex Herman from the jailhouse to the Masonic lodge in the center of the road. Severn had a sawed-off shotgun; Alex Herman had an Oregon boot and chained wrists.

Two-thirds of Coyotero's residents lined both sides of the main thoroughfare. Up at the adobe that housed the Masonic lodge, the crowd was particularly dense.

Brett, Enos, Hale Barlow, and 'Pifas watched from the opposite side of the roadway. The only man missing of this group was the lean, knife-scarred Mexican, Juan Escalante, and he was sitting in a rocker on the hotel porch.

When everyone was inside the lodge hall and the door had been barred from the inside, Marshal Severn impaneled a jury by asking those willing to serve to raise their hands. From the dozens of raised hands he selected twelve people—no females or Mexicans—and read them off the obligations of their office, the legal restriction against preconceived notions, and notified them they would be allowed fifteen minutes to separately reach a verdict after the trial. He then rapped a tabletop and declared the court of the town of Coyotero, Territory of New Mexico, to be in session. No noise would be tolerated from spectators, the roadway would only be unbarred for those requiring an exit for the most basic of needs, and he directed the selected jury men to pay particular heed to the charges, which he read off in a solemn, deep, and loud voice.

"Conspiring with an enemy. Abetting invaders of the United States of America. Treason in the first degree. Contributing to the destruction of propery and the injury and death of those defending Coyotero from a large force or irregular Mexican soldiery called *bandoleros*, as well as unspecified additional charges that will be brought up if needed; at the present time that need does not seem to exist. Alex Herman, rise and state your name."

The liveryman gazed at the sheriff sitting behind an old scarred wooden table with the American flag hanging from a staff that had been firmly jammed into a bucketful of sand. He did not rise, but he stated his name, and Marshal Severn's heightening color had no visible effect upon the prisoner.

"What do you say to the charges?" the marshal asked, effortlessly. He tried to maintain a neutral expression.

The liveryman replied in one word: "Innocent."

Severn's eyes widened. "To all the charges?"

"Yep, to all of them," Herman replied, and perhaps emboldened by the look on the marshal's face, or perhaps the sound of his own voice, he enlarged upon his reply. "You got to prove them charges, Marshal. The more of 'em you put up, the more proof you got to have to each charge."

The large room was so silent a man standing against the back wall could be plainly heard clearing his throat. Marshal Severn leaned on the table, staring at Alex Herman, an individual he'd known for years, had never cared much for, and who, in Severn's opinion, was a weasely, nondescript, slippery son of a bitch from the word go.

Brett nudged Enos, who faintly smiled and nodded as he, too, watched Marshal Severn's face get redder by the moment. But to his credit, the big lawman did not raise his voice as he said, "Alex, this isn't a joke. This here is a trial by law."

The liveryman's reply was curt. "It ain't a trial by law, Bill Severn, because you ain't a legal judge."

For a long moment, the two men eyed each other, and

again the marshal exercised restraint. "There isn't a judge within a hunnert miles, Alex. We been conductin' trials like this since long before you came here. As far as Coyotero's concerned, it's legal."

The liveryman's response was enlightening to the fascinated spectators—and Marshal Severn. "Bill, I got two law books. In my trade, it pays to know somethin' about the law; always someone's tryin' to return a horse, claim I cheated 'em. I read them books from front to back. . . . This here ain't a duly constituted court of law because you aren't no duly constituted judge."

Marshal Severn's smoky gaze wandered around the room and back. "Answer some questions," he told the liveryman. "Alex, we got witnesses that you connived with the *bandoleros*. You gave 'em a key to the powderhouse."

A low gasp came from among the spectators at this revelation.

"You made some kind of deal with Gil Ortiz—maybe your life and possessions in trade for helpin' them overrun the town."

Herman said, "What witnesses?"

Severn pointed. "That feller back yonder. Brett Kandelin. Another one is Juan Escalante. Kandelin was told by Ortiz you sold us out. Juan heard the conversation . . . Alex, that's as bad as murder. It's not only a terrible thing to do to folks you've known for years, it's also treason. I got some law books, too. They say what you did made you an accessory to every killin' those *bandoleros* committed after they come out of Messico."

The liveryman turned slowly to scan the spectators, turned back, and fished for a blue bandanna to mop his face with. As he was stuffing the bandanna away, he said, "Escalante . . . he's a Messican. That other feller . . . he's a free-grazer. Everybody knows what free-grazers are; make their livin' stealin' other folks' grass."

Bill Severn delayed his second question so long it seemed he might not ask it. "Alex, how'd you an' Gil Ortiz come to know each other?"

"He bought a horse off me a year or so back. It was a

good animal. He come down to the barn a month or so back to tell me he'd contracted for a herd of cattle to be brought down here. I asked if he was figurin' on takin' a weight gain while there was grass, an' he said no, he had a market for the cattle over the line down in Messico an' wanted me to round up a few fellers an' sort of mind the herd until he could bring up some friends from Messico to take them over."

Marshal Severn leaned on the table. "When was that?"

"I told you. A month or so back. Well, maybe more like two, three weeks back."

"An' you knew there was an uprisin' down there, didn't you?"

"Hell, Bill, everyone knew that."

"And that's when you an' Gil Ortiz made your swap, isn't it? Your hide for the keys to the powderhouse, and for helpin' the raiders storm the town."

"Bill, I never—"

"You're lyin', Alex. I've known you a long time. Long enough to know when you're lying. I got another question for you. Besides agreeing to make sure you were safe when they overrun the town, how much was Ortiz also goin' to pay you?"

The liveryman fished for his bandanna again and stared steadily at the town marshal as he mopped his face. He did not reply until he'd pocketed the bandanna, then what he said echoed through the totally still room.

"There ain't a word of truth in what you're saying."

Marshal Severn reared back in his chair and gestured toward the spectators. "Jess, stand up." Eames rose. "Now then, Mr. Eames, tell the court what you did."

Eames hesitated, clearly uncomfortable. "It was at the saloon. After we brought Alex back an' locked him up . . . What with you bein' gone an' all, Marshal, bunch of us figured, since Alex was guilty as hell, we'd save the town an' you the trouble—"

"Jess, confound you, I don't want to be here until suppertime. Just tell the court what you did!"

Eames made an uneasy smile as he replied, "You could

tell 'em, Marshal. You'n me cooked up the notion of rummagin' through Alex's house and barn."

Marshal Severn got red in the face again, but he did not interrupt.

"I went down there. Took a long time. Alex lives like a pack rat. You never saw—"

"*Jess!*"

Eames visibly winced at the loudness of the marshal's voice. "I found two hide pouches of gold an' some trinkets looted from some Messican church. Mostly gold, but with diamonds and whatnot set into them."

Marshal Severn leaned on the desk. "Anything else?"

"Yes. That letter I gave you."

"What was in the damned letter, Jess?"

"It said if Alex would hire someone to shoot the feller who brought that herd of cattle down here, Ortiz would pay him a hunnert dollars."

The room was so silent as Eames sat down, his little rustling motions carried. Marshal Severn dropped his eyes to the liveryman. "Why did Ortiz want Mr. Kandelin bushwhacked, Alex?"

"Because he didn't want to pay for the cattle. . . . But I never even considered doin' that."

Marshal Severn gave the liveryman the benefit of the doubt, and did it in such a pleasant way he looked almost benign. "Of course, you never considered killin' Mr. Kandelin, murdering him. . . . Alex, you just admitted that you'n Gil Ortiz had a deal, you two as partners, an' that's all this here court wanted to know. You gave him a key to the powderhouse; you agreed to help him massacre all of us; you took money from him to bushwhack Mr. Kandelin, setting there one row behind you. . . . Tell me something, Alex. What do your law books say about these charges?" Severn did not allow the liveryman, who was white to the hairline and speechless, time to reply. He reared back in his chair, looking around the room. "You jury men," he intoned, "write down your decision on a piece of paper and hold it up as I call your names."

The process of getting a verdict was prolonged because

several jury men had neither paper nor anything to write with. While this was being attended to by spectators, Marshal Severn looked down his nose at the glassy-eyed liveryman, his expression clearly reflecting his feeling of triumph.

Alex Herman found his voice during the lull before the jury men were finished with their obligation. He said, "Marshal, you can't search my place without a writ. That's got to be in your law books, too. You got no—"

"Alex," stated the big lawman, now looking more triumphant than benign, "I'm older than you. Long ago I figured somethin' out about the law. In most cases, there isn't no connection between justice and law books."

The liveryman was fishing for his bandanna again when Bill Severn called out the first name and continued to call them out and write down what he could see written on the scraps of paper that were held up . . . until he came to the last jury man. He squinted, he leaned as far over the table as he could, and finally he scowled. "Tom Sieber, you consarned mule-skinnin', mail-carryin', whiskey-drinkin' scalawag, what you got on that piece of paper? It looks blanks to me."

The answer came irritably back from among the juryman. "You knew darned well I can't read or write, so why'd you put me on your damned jury, anyway?"

"Well," bellowed the red-faced big lawman. "Just yell it out—guilty or not guilty."

"Guilty!"

The town marshal leaned back a little, frowned as he tallied what he'd recorded, and for as long as he was doing this there was not a sound. He finally raised his head, stuffed the tally sheet into a pocket, and looked around the room, where every eye was fixed on him. He said, "Guilty as charged on all counts. Alex, get up on your feet. One of you gents pull him out of that chair. . . . Alex Herman, the judgment of the jury an' this court is that you get hanged by the neck. Court dismissed."

People finally spoke to one another as they started for the unbarred doors and the sunlight beyond. One man remained like a stone. The liveryman did not take his eyes off Bill Severn as the marshal rose, pushed clear of the table, and without returning the liveryman's glassy stare, started past on his way toward the doorway. He had to slow his advance because only a few people at a time could pass out into the roadway. While this was happening, a number of men accosted the marshal to congratulate him. The liveryman twisted from the waist, never taking his eyes off the big lawman—not until the room was almost empty and Marshal Severn turned to order Alex Herman to come back to the doorway, where Severn was waiting to escort him back to the jailhouse. Severn had retrieved the sawed-off shotgun he'd left by the door.

The liveryman, who'd had trouble on his way up here with that Oregon boot, seemed to have even more trouble with it as he started toward the door.

Brett, Enos, Hale Barlow, and 'Pifas were standing in sunlight as the liveryman was herded from the building. He did not look at them. He did not look at anyone as he was escorted to the center of the roadway and directed to walk slowly, which he could not avoid doing, back the way he had come.

People lining both sides of the road watched in silence. Some, perhaps most, felt pity. The liveryman was shuffling along, head bowed, hopelessly dejected.

When they reached the jailhouse and he was herded inside, Marshal Severn leaned the shotgun aside and fished for the key to the Oregon boot and the wrist chains, and Alex Herman finally spoke. "Leave the alley door unbarred, Marshal. Go up and celebrate at the saloon and you can keep them pouches."

Severn kicked the Oregon boot aside, unchained his prisoner, and jerked his head for the liveryman to go back down into the cell room. He did not say a word until he was locking the strap steel door.

He gazed steadily at the liveryman without speaking for a long moment. "Alex, you're still a connivin', worthless son of a bitch, aren't you? Those pouches will go to the town. . . . Just explain one thing to me. How could you agree to get us all slaughtered when you've known every one of us for years? That didn't mean anything to you? What'd happen to the girls and women? You knew every one of 'em, Alex."

Marshal Severn returned to his office, kicked the Oregon boot against the wall beneath his racked-up weapons, tossed the arm chains in a corner, and was about to kindle a little fire for coffee in his stove when Jake, the cafe man, walked in. He hadn't been at the Masonic lodge, but he'd heard of the verdict almost as soon as the jury men returned to the roadway. He nodded, and the lawman nodded back while returning his attention to the stove.

The cafe man did not mention the trial or the verdict. He simply said, "You goin' to use the same big old wagon?"

Marshal Severn turned as he nodded his head.

"Well, it belongs to Alex, y'know."

Severn frowned. "That's not the only rig in town with a long wagon tongue."

Jake nodded about that. "I know. But I've been feedin' a flock of hungry men over at the cafe and that's what they're talkin' about."

Severn went to his table to sit down as he said, "Quarreling about whose rig the town hires this time, are they?"

"No. They're sayin' they don't want no wagon of theirs used for a hanging."

Marshal Severn's brows dropped a notch. "Why not?"

"They don't want to own a wagon that folks'll remember was used for that."

Marshal Severn threw himself back in his chair, eyes rolling. "That's the silliest thing I ever heard. We been using wagon tongues for years."

"Yes, but it was always Alex's rigs. That green-sided old freight rig in particular."

For the lawman, long accustomed to minor exasperations, this did not worry him much—until, sometime after the cafe man had departed, he began to wonder just how many local owners of wagons were involved.

He returned to the roadway without getting his cup of coffee. People were standing in groups over in front of the general store, across the road in front of the harness works, out in front of the saloon, and in shade provided by the cafe's wooden overhang.

Two men slouching on a bench not far from the jailhouse caught and held his attention. He went over to them, sank down, and wagged his head. Enos put a questioning gaze upon him. "You got a conscience?" he asked.

Severn looked indignant when he replied, "For what? For doin' what the law requires and that weasely little bastard deserves?"

"No," the dark man drawled, with a perfectly straight face. "For makin' that feller a jury man who couldn't read or write."

Marshal Severn straightened slowly up on the bench to look steadily at Enos. Both the dark man and Brett Kandelin were grinning. Marshal Severn's sense of humor was buried beneath a host of other things. He did not smile back. He said, "Mr. Kandelin, you didn't happen to have a rig with the cattle did you?"

"No." Haven't had a wagon in years. Why?"

"Seems no one wants their wagon used to hang a man."

Brett and the dark man kept their eyes on Marshall Severn as they tried to make sense out of his statement. Enos finally asked if they couldn't just stand the condemned man on a barrel and kick it out from under him.

Marshal Severn scowled again. "It's not for him to stand on, it's to use in hanging him." At the blank look this comment got, he settled back a little and explained. "No trees, gents," he said and gestured with an arm for emphasis. "Where you boys come from, there's lots of trees. Down here, there's not a decent tree within miles, unless we was to use one here in town, and every time that's come up, whoever owns the darned tree has a fit.

"So, you boys be around tomorrow morning. You'll see how it's done on the south desert."

CHAPTER 19

"Hell, Lad, Don't Feel Bad."

Juan Escalante's recovery was slow. As the haglike local midwife explained to Brett, the wound was healing well, no infection had set in, and Juan would be up and around shortly.

"Loss of blood," she said. "It ain't like water, Mr. Kandelin. It don't just keep on flowing no matter what. It takes time to replace itself, an' if a body's lost very much of it, more'n likely it won't never recover an' he'll die. With Juan Escalante—I'd say a good month before he can get around much. He might try before a month, but if he does he's goin' to feel awful tired. . . . Don't worry, I'll keep my eye on him."

Brett gave the woman two silver dollars, which pleased her, and visited Juan in his room to give him an eyewitness account of the liveryman's trial. Juan was a good listener. "Someday, we said over in Mex town, it was goin' to happen. When will they hang him?"

When Brett told him what the marshal had said, Juan was disappointed because he would be unable to go.

When Brett walked back out to the roadway, someone had hitched a matched pair of twelve-hundred-pound bays to a large old green wagon out behind the livery barn and was now tooling it up through town.

'Pifas and Enos appeared across the roadway to watch. They did not see Brett until he came up behind them and spoke. "You ever see an outfit like that?" Neither of them had. The dark man considered the length of the wagon tongue protruding past the bay horses, which had been hitched as wheelers. "He's either goin' somewhere close to put four more horses on the tongue, or maybe he's only got two horses and don't figure to go far, but that sure looks odd, a wagon tongue sticking way out in front of the horses."

The cafe man came out of his shop drying both hands on a clean flour-sack apron. He scowled, and when the rig came abreast, he called out to the driver.

"Wesley, where you goin'?"

The driver called back curtly, "North of town, to the hangin' ground."

The cafe man continued to scowl. "That's Alex Herman's wagon."

The answer was short. "Sure is, ain't it? He's goin' to hang in an hour or so, in case you want to lock up an' walk out there."

As the cafe man turned to go back inside, Enos and Brett exchanged a look. 'Pifas interrupted their silent exchange of thoughts.

"A man arrived in Mex town last night—early this morning—needing help. He'd been shot." 'Pifas continued to watch the big old wagon as he also said, "They would take him to the *curandera* this morning." 'Pifas's dark eyes came back slowly. "He is a *bandolero*."

Brett returned his attention to the large wagon briefly, then jerked his head and led off in the direction of the nearest narrow slot between two buildings.

They encountered the toothless old man with his walking stick of blood red manzanita. The old man was chuckling when they met him. Without greeting them, he waved with his walking stick, and said, "Did you see the green wagon, amigos? Did you ever see anyone hitch only two horses as wheelers on a six-horse tongue before? They should be hitched up ahead, at the end of the tongue." The old man shuffled away, still chuckling.

When Brett stepped beneath the overhang of the alcalde's

house, three unsmiling young Mexicans rose as though to bar their passage. Brett and Enos eyed them as 'Pifas addressed them in Spanish. One young Mexican shrugged, while the other one spoke in English, shaking his head. "The lady is busy. You come back some other time."

Brett looked at the expressionless and silent third man. "We know who is in there with her."

The stone-faced man's reply was gruff. "Go away. There won't be another hanging."

'Pifas raised his voice to call out in Spanish. Moments later, a woman called back, "*Entran.*"

Under the baleful looks of the three young guards, they walked into the house and had to stop to allow their eyes to adjust to the gloom. There was almost no light, and the place had an odd smell.

Lillian did not appear. The woman who had called for them to enter was the same buxom, assertive woman who had met 'Pifas before but did not know his companions. The woman nodded to Brett and Enos without any great amount of enthusiasm and told them in English that Lillian was tending an injured man in one of the little bedrooms.

They knew this. Brett asked if the woman would tell Lillian they were here, and turned to find a place to sit. Then 'Pifas addressed the buxom woman in Spanish, "*Cariño*, we know who the rider is."

She replied in the same language, eyes sparkling. "You can't hang this one. He's a very sick man."

"We didn't come to hang him, only to talk to him."

The woman regarded 'Pifas through an interval of thoughtful silence before telling him to sit with the others, and walked out of the room.

Brett and Enos gazed at the pockmarked man. He smiled a little. When they continued to stare, he finally said, "Well, her name is Ambrosia Salazar."

Neither of the other men spoke, but continued to gaze at the larger man. He glanced around the room, let his gaze linger long on the niche with the broken door that had held the crucifix, and when he returned his gaze to his companions, they looked gravely back. He flung up his hands.

"She is a friend of mine. I met her not long ago. She is a widow." 'Pifas shrugged. "We have a good friendship."

Enos, whose impression of Ambrosia Salazar had not been helped any by her brusqueness, said, "What happened to her husband?"

'Pifas did not know. "We haven't talked much about things like that."

Enos nodded. "She ate him. Like female spiders eat their mates."

The pockmarked big man was looking stonily at Enos when Lillian appeared in the doorway. The puffiness around her eye was nearly gone, there was what could have been a small scratch under the eye on one cheek, and her mouth had resumed its normal shape. She smiled at them. "You know who this *bandolero* is?" she asked, and when Brett shook his head, she leaned in the doorway regarding him. "He is wounded. He tried to slip back into Mexico twenty miles east, but the *rurales* were waiting. They'd already caught twenty or thirty. This one, his name is Esteven, watched others slip south into Mexico—and was about to leave his hiding place to follow—when there was a lot of gunfire from both sides of the trail. *Rurales* had an ambush down there.

"He watched them strip the men they had killed, take their horses, their guns, even their boots, and ride away. He was coming out of the underbrush to go back the way he had come when two red flaggers, who must have seen him earlier, rode out in front of him. He shot one, and was racing away with the other one in pursuit, when he got shot."

Enos quietly asked if the second *rurale* had given up the chase. Lillian did not know. All the wounded man had said about the chase was that he was in great pain and thought he would be killed, but when he looked back, the *rurale* was no longer back there. "After that, he came here and fell off his horse, out where some old men were herding their goats."

After a long interval of silence, she also said, "He is very weak, but you can talk to him if you like." She looked at 'Pifas. "He knows only Spanish."

They followed her into a small room that was sparsely furnished. Lying in a narrow bed with rope springs beneath a corn-husk mattress was a thin, youngish man, with dark curly hair and tired-looking eyes.

He stared at the men accompanying the *curandera* and spoke softly to her in Spanish. She went to his bedside, murmuring reassurances.

The wounded man looked at 'Pifas and grimaced. He told Lillian in Spanish he had seen that one during the brush battle at the old encampment south of Coyotero.

'Pifas crossed to the bedside and smiled. "You have nothing to fear," he told the wounded man. "Where is your injury?"

Lillian raised the blanket to disclose a thick bandage around the man's upper body. As she lowered it, she spoke in English. "It made a gory rip under his ribs. He bled a lot—twenty miles is a long way to ride dripping blood."

The buxom woman appeared with a mug of hot broth. She shouldered through and leaned over to raise the wounded man and hold his head while he drained the cup. As she straightened up and turned to depart, 'Pifas smiled. She smiled back, and 'Pifas followed her to the kitchen.

With their interpreter gone, Brett asked Lillian to have the *bandolero* tell them what had happened after the soldiers arrived. His answer was a feeble gesture of a hand lying on top of the blanket. "They got around us," he told Lillian. "Many men were leaving, anyway, and rode right into the Yanqui soldiers. It was a very bad fight. Everyone tried to get away. I think most of them did. I don't know any more because I rode away fast."

After she'd interpreted, Brett had another question. "Where is Gil Ortiz?"

This time when she interpreted, Enos and Brett, who were watching her face, had the same impression—she was frightened.

"He heard the gunfire to the east and to the south. All Esteven knows is what he saw: Gil Ortiz and several others rode away from the sounds of battle. He says they rode fast."

"Which way, Lillian?"

She looked steadily at him as she replied, "North."

Brett returned his attention to the wounded man while asking her in English what his chances were. She replied, "I don't know. Fifty-fifty. If he hadn't lost so much blood . . . Still, he's young and healthy." She regarded the youth with a gentle expression. He said something and she smiled at him. "No, they aren't from the law. This one is a friend of mine. The dark one? He is a friend of my friend. Rest, be quiet. Ambrosia will be back."

She herded Brett and Enos back to the sitting room and as before, instead of sitting, she leaned in the doorway. "There are just so many things a *curandera* can do. I've done most of them. Now it's up to God."

'Pifas appeared from the rear of the house slightly flushed. He crossed to the door, and was about to open it, when someone knocked loudly. He stepped back, opened the door, met Hale Barlow's testy look, and stepped aside.

Before Hale saw the handsome woman in the doorway, he glared at his friends. "I been lookin' all over hell for you. They're fixin' to hoist the liveryman. The marshal'd like to have you out there."

As Enos rose to depart, he said, "What for? They short of hands to lean on the rope?"

Hale did not respond, because he'd just seen the woman in the doorway gazing at him. He walked outside and waited. When Enos joined him and told Hale about the wounded brigand inside, Hale glowered but said nothing.

Before Brett left, he offered Lillian a hand, which she took as she said, "North . . ."

He understood. "It would be foolish, but when the hanging is over I'll come back. Maybe north meant he was going due north, along way north, away from this country."

She nodded without much conviction. He kissed her cheek and left.

As the four men were trooping back toward Gringo town, Enos, who had also been thinking about Gil Ortiz, told Hale Barlow and 'Pifas what the wounded *bandolero* had said.

Hale's response was to bleakly hope Ortiz would appear,

but 'Pifas, who knew Gil Ortiz, had served as his companion and aide, hoped nothing of the sort. He told them he knew from long acquaintanceship that Gil Ortiz was a very dangerous individual. He also said he thought that now, having been routed at Coyotero and defeated down near the border, Ortiz's near-insane wildness would make him feel invincible. 'Pifas also thought that the men who were trying to escape with him would not follow him back up here. But he shrugged as he said, "Who can tell?"

When they emerged from the dogtrot into Gringo town, none of the philosophical lassitude that now prevailed again in Mex town was visible. Stores were closed, people were either walking, riding, or driving out of town as though for celebration, not a grisly act of retribution. Some of the women had children with them.

They saw Jess Eames in the company of other men going north in a wagon. Of Marshal Severn, there was no sign. A fully bearded, grizzled man driving a sorrel team on a spring wagon called to them and pointed toward his tailgate. They accepted the invitation. No saddle horseman walked if he could ride.

It was a beautiful day, with a turquoise sky overhead, tiny, shy wildflowers underfoot, and an aromatic scent coming in from the desert. Although the sun was climbing, it was not yet very warm. That would come later, when everyone trooped back.

There was a light skiff of dust above town, where all manner of vehicles were in the procession heading for the hanging ground. There were Mexicans, and even a small scattering of desert Indians, also going in that direction.

Their host on the spring seat twisted to say it was a fine day. Brett agreed. The bearded man then also said, "You boys seen the cafe man?"

They hadn't.

Their driver laughed. "You won't. Jake's a businessman. He warn't at the court hearin' neither. Jake knows, when folks walk out this far an' walk back, they'll be hungry. Same when they got to set through a trial at the lodge hall."

When the wagon driver veered from the road, following the rigs in front, the men in the wagon bed could see the big freight wagon with the faded green sideboards a short distance ahead. A large number of armed men were standing up near the front. The big bay team had been taken off the pole, hobbled, and left to browse. The tongue had been raised almost straight up into the air, with just enough lean to it to provide the exact amount of clearance.

It had been tied back on both sides with an additional length of rope going from above, downward, and into the bed of the wagon, where it was tied fast to a steel ring imbedded into the floorboards.

Hale said, "Where there's a will, there's a way, eh?"

No one answered him. Clearly visible from the top of the wagon tongue to within a few feet of the ground was a stout hard-twist rope with a cumbersomely wrapped hangman's noose dangling at the end.

The tag end of the rope extended over the tailgate, back where ten or fifteen solemn, silent men were idling in wagon shade, awaiting the signal to grab hold and pull.

Their host stopped, tossed down a tether weight, got down and, as his passengers walked ahead and thanked him, wagged his head, his eyes twinkling. "It's a little hardship stoppin' work in the middle of the week, but they dassn't do it on the Sabbath. . . . Anyway, a person needs a little recreation, don't he?"

Everyone else seemed to feel the same way. Several women had brought picnic hampers and were now feeding their mates and their broods.

Brett saw Marshal Severn up near the hoisted pole. He also saw Alex Herman, hands behind his back, distraught in appearance even from a distance. He was rumpled, unshaven, his hair awry, and his body alternatively stiff and loose.

Enos blew out a ragged breath, but said nothing. He watched the big lawman gesture as he spoke to those around him. They didn't lead the liveryman beneath the noose, they lifted him bodily by the arms and carried him over, then lowered him. One of them jumped, caught the noose, and without any hesitation dropped it over the liveryman's head.

Alex Herman didn't move.

Marshal Severn looked at a bushy-headed preacher standing high above, on the seat of the old freight wagon. Given the signal, the preacher began speaking in a thunderous voice accompanied with slashing gestures. When he had finished, he nodded to the marshal.

There was not a sound. Presumably, most of the folks out there had seen other hangings, but Hale Barlow hadn't. His customary slightly vindictive expression was not in place. He stood like a stone, eyes fixed on the men standing around the liveryman. When Marshal Severn asked Alex Herman if there was anything he'd like to say, Hale scarcely breathed as he waited.

But the liveryman did not open his mouth. He seemed to be slightly unsteady, though, as the rope was properly placed and snugged up.

Marshal Severn raised a fisted arm, held it until the men behind the tailgate spat on their hands and gripped the rope, and brought his arm downward in a fierce gesture.

The men behind the wagon had estimated Alex Herman's weight incorrectly. He did not weigh the one hundred and sixty pounds they had thought. He only weighed about a hundred and thirty. When they put all their strength into hoisting a heavier man, Alex Herman shot up into the air as though he'd been catapulted.

As was customary, purely for the benefit of onlookers, his arms had been lashed behind his back and his ankles had also been tied tightly. But he wouldn't have thrashed wildly anyway—because the sudden and powerful jerk had broken his neck.

His body arched, twisted, contorted left and right, and Hale Barlow turned away. It was so still, faint sounds from town were clearly audible.

The shaggy-headed man on the high wagon seat was consulting his watch. When he was satisfied, he snapped it closed, pocketed it, and nodded to Marshal Severn.

The body was lowered to the ground. Bill Severn and others leaned forward for a long time, then turned and gestured. The man with the full beard who had brought Brett, Enos, 'Pifas, and Hale out here, put his tether weight into the wagon then climbed up. He talked up his team and drove carefully through the crowd until he stopped out near the armed men whose backs pretty well obscured the dead man. He climbed down, handed someone a piece of old canvas, leaned to help roll the liveryman into it, then they all boosted the limp carcass into the wagon bed. The bearded man climbed back to his seat and, without a word to the marshal and his companions, turned and drove back through the crowd in the direction of town.

He slowed near Brett and jerked a thumb. "Climb in," he said. None of them accepted the offer of a ride back. The bearded man saw Hale's face, leaned far out, and said, "Hell, lad, don't feel bad. He didn't know anything. Bill Severn loaded him with whiskey on the way out here."

CHAPTER 20

Strangers!

The whiskery individual who drove back with the body had been right; by the time Brett and his friends reached town, the cafe was doing a brisk business, exactly as its proprietor had known it would.

They all went in to eat, except Hale Barlow. He went up to the saloon.

Brett left the others to return to the late alcalde's residence. Lillian was out back with the buxom woman, who made an excuse to leave as soon as she saw Brett coming.

Lillian looked straight at Brett with raised eyebrows. He nodded and sat down on the bench beside her. "It's done," he told her, and pushed out his feet with his back against the warm adobe to gaze up through Mex town in the direction of the old mission church with its leaning cross.

She asked what he was thinking, suspecting his solemn expression was the result of the hanging he'd witnessed. She was wrong. He said, "Those were good cattle. We babied them along until they were in good flesh." He paused to smile a little. "Well, after fifteen years of making a profit, I guess it was time I lost a little."

She asked if he'd like some red wine. He chose black coffee instead, and followed her inside while she put water to boil. He tossed aside his hat, sat at the old table, and said, "I think 'Pifas is sweet on your hefty friend."

Her answer was short. "He could do much worse."

Brett looked over at her without mentioning his personal impression of Ambrosia Salazar. "Maybe in a day or two I'll take Hale and Enos and see if we can find any of the cattle."

She turned. "How long will you be gone?"

An odd sense of understanding had developed between them. He knew why she had asked that, and pondered his reply until she put a cup of coffee before him; then he said, "Maybe Hale and Enos could do that. I'll sort of stay around town."

She sat opposite him without coffee, for which she'd never formed a liking. "You should go, too, Brett. Maybe the three of you can find most of the cattle."

He doubted that. "Maybe we can find some of them," he replied dryly, and raised the cup. As he lowered the cup, he smiled ruefully. "This close to the border, with hungry Messicans below it . . ." He shook his head and changed the subject. "Lillian, what will you do now?"

"The same as I've always done. But without my grandfather to look after. Stay here. I told you, I was born here."

He gazed into the cup. When this topic had surfaced between them another time, he'd thought that belonging probably had its value, even though he had never felt as though he belonged anywhere.

She cut into his thoughts. "And you?"

He hadn't thought much about it. "Go back up to the grass country, I expect. Start out small again and build up to where I can buy lots of cattle. Except . . ."

"Except what?" she asked, slightly breathless.

"Except that free-grazin' is getting harder and harder. If it's not cattlemen on deeded land it's homesteaders putting up fences." He raised his gaze to her face. "Maybe I ought to consider going into some other business."

She asked if he wanted more coffee, then got it for him. As she was pouring, she said, "I'll miss you."

He waited until she's returned from the stove to the table before speaking again. "I sort of had in mind taking you along."

She smiled fondly at him. "Where? Wyoming? Colorado?" When he nodded, her smile lingered as she said, "I've been to those places. That's how far I went when I ran away from my husband. I don't like snow. Five months of it every year, bitter cold. And ice. Even the summer nights are cold."

He continued to look at her after she'd said that, did not speak until he sipped more coffee and put the cup aside. "For a fact it gets cold up there."

She leaned on the table. "There is nothing to do for all those months but try to keep warm."

He nodded about that.

"And when the grass comes, it doesn't last long enough."

He nodded about that, too.

"Brett?"

He raised his eyes.

"Stay here."

His eyes widened a little. "And herd sheep? Lillian, I don't like the smell of sheep."

She did not drop her eyes. "I didn't think you would. But there are other things. This morning, while you were gone, I thought of other things you could do."

"Name one, Lillian."

"Do you like horses?"

"Yes. I've been around horses all my life."

Her expression brightened toward him. "There is no one to run the livery and trading barn now."

He stared at her.

She permitted him no time to speak. "It is a good business. My grandfather told me it's the best business in Coyotero, after the general store. There are always people who need horses. There are . . ." She waited until he drained the cup and put it down before continuing. "There are freighters and stockmen, even Mexicans from below the line always wanting horses and mules."

Brett leaned back and laughed at her earnestness. She leaned away from the table a little, listening to a distant sound.

Their discussion ended abruptly when Ambrosia Salazar

appeared at the back door to say some vaqueros who had arrived in town from the south were telling patrons of the cantina that they had had to flee for their lives from a band of *rurales*.

Lillian's eyes widened. "Up here?"

Ambrosia nodded. "Not five miles from Coyotero."

A set of hard knuckles rattled the front door. The noise startled the women as Brett left the table to pass through the sitting room.

Enos was standing out there. "There's something going on. Some Messicans came to town a while back and told Marshal Severn they saw some of those Mex constabulary soldiers not very far from town. He's gong to make a posse an' wants us to go along." Enos peeked over Brett's shoulder, heard women's voices, and said, "You don't have to go."

Brett left him in the doorway, returned to the kitchen to tell Lillian he would ride with the lawman's posse to hunt for *rurales*. She nodded soberly as he went back to the front of the house to join the dark man heading for Gringo town.

Evidently the news had traveled throughout town because people were in little groups on both sides of the road, looking as solemn as owls as they talked.

When Brett and Enos reached the lawman's office, Hale and 'Pifas were just leaving. They said they were going for their animals and hurried on their way.

A number of armed men were in the marshal's small office. When he saw Brett and Enos, he paused in what he'd been saying to include them in the rest of it.

"Maybe them vaqueros saw some riders and thought they was red flaggers—and ran like hell for home."

"And maybe," drawled a lean, weathered man with the accent of Texas, "maybe they really did see red flaggers. With all the commotion goin' on down yonder, it sure as hell wouldn't surprise me if they did."

"What for?" another man asked, pointing out that only a handful of Mexicans from below the border couldn't expect to accomplish much with the entire Coyotero countryside still in arms after what had happened.

Marshal Severn's reply was almost the same as the reply he'd offered before. "Maybe they got something in mind. Maybe they're scoutin' for a bigger force. Whatever in hell they're doin' up here, they got no business crossing the border. How many of you gents are ready to ride?"

They all were. So were another fifteen men who hadn't bothered visiting the marshal in his office but who had already brought in their horses to be rigged out and themselves fitted for Winchester boots.

When Brett and his companions got down to the livery barn, where the scarecrow day man was acting like a flea in a hot skillet, armed men were converging from all over town.

The day man handed over horses and tried to be everywhere at once, which resulted in his being of almost no help to anyone as posse men saddled up, mostly in bleak silence.

Brett had the impression that this time no border-jumpers were going to be allowed within miles of Coyotero.

When the posse left town, heading south at a dead walk, Brett counted twenty-two armed men, not including Marshal Severn out in front. Enos leaned toward him to say, "Severn's army," and jutted his jaw at the way the big lawman was riding ahead like a soldier-officer.

There was rising heat, but not enough to create the customary desert heat haze that limited visibility. Brett wondered aloud how the marshal knew which way to ride, and the affable man who had owned the wagon that had brought Alex Herman's body back in from the hanging ground spoke from behind.

"One of them Messicans who seen 'em down there told him they was south—about a couple miles where there's an old *jacal* without no roof that a preacher built."

Brett and Enos knew the place. So did 'Pifas, who was riding up ahead with Hale Barlow.

Marshal Severn raised an arm to halt his column, turned in the saddle, studied faces until he saw 'Pifas, and detailed him to scout ahead.

The land was clear for a considerable distance. There was

underbrush, but it was east and west of the area Severn's posse men were passing over.

Someone muttered that with the dust the posse was raising, if the red flaggers weren't blind they'd see it, guess they were outnumbered, and ride hell for leather back down into Mexico.

Another man said, "I sure hope so. I'm goin' to leave this country, find a place where there ain't no revolutions an' no Messicans."

Enos put a cold eye on the speaker. "What's wrong with Messicans?" he asked, and saw the man who had spoken look quickly away without answering. When Enos faced forward, Brett was staring at him. Enos scowled. "Well, what's wrong with 'em?"

"They all look alike," Brett stated, with a straight face.

For a moment the dark man looked straight at Brett, then looked up ahead where 'Pifas was loping, and shrugged.

The surprise came from the east, not the south, where 'Pifas had slackened to a walk, trying to make sense out of all the horse tracks that had been left down there over the past few days.

The same resentful individual who had said he was going to leave the south desert yanked down to a halt so abruptly the rider behind him bumped his mount. The resentful man was pointing eastward with a rigid arm. He did not say a word, but someone else did; they yelled up to Marshal Severn that there were *rurales* watching them to the east.

The riders halted and stared. Enos grunted and said to Brett, "Don't look like they're going to run. How many do you make out?"

Brett counted what he could see. "Six in sight. In that damned brush there could be a hundred more."

Evidently Marshal Severn had some similar idea as he sat his horse like a wooden Indian. Eventually he looked back and summoned Brett with a gesture. As Brett rode to a meeting, Enos trailed after him.

Marshal Severn said, "You never know with them. Could be a bunch more over there. Mr. Kandelin, you're lookin' at some of the best bushwhackers in the business." He told the other men to remain where they were, took Brett and Enos, and began slowly walking his horse toward the motionless, dark riders in their tight short jackets of very dark blue with red piping, sitting typically Mex saddles with huge saddle horns. Closer, guns were visible on every saddle and around every middle. There were also long heavy knives in saddle scabbards.

The men were lean and dark. They were also motionless. Brett and Enos were curious as well as cautious. Everything they'd heard of these men had been uncomplimentary.

As they rode closer, one Mexican, a fairly tall man, eased his horse out to meet Marshal Severn. He stopped, rested his hands on top of the saddle horn, and smiled as Bill Severn, nearly twice the *rurale*'s size, drew rein and nodded.

Severn said, "You're a long way from home, señor."

To which the smiling man with jet-black eyes, a nearly lipless mouth, and a hooked nose replied, also in English, "We came to talk." The smile turned rueful. "We came up here last night but were afraid to approach your town."

Severn nodded about that. "Not in darkness," he said dryly, "and maybe not in broad daylight. What do you want?"

"You have some artillery that belongs to the Mexican government."

Marshal Severn's brows shot up. "You want those guns?"

"Yes. The Mexican Army lost them during the battle of Ciudad Morales. We have been sent up here to ask you for them."

"That's all you want?"

"*Sí*. Yes."

"How are you goin' to get them back to Messico?"

The lean man with the menacing smile gestured. "We brought mules. They are back in the underbrush."

Severn looked at Brett and Enos. The other *rurales*, farther back, as still and silent as stones, had also been studying the dark man. The spokesman for the *rurales* broke the silence. "We will ride back with you, get the guns, and go back into our country. All we ask is that you send someone ahead . . . to avoid trouble."

Marshal Severn nodded about that. "I suppose that'd be best, señor. Tell me something. What happened to the *pronunciados*?"

The Mexican showed strong white teeth in a broad smile. "The same thing that usually happens to rebels. They were put to death. A few may have escaped. Not many, I think."

Enos blurted out, "Without no chance to surrender?"

The smiling Mexican swung his attention to the dark man. "Some surrendered,'" he said, and shrugged. "At discretion. Under Mexican law, señor, at discretion means men who surrender can be disposed of at the discretion of the capturing officers."

"So you shot them?"

The Mexican continued to smile at Enos. "It is the law. Anyone taken in arms is to be put to death within fifteen minutes of their capture—or their surrender."

Enos looked steadily at the lean, dark, smiling man. "An' I thought lynchers were a bunch of bastards," he muttered.

The Mexican's smile broadened as he spoke quietly. "Someday, señor, maybe you will visit Mexico." The menace was glaringly clear.

Marshal Severn interrupted what promised to be increasing unpleasantness. He asked Enos to go find 'Pifas and bring him back. After the dark man had ridden away, the lawman rolled his eyes at Brett before addressing the *rurale* again.

"I guess you can have the guns. I don't think it'd do any good for me to say you can have 'em on condition you don't let any more *pronunciados* come over the line."

The Mexican agreed. "It would do no good, señor. We try to prevent it, but there will always be some who do it."

Marshal Severn asked if the *rurales* he could see were all there were and, when the Mexican said they were, Severn asked the Mexican to call them forward and they could ride back to Coyotero with his posse men.

As the Mexican turned to call to his waiting companions,

Marshal Severn and Brett rode in the direction of the men from Coyotero.

When they got back there, Enos and 'Pifas were loping up from the south. The marshal explained about the *rurales* to his posse men and, knowing these men, he warned them against saying or doing anything that would cause a fight. One man growled, "That's what we come down here for, ain't it, Mr. Severn?"

When Enos and the pockmarked Mexican came up, Brett turned aside to ride over where they stopped. Marshal Severn was laying down the law to the others in a dead serious tone of voice.

Enos shook his head at Brett. "At discretion," he said sarcastically. "It's a wonder anyone's left down there." He faced 'Pifas. "Do they really kill people like that—just for having guns on 'em?"

The big Mexican was gazing out where the red flaggers were riding at a slow walk in the direction of the posse men. He did not answer the question. He said instead, "I know that one out in front. His name is Geraldo Suarez. He was with Gil Ortiz before the rebellion. They were friends."

Brett turned in the saddle. The posse men were watching the *rurales* approach without a word passing among them. The Mexicans, too, were silent. They were also wary—and clearly apprehensive.

CHAPTER 21

Rumors

Marshal Severn put the *rurales* out front and sent Brett ahead with Enos to let people in town know who was coming back with the posse. Hale would have gone back with them, but he hadn't been asked to do so. As he slouched along beside 'Pifas, regarding the backs of those *rurales* up ahead, he asked questions that 'Pifas answered curtly because he had no liking for red flaggers, hadn't since he'd witnessed their first visit to his village in Mexico . . . and what they'd left in ashes as they rode out.

The other posse men, with either first-hand knowledge or hearsay information about the lean, dark, graceful men up ahead on their unique saddles, spoke very little. If the red flaggers felt the mood of the men behind them, they gave no sign of it. They talked, laughed, smoked little foul-smelling black cigars, and those among them who were leading Mexican mules rattled snippets of information about the *pronunciados*, which made the others laugh.

'Pifas made no attempt to interpret. For most of the posse men, excluding Hale Barlow who understood Spanish, what seemed hilarious to the red flaggers was not the least bit amusing to them.

By the time they had Coyotero plainly in sight despite the mild heat haze, most of the laughter and talk had ceased. The *rurales* were particularly wary. They knew how *norteamericanos* viewed them, and while in Mexico they liked to be feared, north of the border the grisly tales had produced an entirely different attitude. The lean, tall Mexican up front said something curt in Spanish, and this time 'Pifas interpreted. "He said to watch for ambushers."

As they came to the outskirts of town, where only a few people were in sight along the roadway, Marshal Severn eased up beside the *rurale* leader. He rode stirrup with him, declined the offer of one of those little black cigars, and asked if the red flagger had ever been to Coyotero before. The reply came back while the *rurale* was watching the town up ahead.

"Yes. Twice. Once to buy horses and another time to visit a friend of mine."

"A gringo friend?"

The lean man looked around. "No. Not a gringo."

As they looked at each other, Marshal Severn said, "Gil Ortiz?" and the Mexican's quick smile flashed as he nodded. "*Sí.*"

"Where is he now?" Severn asked, and the Mexican's smile remained as he replied.

"I don't know. He has a few men with him. Maybe he stayed up here. We hunted very hard below the border. Some *pronunciados* said they saw him riding toward your town—in that direction, anyway—up north." The *rurale* shifted his attention back to roadways and rooftops as he finished what he had to say.

"My government has a price on each leader of the rebellion. On him, too. If I found him up here, I was to kill him and return with his head for identification." The *rurale* returned his attention to Marshal Severn. "We grew up in the same village together, like brothers."

Bill Severn did not ask the obvious question: How could a man who had grown from childhood to manhood with another man put the other's head in a sack to collect a reward? He rode beside the *rurale* to the southernmost end of town, then veered to the west, beckoning for the others to follow along, and led the way up the alleyway to where the small artillery pieces had been dragged behind his jailhouse.

The mounted men sat for a moment regarding the guns before the officer gave orders and his men swung to the ground to help hitch the Mexican mules to the Gribeauval sleds. When everything was ready, the chief *rurale* went over to inspect the guns. He said nothing, just examined them with the kind of interest an artilleryman would have, then went over to offer Marshal Severn his hand.

The men around Severn continued to wait. They would escort the Mexicans out of town, beyond rifle range.

Brett Kandelin appeared around the side of a building. He was alone until Enos came up north beyond the jailhouse. He, too, was alone. Neither of them moved closer nor returned the apprehensive stares of the *rurales*.

'Pifas disrupted the discomfort by kneeing his horse up near the lawman and the *rurale* and speaking to the Mexican. "*Teniente* Geraldo Suarez. Do you remember me?"

The *rurale* was releasing Marshal Severn's hand when he looked at the large man with the pock-scarred face. "I thought I knew you back where we all met. I couldn't remember. Epifanio . . . ?"

"Epifanio Valdez, the aide to Gil Ortiz."

The *rurale* nodded. "I remember," he said in Spanish. "And you are now with these people?"

'Pifas brushed the question aside to ask one of his own. "Where is Gil Ortiz?"

"I just told the lawman here, I don't know. If I knew, I'd find him and kill him. All I can tell you is what some of the prisoners said, that he took some men with him and rode northward." The *rurale* shrugged. "By now he could be very far north. . . . He was your friend, wasn't he?"

'Pifas offered no denial. "Yes, for two years."

"But not now?"

"Not now, and not for a long time. He began to change until he wasn't the man I'd known. He was bad, *Teniente*. Did you know the *pronunciado, Coronel* Diego Rivera?"

"Yes. I knew him very well."

"Gil Ortiz shot him in his tent when a herd of cattle stampeded through the camp ruining everything, scattering the men."

The lieutenant looked closely at the big man when he asked how 'Pifas knew this. The answer he got surprised even Hale Barlow. "I saw the general's body. The bullets that killed him came from behind. . . . Very small, neat wounds, *Teniente,* the kind made by the French pistol I gave Gil Ortiz as a present his first name day after I became his aide. I'd seen holes like that before. It was the only pistol I knew that made such nice, clean little holes."

The lieutenant responded to the soft hiss of a squatty, barrel-shaped, very dark man back near the sleds. He did not look around, but he smiled at 'Pifas and said, "I'll find him. Someday, amigo, I'll find him."

Brett spoke from the corner of the building where he was leaning. "When you find him, friend, he'll be under the ground."

The *rurale* turned, said nothing as he eyed Brett, then gave a curt order in Spanish. The mules leaned into their collars and the sleds began to move. People appeared here and there, not very many and not enthusiastic enough to walk boldly forth. The *rurale* reputation on both sides of the border had inspired a lot of justified dread.

Brett and Enos came together out where the guns had been to watch the procession start southward; Mexicans in front with their little guns, local posse men behind.

No one questioned Marshal Severn about giving the guns back. That would come later, much later, when all that was left was to dissect events, criticize, place a little blame, and in general denigrate the only man in Coyotero who'd taken charge and had done his best. It was human nature at its least admirable, but it never prevented belated criticism from surfacing.

An hour later, after the lawman had detailed two wiry young men from Mex town to hover like vultures in the wake of the *rurales* to make sure they did not turn back or delay their departure from the north to the south, he met Hale and Enos at the saloon. He accepted their offer to join them at the table and share their bottle. He asked where 'Pifas and Brett were, and got back a blank stare and no reply.

Marshal Severn was not offended. He drank from the bottle as Enos spoke while getting more comfortable in the chair. "Juan's up and around. That midwife who's been lookin' after him—by any chance do you know her, Marshal?—there is a woman who can swear. I'm here to tell you when she caught Juan walking around she cussed him out for at least three minutes without repeating herself."

Marshal Severn put the bottle in the center of the table, let go with a flammable breath, and gazed at his companions for a moment. Then he laughed for no reason either of his companions understood until he leaned back in his chair.

"It just came to me, gents. While we been busy as kittens in a box of shavings. . . Here's a Messican, a black man, and a gringo. Countin' the others, there's Escalanate, Kandelin, and the big Messican, 'Pifas." At the steady looks he was getting, Marshal Severn explained further. "It didn't matter who was what, did it? What mattered was that we had common interests. *That* mattered."

He continued to get the unwavering looks until his companions caught what he meant, then Enos reached for the bottle, drank, shoved it in front of Hale Barlow, who did not touch it until after he had spoken. "Never thought about it," he said, and reached as Enos, with a twinkle in his eyes, gazed over at the big lawman.

"Maybe they don't all look alike, Marshal. Unless they're *rurales*. Now those fellers *do* look alike."

Marshal Severn did not take this up. He'd made his point, and beyond that he was not particularly interested. Because what could conceivably have ended in an argument was interrupted by the arrival of Jess Eames, who didn't wait to be invited, just dragged a chair up, swung it, straddled it, and said, "I was on the porch at the hotel when Juan had a visitor from Mex town. A rickety old gent with only two teeth, an' they didn't mesh, who walks with a manzanita stick."

The big lawman nodded. "I know him. He's older'n dirt. Can't recall his name offhand. He don't sound Mex, but he sure looks like one."

Eames waited until Severn had finished to drop his bombshell. "Well, this old gent's got his ear to the ground about everythin' that happens in Mex town. The winder was open in Juan's room. I heard the old gent tell Escalante a couple of strangers rode in down there and was askin' questions at the cantina."

Severn asked what kind of questions, and the hotel proprietor answered curtly, "All kinds of questions—like was all the soldiers gone, an' did we still have prisoners in Coyotero, an' was the feller who stampeded the cattle over the raider camp still in town."

Enos dropped his gaze to the label on the whiskey bottle without commenting. Hale Barlow studied Jess Eames's face during the interval of silence, until Marshal Severn placed both hands on the arms of the chair to rise as he said, "I guess it wouldn't hurt to amble down there."

Eames said, "They left town a while back."

Enos had a question. "Did the old man say which way they rode?"

"North. Like I told you, that old man don't miss anything."

Enos and Hale also rose. When the big lawman nodded to the hotelman and started for the door, Enos put the bottle squarely in front of Eames, then also headed for the door.

Roadway traffic was beginning to thin out. There were soft shadows beginning to make a stealthy approach as three vaqueros came slowly up in the direction of the saloon where the lawman was standing. He halted to watch. One of the riders made a gesture with his hands as he spoke from the saddle. "They were still going south when we turned back."

"Any other *rurales* join them along the way?" Severn asked.

"No."

Severn thanked the vaqueros, turned toward Hale and Enos, and said, "Well, that part of it's ended. By the time they get back to Mexico draggin' those little guns, their damned war will more'n likely have moved deeper into the interior."

He led all the way down to Mex town. At the cantina,

customers were departing because it was almost suppertime. Otherwise, except for two middle-aged women drawing water in the center of the plaza, there was no particular activity. Enos wagged his head. "Maybe they don't all look alike, but they sure all act alike. They came within an ace of gettin' shot all to hell yesterday, and today they act like nothing happened."

Severn's only comment was, "It's the Messican way. They been raided so many times over the last hundred years it's like water off a duck's back."

There was no light at the alcalde's *jacal*. When they stepped onto the porch and knocked, only an echo came back from the empty interior. Enos stepped around the marshal, flung the door open, and squinted into the darkness.

The house was empty.

Hale did not like this. "If those strange Messicans was Ortiz's men, maybe they carried Brett an' the lady off with 'em."

He got no response as Marshal Severn followed Enos on a search of the house. Hale lit a kitchen lamp while the others were searching. He felt the coffeepot, which was cold, and sniffed at the stove, where he detected a faint scent of dying coals. When the other men joined him in the kitchen, he stirred ash, blew, and all three of them watched coals begin to glow. Hale turned toward Marshal Severn. "How long ago do you reckon those strangers was down here?"

The answer had to be a guess, because Jess Eames had not mentioned time. "I'd guess maybe early afternoon."

"Then I don't think they took the woman and Brett away with 'em. Someone cooked on this stove not more'n two hours ago. That'd be after the vaqueros left, wouldn't it?"

He could have been right, but since they did not know exactly when the strangers had departed, Hale's idea, while it boosted their spirits, was unverifiable.

Without a sound, Ambrosia Salazar appeared in the kitchen doorway, hands on hips, lips drawn flat as she regarded the marshal and his companions.

"Well," she exclaimed in Spanish, "what is it for men

to go sneaking in the night, breaking into houses! Marshal . . .?"

"We're looking for Mr. Kandelin and the alcalde's granddaughter."

Ambrosia flung her arms wide. "Do you see them? No? Then they aren't here, are they?"

"Where are they?"

"Why should I know? The last I saw, they were walking."

"Where? Which direction?"

"North. Toward the old mission," the sturdy woman replied, and looked from man to man before also saying, "What is it? No! He hasn't come back! Is that it, Marshal? Gil Ortiz is back?"

Enos and Hale were regarding the woman from expressionless faces. Marshal Severn did not answer her; he shouldered past to reach the dusty yard beyond. Out there, Ambrosia Salazar said nothing until the three men were walking in the direction of her *jacal*, then she ran in front of them to stand very dramatically in her own doorway, arms flung wide to prevent an entry.

They walked past without a glance in her direction. Up ahead the massive old adobe mission structure loomed solidly. "He's not goin' to be in there," Hale said sourly, and stopped in his tracks when a familiar voice called from behind.

'Pifas came hurrying forward where the others had stopped. He asked where they were going. Enos answered in a very dry tone of voice, "To that old church. Brett and the girl are missing."

'Pifas drew to his full height. "Missing? How can they be missing? I saw them not half an hour ago."

"Where? Are you sure it was them, because we think some of Gil Ortiz's renegades were here, in Mex town."

'Pifas's eyes widened in disbelief. "Who told you such a thing?" When Marshal Severn replied, the large man looked apprehensively around, then gestured for the lawman to resume his march toward the old church, although he did not believe Brett or the handsome woman would be there.

Hale interrupted 'Pifas to mutter a question. "You goin' to marry that hefty lady?"

'Pifas widened his stride to get away from Hale Barlow.

Several elderly women emerged from the church. One was carrying a small candle, which she shielded with her fingers. The men waited until the women had gone, then left it up to the lawman to find the doorway; he was the only one among them who had been inside the old church.

Severn did not use the big double doors in front. He led them around back, where a *ramada* ran the full length of a worn old tiled walkway.

The door he sought was much less impressive than the massive double doors in front, but it opened into what had once been some kind of small room with a veil hanging between it and the much larger, cavernous main chapel.

This evidently was where in better times the priest had been able to see out without being seen himself and make his tally of the number of people in the main chapel.

Two doorways leading from this room were on opposite sides of the wall. Marshal Severn did not like the idea of dividing his companions, so it took more time to complete their search.

They spent a lot of time poking into long unused kitchens, small cells, niches, and crannies, as well as a very large underground room with a huge wine vat in it and a series of what once must have been dressing rooms for priests, and their spartan living quarters and offices.

When they were back outside, with fresh air instead of the residual aroma of centuries of ceremonial incense to smell, Hale complained that they'd wasted a full damned hour and did not wait to see if the others would follow as he turned to retrace his steps to the alcalde's house.

Brett and Lillian were waiting side by side, along with the buxom woman, when Hale got back to the alcalde's house, where he stopped in his tracks, staring at them.

Enos came up, grunted in exasperation, and asked if Brett hadn't heard that some of Ortiz's man had been in town asking questions.

Brett shook his head while gazing at the searchers. ''What kind of questions?''

''Where you an' the lady was—along with other questions.''

''How do you know they came from Ortiz?''

For a few moments no one replied. It struck Marshal Severn at the same time it seemed to strike Enos and Hale that retelling the Eames story was going to sound foolish. Who was the old man with the manzanita cane? Old men had wandering minds. Enos said lamely, ''Somethin' goin' on over in Gringo town. . . . Come on, Marshal, Hale.''

Bret, 'Pifas, and the women watched Marshal Severn lead his two companions away. Ambrosia asked if it was possibly true, that tale of Ortiz sending men into Coyotero? Brett shrugged, took Lillian's hand, and led her toward the alcalde's adobe.

CHAPTER 22

A Plot

The following day, an unexpected event occurred that was mildly puzzling to the residents of Coyotero and also quite reassuring—the army came through. Three companies of the Fifth Cavalry, dusty, thirsty, glad for the respite Coyotero provided.

They did not stay in town, but pitched camp at the lower end—and after nightfall gave the town's economy a slight boost at the saloon, the cafe, and the pool hall, among other places.

Marshal Severn smoked a fat cigar with the commanding officer, a large, red-faced man with the kind of formidable mustache cavalrymen liked to cultivate. His name was Austin Campbell. He was originally from New York, had served at a variety of posts, camps, and stations, and explained that he was making a routine sweep along the border in consequence of the trouble down there. He also said that so far, although a few individual horsemen had appeared to pop up out of the ground in the distance, they vanished the moment he swung in their direction. Beyond that, he'd encountered nothing interesting and was on his way back to the barracks with the summer's heat crowding him a little.

The following morning, Captain Campbell sent out a strong detachment to scout north of town, with orders to bear southerly after completing the sweep in order to meet the rest of the column on its way eastward.

The fact that the soldiers had made a miles-deep patrol without encountering *bandoleros* or other varieties of possible trouble was reassuring. The few people who still went to bed without lighting lamps, as well as some who had traveled up toward the mountains to scan the countryside, abandoned their wariness and their vigil.

As Marshal Severn stood in front of the jailhouse watching the horse soldiers leave town, he was joined by Jess Eames and several other men. Somebody mentioned a rumor they'd heard about strangers being in Mex town, and Eames scoffed. "There's always strangers over there. They got a regular trail between some of them little villages south of the border and Mex town."

If the original spokesman had intended to mention the rest of what he'd heard, the scoffing discouraged him and nothing more was said until the cavalry column was no longer in sight. Then, the small party of idlers broke up.

The lawman was at his untidy old table an hour or so later when the owner of the general store walked in. He was still wearing his flour-sack apron. He commented about the army. Severn said it was not the same officer who'd joined in the south desert *bandolero* hunt, which the storekeeper knew because he'd been on that earlier foray. What had brought him across the road was something an outlying resident had told him while buying supplies. "He saw some Messicans north of town. Figured, as near as he could make out, maybe four of 'em."

Severn looked down his nose. "There's always Messicans around. Far as I know they always been around, part of the landscape."

"Wearing crossed bullet belts?" the storekeeper asked quietly.

Severn had one of his lapses before speaking. "Who saw them? Where did he see them?"

"North of town, up the stage road a few miles, where he herds his goats and sheep. I know him pretty well. An old Messican named Augustín Iturbide."

Marshal Severn nodded slightly. He, too, knew the old Mexican. What began to bother him now was that among all the Mexicans he knew, old Iturbide was probably the least likely to exaggerate.

He sat gazing at the storekeeper for a long time, then rocked forward to stand up as he said, "If you'd told me sooner, I could have got the army to make a sweep."

"They made a sweep northward this morning."

"Yeah, so they did. Well, they'll find your *bandoleros.*

"I don't think so," stated the merchant.

"Why?"

"Because old Augustín told me yesterday what he'd seen, and it was three or four days before that when he saw them."

Marshal Severn stood in silence for a moment, then sat back down. "If they wasn't gone by today and saw the soldiers, they'll sure as hell be gone now."

The storekeeper rose. "Thought I ought to let you know, is all," he said, and departed.

For the town marshal the tendrils of the recent trouble were annoying. He had been ready for things to return to normal several days ago. There could be wandering raiders still around. For a fact, they were safer north of the border than south of it. He might even continue to be told of sightings for another few weeks or a month, but to his knowledge there could not be very many, certainly not enough to threaten the town.

He went over to the cafe for breakfast and encountered Juan Escalante over there. At his surprised look, Juan smiled. "The midwife had to go somewhere and deliver a baby. If she hadn't, I wouldn't have walked down here."

Marshal Severn thought about that before speaking. "Are you that much better? You look a mite peaked."

Juan leaned back as the cafe man placed a platter in front of him. "I feel fine. Still a little weak, but fine." He gazed fondly at the steak, potatoes, coffee, and toast. "This is what a man needs, not vegetables and broth and so much water."

Hale Barlow and Enos walked in, saw the marshal and Juan Escalante, sat down beside them, and Juan had to repeat what he'd just told the lawman. Enos looked at Hale

Barlow and rolled his eyes. Escalante was crowding his luck.

An old Mexican, walking with the aid of a red cane, shuffled by the steamy window, cupped his hands, and peered in. The cafe man saw him, attracted the lawman's attention, and pointed.

The old man's wrinkled face split into a wide grin. He made a beckoning gesture, and Marshal Severn swore under his breath as he rose.

Outside, with the pleasant morning sunlight beginning to bring cool warmth into the new day, the old man led off toward the nearest bench, sat down with the cane between his knees and, still smiling, fixed his gaze on something across the road as he said, "Did you hear about *bandoleros* north of town?"

Marshal Severn sighed, sat down, and nodded. "Yeah, I heard. Three or four. It'll take time; they got scattered and'll be afraid of going back to Messico for a while."

The old man patiently listened while ever so slightly nodding his head. He'd known *norteamericanos* for more years than most men had lived. Some were different now than most had been when he'd been young, but all of them were opinionated and stubborn, so the old man was discreet when next he spoke.

"You must be right, *jefe*, but it seems to me fugitives do not ride into a town just to ask questions. Right now in Coyotero that would be very dangerous. Not in a few months, no, but right now."

Marshal Severn looked at the old man for a moment before speaking. "Abizu, how long have we known each other?"

The old man continued to gaze across the road. "I don't know. I stopped counting years long ago. A long time."

"And you understand me?"

The old man chuckled. "Yes."

"And I know you. . . . So, just what is on your mind?"

"*Jefe*, some of the men in the cantina who saw those strangers recognized one of them. He was always with Gil Ortiz."

Bill Severn settled back on the bench. The damned mess wasn't over with, after all. "He was sure, Abizu?"

"Yes, he was sure," the old man said, and finally turned to face the big lawman. "What I think, *jefe*, is that Gil Ortiz escaped down there. He ruined everything by stealing the alcalde's daughter—his wife, of course, so maybe he had the right to do that. But she got away. Gil Ortiz is not a man to overlook something like that, especially since he has no one else to take out his anger on now. You understand what I'm saying?"

Bill Severn understood perfectly. "An' you think those strangers asking questions were his men?"

The old man spread his hands, palms up. "Who else would want to know if she was here in Coyotero? Her and the gringo who brought her back? One of them was recognized. *Jefe*, I know you would have figured this out in time, but maybe not for a long while—because you don't live in Mex town. Not until after he had killed her. Maybe not for a little longer even then, because he wouldn't shoot her. Too noisy. He'd slit her throat."

Marshal Severn saw Juan among others leaving the cafe looking replete. His own breakfast would be cold by now. He patted the old man's shoulder, rose, and returned to the cafe.

For old Abizu Corales, the "Mexican" who was not a Mexican, there was nothing more to be done. He rose with some difficulty and went between two buildings, back down into Mex town. Gringos: opinionated, stubborn—and sometimes very unpredictable. A man could eat any time; what the old man had confided to the town marshal needed immediate attention.

Maybe the old man was right, but he was no longer in Gringo town when Bill Severn left the cafe to hunt up some riders to scour the north country with him.

He didn't encounter much difficulty. It was a beautiful morning: clear, softly warm, and pleasant. He rode out of Coyotero with six posse men. Hale and Enos watched the procession from the porch of the hotel. They'd just emerged from visiting the lean, calm Mexican with the scarred face—Juan Escalante.

Hale said, "Now what the hell you reckon they're up to?"

Enos replied curtly. "*Bandolero* hunting. Let's go find Brett."

"Finding" Kandelin consisted of hunting for the nearest dogtrot and ducking down through it. He was sitting on a bench out in front of the alcalde's house with 'Pifas. He saw Enos and Hale coming, frowned faintly, and murmured to the big Mexican that when Enos walked like that, with long strides, he was concerned about something.

They exchanged greetings before Enos related what he and Hale had just seen—the big lawman and six heavily armed men leaving town on the north stage road.

Brett nodded and asked if they'd care for coffee. They would, so he went inside to get it, and told Lillian in the kitchen what Enos had said. He also told her that evidently those question-asking strangers who'd been at the cantina were strongly suspected of being Ortiz's men, and she nodded in silence, wearing the philosophical expression he'd seen on her face before.

She said, "And you want to go after them."

He filled two cups with coffee as he replied, "No. . . I want you to go with Hale and 'Pifas—after them."

She turned, wide-eyed and speechless.

He put the pot down. "He wants to kill you."

"And you want me to make it easy for him?"

"No, Lillian, to make it impossible for him."

"What are you talking about?"

"He isn't going to let up, and we can't forever be looking over our shoulders. You'll wear my clothes. The three of you will trail the posse. Stay well behind, but keep it in sight. That will be your protection."

Her eyes were fixed on him. "And you?"

"I'll wait here. Enos and I."

Understanding was dawning when she asked her next question. "Wearing my clothes?"

He grinned at her. "You're pretty quick. . . for a woman."

Another time she might have made a tart remark, but

not now. She went to the back door, opened it, and looked out as she spoke over her shoulder. "That coffee will get cold."

He took the cups out front, leaving her standing in the doorway. Of course, he was right; they couldn't spend the rest of their lives looking over their shoulders. But she knew Gil Ortiz better than Brett Kandelin did. In fact, if he came in darkness and saw someone dressed to look like her, he wouldn't even think about a trick—but he was a dangerous and deadly man, especially with weapons.

She was turning back around when Brett appeared in the doorway. "Hale and 'Pifas have agreed. They think it's a crazy idea, but Enos don't."

She said, "When?"

"Right now." He led her toward the back of the house and, as they were exchanging clothes, she wondered aloud if Ortiz would come this night, or maybe later, some other night.

Brett's reply to that was brusque. "If he's up north somewhere, hiding probably, and by now's got the report of the spies he sent to find out if you and I were in Coyotero, then my guess is that he's sitting in shade watching Marshal Severn and his riders. Maybe that's the way he planned it, except I don't think so. But I know one thing about Gil Ortiz—he knows an opportunity when he sees one. . . . Tonight, Lillian."

They faced around to look at each other, and she laughed without saying why. His clothing was not loose; in fact, she did a better job of filling his clothing out than he did, but the trousers were a little too long, as were the sleeves. He shrugged that off. "Hale and 'Pifas will get the horses and bring them here. The three of you can ride north from Mex town and angle over until you reach the stage road. They won't see you in town that way. On the road, it won't matter."

She put her head slightly to one side. "I know all of that. Even if someone does see me on the stage road, we can simply turn off for a short distance until they pass."

He nodded at her. "I think from a distance you'll fool

him. He's not going to be interested in three riders behind the posse. He's going to be interested in the posse."

"I said I'm not worrying about fooling people. I'm worried about you. Suppose he comes with many riders?"

Neither of them really believed this would happen. Not after all the other things that had happened. He would come either silently alone in darkness, or perhaps with a companion. Despite Coyotero's swift recovery from menace and fear, gunshots in Mex town would rouse everyone. But neither of them believed Ortiz would use a gun.

He took her back to the kitchen, poured them both wine, and told her to wait. He went out front—where the slouching men on the bench looked, looked harder, then burst out laughing. He sent Hale and 'Pifas for three mounts, left Enos sitting out there, and returned to the kitchen, where Lillian watched him walk and raised a discreet hand to her lips.

They looked steadily at each other over the rims of their cups, drank wine, stood a moment, until Brett said, "Be careful. You'll be in good hands, but be careful."

Her reply was direct. "I'm not going to be in much danger. If he is really out there, *you* are. . . . Brett?"

"Yes'm."

"Have you thought about buying the livery barn?"

He had thought about it, not seriously, but he knew that at this moment she wouldn't want to hear about his casual thoughts, so he nodded. "We'll talk about it when you get back."

Hale poked his head inside from out front. He and 'Pifas were back with three horses. Brett looked long at the handsome woman and opened his arms. She came into them, pushing her head against him, holding him firmly for a moment, then breaking clear with moist eyes. "I haven't had time to talk to the relic," she told him, and gave an uncertain smile. "When I get back I will."

He took her to the door and watched as she went out to mount his animal. As the trio rode away, up through Mex town, Enos, who had been dozing until the handsome woman appeared in Brett's clothing, wagged his head and looked around. "You better get back inside before some rutting buck sees you and wants to come courting."

They went to the kitchen, had some wine, and Enos moved to the stove to make a meal. He was quiet for a long while. Brett did not notice; he had his own thoughts. When the meal was ready and the dark man placed their plates on the table, he said, "Y'know, they aren't much different, are they?"

Brett looked up smiling. "No." Then he gazed at the plate in front of him and also said, "But they all look alike."

Enos's teeth flashed. "You're never goin' to let me forget that, are you? Why didn't you just change clothes with her and let her stay here?"

"Because this house isn't going to be the safest place in Coyotero when that son of a bitch comes back."

"Maybe he won't. Maybe he'll be scairt to after seeing the soldiers."

Brett paused at his meal and spoke without looking up. "What the hell is this?"

Enos had no idea. "It was lyin' there in a dish with flour all over it. I thought it was fish; the shape was about right."

"Did you ever eat a fish made of ground corn?"

"It's not bad. I've sure eaten worse." Enos picked up the somewhat elongated, fish-shaped thing from his plate and studied it. "I think she was fixin' it to be filled with something."

Brett's expression changed. He took another mouthful, then said, "Hell, it's a *relleno*. She made some for supper the other night. Only they had cheese and whatnot inside 'em."

Enos topped up their cups with red wine. "I wish I had a shotgun," he said. "The way I hear it, he'll have three or four gun hands with him."

"He'll need more'n that, Enos. He's going to come into a dark house expecting one woman to be here, asleep."

They finished their meal, cleaned up after themselves, and Enos said he'd never dried dishes with such a handsome something or other, in a nice dress like—it—was wearing!

There was no time for a retort; someone knocked on the back door. They exchanged a look, and Enos jerked his head in the direction of the bedrooms. Brett hastened, had closed the door to within a couple of inches of its jam when he heard an unmistakable female voice ask in obvious surprise what Enos was doing in the late alcalde's house.

He answered in a mild tone of voice, "Wipin' up some dishes."

"I'm not blind," the woman exclaimed. "Where is Lillian?"

"She ain't here, an' that's about all I can tell you."

The woman said, "My name is Ambrosia."

"Yes'm. I know who you are."

"Is 'Pifas with you?"

"No ma'am."

"Do you know where he is?"

"Yes'm. He went horseback riding."

There was a brief lull, broken finally when Enos asked Ambrosia to come inside and she refused, although she leaned in to peer around before she turned and departed with quick, hard steps.

Brett returned, and Enos rolled his eyes at him. "If 'Pifas gets into double harness with her, he's goin' to spend the rest of his life regrettin' it." He draped the dishtowel and said he thought he'd amble up to the hotel to see how Juan was.

As he was departing, his last words were, "Don't fret. I'll be back before sundown."

Brett didn't fret, but he was not accustomed to being cooped up inside a house with a long wait ahead. He found two old dog-eared books. Both were in Spanish. He left them where he'd found them and poured half a cup of red wine at the kitchen table.

Things, he told himself, had a way of turning out, not as someone expected them to, but as some unknowable fate made them turn out.

Lillian would be safe. As safe as it was possible for her to be under the circumstances. Not even a madman would attack her in sight of a posse.

He sat dozing for a long while, until he was roused at the sound of boots coming up onto the porch out front.

It was Enos. Juan Escalante had told him there were rumors around town, thick as the hair on a dog's back, about Marshal Severn leaving town with an armed posse. The only one Enos thought worth repeating was to the effect that over in Gringo town people were saying the reason Marshal Severn had taken a posse out of town was because he'd heard a large band of *bandoleros* were going to attack.

Enos sat down, tossed his hat aside, and considered the bottle of red wine. Brett pushed his cup across as Enos reached for the bottle.

"If they try it," he told Brett, "I got to change my opinion about Messicans. I thought they might be just as savvy as you'n me. If they try anything like that, they're downright crazy—unless it's another big army of 'em. You believe that?"

Brett shook his head.

CHAPTER 23

Huevos con Carne

As the day waned, they saw the old man with the red cane out front in the middle distance, standing in tree shade and grinning at the alcalde's house.

He was still there when they looked a half hour later, so Enos asked if the old man spoke English. When Brett confirmed this, the dark man flung open the door, walked straight toward old Abizu Corales, and halted with his head tipped challengingly. "*Buenas dias, viejo,*" Enos said, and learned something. Never address someone in their native tongue unless you are fluent in it. The old man spouted Spanish until Enos held up a hand and reverted to English.

"Señor, I just used up all the Spanish I've learnt down here. Almost all, anyway. Tell me something. Why are you standing over here like you're goin' to bust out laughing?"

The old man settled his back against the tree and leaned on the manzanita cane as he replied, eyes twinkling, "I wanted to see your friend in Lillian's dress."

Enos considered the shrewd old eyes in their setting of spiderweb wrinkles. "Why would he be wearing her clothes?" he asked, and got a dry chuckle.

"Because when I was sitting in shade up at the mission, I saw the alcalde's granddaughter riding toward the road with two men . . . and she was wearing your friend's clothes."

Enos was silent a long time. It might have been a very

long time if the old man hadn't spoken again, this time a brief murmur in Spanish, which he immediately interpreted. "Be tranquil, friend. It was the wrong time of day. The heat was coming. People in Mex town go indoors when the heat comes. If some others saw the three riders, I was the only one close enough to recognize the alcalde's granddaughter."

Enos finally arrived at a decision. He gestured in the direction of the adobe house and jerked his head by way of inviting the old man to accompany him back there. Old Abizu Corales went along agreeably—slowly, shuffling, but agreeably.

Brett opened the door for them. The old man's eyes widened briefly, then squinted nearly closed as he made a keening, high laugh.

Enos closed the door as he related to Brett what the old man had said. The two of them stood looking at Abizu Corales until he said, "The alcalde always had cool wine, señores," then they took him to the kitchen. It seemed to Brett the old man wanted the wine less than he needed to sit down.

He tasted the wine, nodded as though in approval, and said, "The alcalde made very good wine. Only once, when he was young—that time it became vinegar. . . . This is from the last he will make, no?"

Enos was worried about what the old man had said about recognizing Lillian. But Corales put the dark man's mind at rest. "No. I told you, there was no one else at the mission. Not even the old grandmothers. When it gets hot, they don't stay to talk to God."

Although the dark man seemed relieved, he and Brett now had a new worry. What if the old man was wrong?

They refilled his cup, after which he leaned his red cane aside and became expansive. It clearly required very little wine to bring old Abizu Corales to this condition.

"I remember the first gringo I saw," he told them, wiping wet eyes with a soiled cuff. "It was soldiers, with a red-faced man out in front and a young boy who was carrying a little flag. It was a very nice little flag with a number on it. That was some time ago, when Santa Anna lost most of Mexico to the gringos of the north. Neither of you had been born then. Later, you had your own war.'' Corales's eyes drifted to Enos and remained there.

''That was your war, amigo.''

Enos tipped wine into his own cup. It hadn't been ''his'' war, it had been his father's war.

''After that, they came with huge wagons, and some natives moved south. Well, there were massacres before that; men like Diego Rivera and Gil Ortiz ruled. The Mexican Army, when it was here, could do almost nothing. The *bandoleros* in those days did not have to fight much; they had only to know whose palm to pour gold into. Afterward, it was different. Not a lot different, but there were fewer massacres—and the gringo soldiers did not turn back as the Mexicans had done. They did not give up until they'd cornered someone. Apaches, Texas Indians, *bandoleros*, parties of renegades. They never gave up. . . . I knew this was the alcalde's wine. It has special flavor, no? A little more in the cup, if you please?''

Enos looked at Brett and got back a shrug, so he poured. At the same time, he brought the conversation forward fifty years. ''You know Gil Ortiz?''

The old man's eyes were not focusing well when he nodded. ''*Sí*. Yes. I know Gil Ortiz y Duran. I knew his father, even his grandfather. Bandits. Every man comes to a profession. On the south desert, *bandidos* are born. If you work, you live, not well, but you live. If you rob and kill, you live much better. Sometimes not as long, but I can tell you, friends, living can go on too long.''

Brett murmured, ''Gil Ortiz,'' and the old man's mind reverted back to where it had digressed.

''Gil Ortiz learned from the Yanquis, who don't kill for sport, only for profit. He learned well.''

Brett murmured again. ''And his wife?''

Abizo Corales peered into his empty cup and, when neither of his companions moved to refill it, he leaned back and said, ''She was very pretty. Her mother was very pretty. Her father . . . I don't remember him very well, but I knew her grandfather all my life. He—''

"Lillian . . . ?" Brett interrupted.

"Yes. She could have married many times." The old man shrugged. "Someone with a mud house and some goats. Gil Ortiz came—on a golden horse with silver on his saddle and bit, with money and his big smile. Well, it lasted a few years, maybe that long because he was away much of the time. . . . She ran away. One night her grandfather told me he had heard her crying in her room. The next morning she was gone."

The old man leaned on the table in silence, leaned lower, and finally, when his head dropped to the tabletop, Enos sat a while gazing at him. Without a word, he went around, picked the old man up in his arms like he was a child, carried him to a bedroom and placed him flat out and returned.

Brett was gazing at a blank wall. Enos put the cups and bottle away and was turning to speak when a fist rattled the kitchen door.

Brett jerked upright, crossed glances with Enos, and left the table. Enos waited a decent interval, then opened the door. Ambrosia Salazar was standing there, this time without hands on her hips or the challenging look on her face.

She said, "I can't find 'Pifas."

Enos nodded about that. "I told you, he went horseback riding."

"Where? He didn't tell me he was going away."

"He'll be back, " the dark man told her.

"He went with somebody. Maybe a woman?"

Enos shifted stance; this was likely to take time. "Why should you worry about another woman?" he asked the buxom woman. "You can hold your own."

She gazed a trifle skeptically at him. "What do you know about men, eh? Their eyes wander."

"Lady, take my word for it, he'll be back. Maybe not today, but by tomorrow."

"You know where he went!"

"Yes. An' I know he'll be back."

"It is a secret?"

"Lady, 'Pifas will be back. I promise you he will."

"It is a secret, then," Ambrosia said, and put both hands on her hips. She glared. "Tell him, when he comes back, my house is locked. Tell him I know men are liars; I don't want to see him again!"

She spun on her heels and marched away with Enos's calm gaze fixed on her until he closed the door.

Brett came out of hiding. There were shadows beginning to form on the east side of buildings; the heat had been increasing for some time. Springtime on the south desert did not last long, and once full summer arrived, the daylong heat, stored by rocks, the earth, the walls and roofs of buildings, continued to increase even after sundown. If the walls were very thick, as they were with most adobe houses, three to four feet thick, inside where the heat could not reach, it was pleasant, as it was in the alcalde's house.

As Enos was closing the door and Brett returned, the dark man repeated something he'd mentioned before. "If 'Pifas marries that woman . . ." He let it trail off on his way to the table, where he sat down, lifted out his six-gun, and began to methodically clean and examine it.

Brett sat on the opposite bench and also took out his six-gun to clean and examine it, but he had reached a different conclusion, so he said, "I don't know, Enos. Since we been down here, I've seen 'em screamin' at each other like there was goin' to be murder. The next morning, they were pleasant as can be."

Enos was silent a long time after holstering his weapon and going to stand where he could see out. "If we come out of this," he said, without facing the table, "what then? Go back up north, wait until late winter, an' buy more cattle to free-graze for a weight gain?"

Brett gazed at the back of the dark man. "It's harder every year, Enos. You know that."

"Yes, I know it. That's why I asked. When we leave here, what then?"

Brett was getting hungry. He went to the stove, stood looking at it, and said, "You hungry?"

Enos turned. "What then, Brett?"

Brett continued to stand in front of the stove, looking at

it dubiously. He wasn't a very good cook even over an open fire. Using a stove, particularly one he'd never used before, was daunting. He continued to look at it as he replied to Enos's question.

"I don't know. But I do know if we go back to free-grazing, one of these years someone's likely to run off our cattle an' maybe shoot us."

Enos waited patiently for all this to be said, then repeated it for the third and last time: "Then what? Life don't end because some son of a bitch invented barbed wire."

Brett looked straight at the dark man. "You ever work at the livery and trading business?"

Enos's eyes widened. After a moment, he asked a question. "Here? The dead liveryman's barn?"

"Maybe. Coyotero's on the north-south roadway. I was told he did a hell of a business, mostly in buying and selling."

Enos returned to the table, sat down, clasped both hands, and regarded his partner. "How long you been thinking about this?" he asked, and got as evasive a reply as Brett had given the handsome woman.

"It's worth thinking about, Enos. The choice is to be saddle bums, or get tarred and feathered for free-grazing over some big cow man's grass. And there's somethin' else. Always drifting behind a bunch of cattle will someday end us up somewhere where everyone belongs—and we don't."

"You sound sort of dissatisfied with life, Brett."

"I don't think that's it, Enos."

The dark man rose from the table. "I think I know what it is," he said, and grinned a little. After a while, he said, "I figure you're right about the livery and trading barn."

Brett said, "You like the idea?"

"Maybe, but I haven't thought about it as much as you have. You figure out how to work it?"

Brett shrugged. "Partnership."

Ambrosia returned to knock on the door again. Brett went for cover, and this time when Enos opened the door he did not give her a chance, he spoke first. "Lady, he's not back yet. I told you—tomorrow."

Ambrosia snapped her fingers in his face. "I told you—my house is locked to him." She lowered her hand and softened her tone. "I'm making some peppered meat for supper. More than I can eat. And I make the best *cerveza* in Coyotero."

Enos looked doubtful. "What's *cerveza*?"

"Beer. Supper will be ready in two hours." Her expression became scornful. "You can't cook. My uncle could cook, but my husband couldn't; most men can't. If you are going to stay in here all day, you need company, a decent meal . . . Two hours, señor?"

An angry yellow jacket dived out of nowhere, aiming for Enos's face. He saw it from the corner of his eye and bobbed his head. The yellow jacket missed and took his fury elsewhere, but Ambrosia Salazar made a smile that showed beautiful white teeth as she tossed her head, flung around, and walked in the direction of her *jacal*.

This time as Enos watched her go, none of the calmness that had marked his earlier facedown with her showed. When he'd closed the door and Brett emerged from hiding, the dark man said, "I hope to hell Ortiz gets here a little early," and refused to say anymore, although Brett gazed inquiringly at him.

Dusk arrived; the heat continued to increase—and would do so for another couple of hours. Herders brought their goats and sheep into Mex town, some with dogs along, some using nothing more than very long staffs and colorful profanity to accomplish what dogs would do.

The community was coming to life; siesta time had passed. Children ran yelling, dogs barked, people hailed one another, there was a pleasing aroma of cooking fires in the air.

Enos started a meal while Brett went to look in on their uninvited guest. The old man was snoring. It sounded like an asthmatic shoat caught under a gate. Brett returned to the kitchen.

Their wait would not be for much longer. The man they were waiting for could come anytime after full darkness arrived—or, he could not come at all. Not this night, anyway, and Enos was not sure he could go through another day cooped up with that Salazar woman living close enough to come banging on the door every time she ran out of something to do, or someone to pester.

When Enos put supper plates on the table this time, Brett eyed what he thought were eggs, but something had been added. As Enos eased down across the table, he said, "Eat."

"What is it?"

"Eggs *con carne,*" Enos replied a trifle stiffly. "If you figure to stay down here you'd better—"

"What the hell does *con carne* mean?" Brett raised his head. "Where'd you pick up Spanish?"

"*Con carne* means somethin' cooked with meat. . . . Everybody speaks Spanish down here. The storekeepers, the town marshal. Haven't you noticed that? Brett, if you're goin' to stay down here, you're goin' to have to pick it up like I do—listen, figure out what words mean, ask questions. I thought it'd be hard. Hell, it's not hard at all. Quit starin' at it, just eat it."

Brett's brow remained furrowed. "What kind of meat?"

"I got no idea. Meat." Enos paused before maliciously saying, "Maybe goat meat, an' that's something else. They eat lots of sheep an' goat meat down here."

He ignored Brett and went to work on his supper. From the corner of his eye, he saw Brett try a tentative forkful, wait a moment, then try another forkful. Enos had cleaned his plate before Brett had half emptied his. The coffee was black; at least on that topic everyone in the southwest seemed to be of a mind.

When Brett finished, he asked what Enos had flavored their supper with. The answer was again indicative of the south desert life-style. "Peppers—not much—garlic, an' salt. Not bad, was it?"

Brett looked resigned. "No," he said and pushed the plate aside to pull the coffee cup closer.

Enos cleared the table before returning to nurse his cup of black coffee. He said, "You looked into this tradin' and livery business?"

Brett hadn't. "No. But it would bear lookin' into. You interested, Enos?"

"Might be," the dark man replied guardedly. "Who'd we buy the business from?"

Brett didn't know that either. "If he's got heirs, from them I guess. If he don't . . ." Brett shrugged.

"How much money?"

Brett was beginning to feel exasperated because every question Enos asked, he could not answer. He said, "It was just an idea. I don't know any more about the business than you do. It seems to me it's an opportunity. We need one, Enos. We're out of the cattle business."

Enos startled Kandelin. "If it takes more'n two thousand dollars for my share, I can't buy in."

Kandelin stared. "You got two thousand dollars?"

"Yeah. It's taken me fifteen years, but I got it."

"That's a hell of a lot of money.

The dark man smiled enigmatically and said nothing.

"You didn't rob a bank or something like that, did you?"

"I never stole a cent of it. I been weaselin' it away since long before you went to work for me."

Brett got the wine jug and they used the same cups they'd emptied of coffee for it. A night bird sounded somewhere. Brett and Enos sat looking steadily at each other.

There was no reply, so they assumed it was a genuine night bird—until some dogs between the alcalde's house and the mission began to furiously bark. They had a stubby little candle lighted in one of the wall niches and made no move to douse it. What light it gave off was barely enough to see by. Without it, they would be in total darkness.

A groan came from the back of the house. They left the kitchen to go stand in the darkness of the bedroom where Enos had put the old man. He wasn't awake; he had shifted position and had groaned while doing so.

Brett shook his head. "He's goin' to feel like hell in the morning."

They returned to the kitchen. A few dogs were still barking but not as many as before. From the night bird there was not a sound.

Brett went through near blackness to crack the front door. There was no movement that he could see, so he rebarred the door and returned to the kitchen.

Enos had peered past a slit in the rear door. He, too, had seen nothing worthwhile. His teeth shone white in the gloom. "Dogs'll bark about anything." He nevertheless tugged loose the tie down on his holstered weapon and watched Brett do the same.

CHAPTER 24

Dawnlight

Endangered people seem to have an affinity that allows them to sense peril with no visible evidence it is approaching.

In the case of the two men waiting inside the dark house, it may have arisen as a result of their subconscious belief that it was coming.

The continued to wait. Once, they heard someone call out in a startled tone of voice. After that, the silence returned deeper than ever.

The dogs only barked intermittently now, but they wouldn't have barked even that much if whatever had aroused them was not still out there.

Brett said, "Coyote after chickens."

Enos agreed, using a different simile. "Raccoons raiding someone's garbage pit." After a moment, he also said, "How many you reckon?"

Brett guessed. "Three. If we're unlucky, maybe more."

Enos's response was dry. "I don't feel unlucky, but I been wrong before."

Until a woman's fierce torrent of Spanish broke the stillness, the silence had been running on for almost an hour.

Brett said, "You're right, we got to learn Spanish. I got no idea what she said, but she was mad. Voices sound alike in any language when someone's mad."

Enos made another dry remark. "It was the Salazar

woman. Hell, she's mad all the time, anyway. . . . Only, don't it seem kind of late?''

Brett went to the rear of the house to look in on the old man. He was sleeping like a stone. Brett returned to the kitchen as Enos raised a warning hand. Brett heard nothing, and after a few moments, Enos shrugged to indicate that he'd probably been mistaken.

Time passed; Mex town's traditional noises diminished, a new moon arrived and began its ancient tour of the cobalt heavens. Distantly, from the direction of Gringo town, loud voices erupted, but evidently it was not a fight because they stopped and no further racket reached the men in the late alcalde's kitchen.

Brett said, ''I figured it would be later, after everyone was asleep.''

Enos nodded absently, a movement that was scarcely visible to his companion. ''Maybe it's not them,'' he murmured. ''Maybe it's someone lookin' for the old man.''

Brett had doubts. ''Would those dogs keep on raising hell about someone down here they saw every day?''

Enos mentioned something he'd spoken of before. ''I wish I had a shotgun.''

Brett grinned. ''As long as you're wishing, wish for a cannon.''

Something more like roiled air, something sensed rather than heard, seemed just beyond the kitchen door. Enos and Brett, sensitive to anything unexpected or unusual, moved apart, facing the door. A scrap of sound, like someone's stormy breath being expelled under pressure, was barely audible outside.

Brett whispered, ''A woman!'' and immediately thought of Lillian.

Enos's reply, also whispered, sounded mildly disgusted. ''Ambrosia. I thought that was her a while back. Darned fool female. What was she doin' outside her house, anyway?''

Brett offered no response as he strained to hear the sound again. There was only silence, and now the more distant dogs were no longer barking, only one dog, nearer to the center of Mex town, continued to bark intermittently.

Brett said, "Gettin' closer," and Enos nodded in the darkness.

The sudden violent knocking of a fist on the door made echoes inside the house. Brett shook his head, and once more Enos nodded. He also rolled his eyes in the direction of the back of the house, but Brett missed this, not entirely because of the darkness, but also because he was watching the door.

The knocking was repeated. This time it was accompanied by a strained-sounding female voice. "Open! It is Ambrosia. There is something I must tell you!"

Enos sighed and wagged his head. "She never sleeps." But Brett had paid less attention to the words than to the way they'd been spoken. "Someone's out there with her, Enos."

Silence returned for a few moments, then the knocking was resumed, but with more force this time. They waited for the woman to speak again, but after the knocking ceased, silence settled again.

Now, the silence was not broken for a long time. Only the barking of the one dog was audible inside the house.

A slight scraping sound from out front somewhere brought both men around. Before Enos could get untracked, Brett crossed into the sitting room—and saw pale, watery light reflected off a long, thin knife blade that had been inserted between the warped old doorjamb and the door. It was rising upward very slowly, groping ever so gently for the bottom of the *tranca*, which barred the door from the inside and rested in a metal hanger.

Brett's gun barrel moved upwards as slowly as did the blade of the knife. When the blade touched the *tranca*, it hesitated. Brett's gun stopped moving, too. If the old door hadn't been thick, ancient oak, he might have tried shooting through it.

His gun palm was sweaty. He was concentrating so hard on the knife he did not know Enos was behind him in the doorless opening between the sitting room and the kitchen.

The blade began pushing upward, finally lifting the *tranca* gently, silently clearing it from its hanger. Brett took one step closer in order to be able to see exactly when the *tranca* cleared the hanger.

He moved again, slightly to the right, where he would, hopefully, not be as noticeable when whoever was outside sprang into the house.

The wooden bar cleared its hanger. Now it stopped with the blade holding it motionless. Brett's thumb, on the gun's hammer, settled very firmly. If he cocked the six-gun before the intruder jumped inside, the man would hear it. Over in the intervening doorless opening, Enos raised his weapon chest high and waited. He'd cocked his weapon in the kitchen during Ambrosia Salazar's harangue.

Seconds seemed like hours. Neither of the waiting men breathed very deeply. Part of Brett's little plan had already unraveled. He wasn't going to have to look like Lillian; force, not a ruse, was going to settle the affair.

The door wasn't kicked open, it was eased very gently inward, knife blade still supporting the *tranca*, which otherwise would have fallen. Brett had seconds to realize it couldn't be the same man who opened the door who was also holding the *tranca* aloft, so there were two of them. At least two.

He and Enos had an agonizingly long moment to sweat and breath shallowly before the door was open enough for someone to come inside.

The man who moved fluidly sideways to enter was thin, attired fully in black, and hatless. He was holding a cocked six-gun in one hand. The other hand was raised slightly, pushed forward.

The second man, still holding the door bar aloft with his blade, began easing the blade and the *tranca* silently downward.

Enos fired.

The sound was deafening, the muzzle blast lanced like fire, and the man holding his cocked pistol struck the door violently under impact, slamming it closed as his trigger finger jerked and the second deafening shot and flame nearly blinded and deafened both Brett and Enos.

That bullet made a groove in the floor no one would remove for many years.

Behind Enos, the kitchen door was nearly wrenched from

its hinges by a shotgun blast at close quarters. It absorbed most of the buckshot.

Enos ducked, sprang toward the nearest place of protection, which was the doorway of the old man's resting place, and fired three times, very fast, at a pair of moving black shadows that sprang past the broken door. One of the shadows was solidly hit at close quarters, fell back out through the doorway, and a woman screamed as his lifeless body knocked her down beyond the doorway.

The second of Enos's shots missed completely, but the man in black dove flat to the floor and rolled before firing at Enos's muzzle fire.

Brett shot the man from the sitting room where, down on one knee to provide a smaller target, he had seen the intruder drop, roll, and fire. He did not miss. Impact punched the prone man a foot before he stopped moving.

A man's harsh cry from somewhere out front ended abruptly as a rifle or a carbine almost caught him in full flight.

Another gunshot outside the house followed a string of profanity in Spanish. The fleeing man's outcry ended too abruptly to have been voluntary.

Now it seemed that every dog in Mex town was barking, and through that racket, the sounds of a woman crying were audible.

Brett and Enos moved warily in opposite directions, Enos to sidle behind protection as he peered out into the late night behind the house where the sobbing came from. Brett began to ease open the front door to peek out.

After a period of time that seemed to the men in the house to be an eternity, a deep, booming voice called out in English, and Brett leaned on the wall for a moment before calling back.

" 'Pifas! What the hell are you doing out there? You're supposed to be—"

"Hey, *pistolero*! I got one!"

At once a cranky youthful voice spoke out loudly and indignantly. " Like hell you did! You missed when he was in front of the house. I nailed him on the run!"

Enos came through to the front door, stepped over the man Brett had shot, stood just inside until he'd reloaded, then leathered his weapon, and looked solemnly at Brett. "The old man's dead." At Brett's blank stare, the dark man also said, "When that feller shot at me while he was tryin' to roll, the bullet hit the old man plumb through the brisket. He never knew what hit him."

"How in hell could someone shootin' from the floor hit the old man on the bed?" he asked.

"The old man was standin' up. Maybe the noise wakened him. Go see for yourself. He's lyin' half across the bed, dead as a rock."

'Pifas and Hale Barlow appeared on the porch, still gripping guns. Brett had to roll the man he'd shot out of the way before he could open the door fully for them to enter.

They looked at the corpse, at the man who had shot him, and wrinkled their noses; the smell of spent gunpowder was unpleasant.

Enos took all of them to the bedroom door, where the old man was lying sprawled on his back across the bed. It was too dark to make out details, but none of them moved inside to look closer. 'Pifas, who had known the old man, crossed himself, breathed a prayer, and went out to the kitchen.

Brett lingered as the others went to the kitchen. Out there, the moment 'Pifas stepped into the rear opening, something struck him with enough force to compel him to brace one leg back to avoid being bowled over. Ambrosia Salazar clung to him with frantic strength; for once, she was speechless. He closed his arms around her as the sobs came, half carried, half escorted her back to her own residence, and disappeared inside with her.

Brett was still in the bedroom doorway when someone came silently up and, looking past, softly said, "Why was he here?"

Brett turned, met the solemn dark gaze of Lillian, and did not ask what she was doing here when she was supposed to be miles away. He told her how the old man happened to be in the house, and thought of something Abizu Corales had said at the kitchen table: I can tell you friends, living can go on too long. She returned her gaze to the barely visible outline of a frail old dead man.

The commotion in Mex town had aroused people in Gringo town. One of the first to arrive was Juan Escalante. He joined a group of wary Mexicans, nearly all wrapped in hastily snatched-up blankets. No one could tell him what had happened.

Marshal Severn came lumbering up, fully but hastily attired, carrying a sawed-off shotgun and looking angry. They were lining up the dead raiders out front when he arrived and halted to look at them with bitter eyes. He used the barrels of his scattergun as a pointer as he said, "Gil Ortiz—the damned fool!"

Brett ignored the dead man. "When did you get back to town?" he asked.

He got a curt reply, "About ten o'clock. We didn't find no trace of raiders." He looked again at the corpse. "No wonder. He was sneakin' back here." Severn's gaze went to Lillian. "I guess you can sleep nights now."

She nodded and took Brett's arm to lead him around back, where the shotgun blast had nearly torn the rear door off the wall. There was candlelight in the Salazar *jacal*. She said, "The noise wakened everyone."

Brett's reply was revealing. "Not her. I think she must have been outside and saw them. Anyway, however they did it, they were using her to try to get us to open the back door."

Lillian turned. "Are you all right?"

He could not answer very well, so he asked why she had come back. Her reply was simple enough. "I was worried about you. Just the two of you. 'Pifas and Hale didn't want to ride away, either. But we did as you said; we saw the posse ahead and followed it—for a short ways, at least. You didn't say we couldn't come back."

People were still arriving, some from Mex town, an equal number from Gringo town. The friendly whiskered man who owned the light wagon in which he'd taken Brett out to the hanging ground arrived to seek out Marshal Severn and speak quietly with him for a few moments, then he headed briskly back the way he had come to hitch his horse and return with the wagon. Coyotero did not have an official undertaker, at least not in Gringo town. Folks buried their own; the unknowns were buried at community expense.

Mex town had a *cajónero*, but he rarely did undertaking outside of Mex town. The whiskered man was not an undertaker, he was simply a man with a light wagon who had taken the dead in one direction or another for years. As had been said, ekeing out a living on the south desert required ingenuity and an opportunistic outlook.

By the time dawn arrived, most of the aroused townsfolk had returned homeward. Lillian and Brett had placed the old Basque in a comfortable position on the bed, had covered him, placed his manzanita cane beside him, and had lighted two candles in wall niches. Old Corales looked completely at peace.

Lillian remained with the old man when Brett went to the kitchen, where Hale and Enos were drinking the alcalde's red wine with Juan Escalante. As he sat down, Juan pushed the jug toward him, but right at this moment Brett was not ready to drink the wine of one dead man after having just left another dead man, the friend of the maker of the red wine.

They could hear creaking wagon wheels out front. The sound grew fainter as predawn chill crept past the ruined rear doorway.

Lillian appeared soundlessly. Brett rose to go outside with her. There was a hint of pale pink in the east; another day was arriving. They walked out a short distance, stopped at an old faggot corral to lean and say nothing for a while, until he lifted a heavy coil of dark hair and gently placed it behind her ear. Then she said, "I owe you everything," and turned slightly to gaze at him.

"You owe me nothing," he exclaimed.

"And the town owes you everything, too."

She meant his lost herd of cattle, and he shrugged about that.

"And now you will leave."

He looked at her. "Do I have to?"

"Don't you want to?"

"No. Well, only if you'll go with me. It'll be tough sledding. I don't have much."

"That wouldn't matter, Brett. I'm not used to much."

An awkward silence settled, broken eventually by two old men driving a band of mixed sheep and goats northward out of town in order to reach some graze ahead of sunnrise, which would evaporate the dew. Both the old men saw them leaning there. One of them touched his hat brim and smiled. The other was more bold. He called something in singsong Spanish as he grinned and kept moving, obviously expecting no reply.

Lillian was looking uncomfortable when Brett looked back from watching the old men. He had a flash of intuition. "What did he say?"

"Just talk. An old man's joke."

"About me?"

"No, about me."

Brett considered the brightening distant horizon for a while before speaking again. "I talked to Enos about the livery barn."

"Did he like the idea?"

"I think so. Sometimes Enos is kind of hard to figure out." He faced her again. "He'll partner up with me in it."

"You're sure?"

He smiled at her. "Yes, I'm sure."

"Then you will stay?"

He continued to smile at her, eyes fond but shrewd. "If you'll tell me what that old man said."

She also turned to study the distant dawn. "He said . . . his wife is sixty and still bears children."

He hadn't expected that. A sliver from the top of the old faggot corral was sticking him. He became very busy searching for it.

ABOUT THE AUTHOR

Lauran Paine lives in Fort Jones, California. He is an accomplished western writer who has published dozens of books under various pseudonyms and his own name.